Praise for *Wyrmhole*

"Fascinating and well-imagined . . . a terrific read, combining all the elements of great science fiction: originality, speculation, and consequence."

—Julie E. Czerneda, author of
In the Company of Others

"Jay Caselberg is Philip K. Dick gene-spliced with Raymond Chandler. Complex, layered, black as night, unputdownable."

—Stephen Baxter, Hugo Award–nominated
author of *Evolution*

"Jay Caselberg weaves SF with mystery for a new spin on the PI genre. In a fluid, dreamlike world where everything is changing, Jack Stein, psychic investigator, uses sharp edged dreams to solve a case of miners vanished off a distant planet. An adventurous romp of a first novel, *Wyrmhole* keeps you guessing. The Philosopher's stone and alchemy shift into the digital age."

—Wen Spencer, Compton Crook
Award–winning author of
Alien Taste and *Tainted Trail*

Jay Caselberg

WYRMHOLE

A ROC BOOK

ROC
Published by New American Library, a division of
Penguin Group (USA) Inc., 375 Hudson Street,
New York, New York 10014, U.S.A.
Penguin Books Ltd, 80 Strand,
London WC2R 0RL, England
Penguin Books Australia Ltd, 250 Camberwell Road,
Camberwell, Victoria 3124, Australia
Penguin Books Canada Ltd, 10 Alcorn Avenue,
Toronto, Ontario, Canada M4V 3B2
Penguin Books (N.Z.) Ltd, Cnr Rosedale and Airborne Roads,
Albany, Auckland 1310, New Zealand

Penguin Books Ltd, Registered Offices:
80 Strand, London WC2R 0RL, England

First published by Roc, an imprint of New American Library,
a division of Penguin Group (USA) Inc.

First Printing, October 2003
10 9 8 7 6 5 4 3 2 1

Copyright © Jay Caselberg, 2003
All rights reserved

Cover art by Christian McGrath

For P.

Acknowledgments

I would like to express my gratitude to all those who made this book a reality. First, to my editor, Jennifer Heddle; my agent, Linn Prentis, and all those at the Virginia Kidd Agency; to fellow writers Charlene L. Brusso, Lynn Flewelling, Laura Anne Gilman, Devon Monk for their input; to the IMPs of CompuServe for pointing the way; to the Clan for ongoing support and encouragement, especially when things became dark; and to my mother, Jennifer, for her unflagging love and belief.

One

Stein woke that morning with blood in his piss and the taste of something more insidious deep within his brain. Strangely innocuous, deadpan—that was how it felt. As if none of it really mattered. Heavy grav, that was what did it. Too much weight and too many stims to keep him going. Heavy grav got you down.

He grunted, shook the last few drops of the accusatory pink-yellow stream, then dry-flushed. Maybe he was just becoming paranoid. Too many stims would do that to you. He was going to crash big-time without them, but his kidneys wouldn't take it much longer. He peered blearily at himself in the mirror, then shook his head. *What the hell?* He reached into the cabinet and slapped on another patch. *Time and tide wait for no man.* Now where had that come from? Jesus, where did he get this crap? He was having too many random thoughts like that these days, stuff just popping into his head.

Back into the kitchenette to brew a cup, one foot planted ponderously after the other, every step an effort. The stuff didn't even smell real. By the time he'd finished the lukewarm nothingness that passed for coffee out here on the Rim, and tossed the plastic cup into the disposal, the stims had started to kick in. He was starting to feel barely human again—sort of like strung wire—but at least human. He scratched at the stubble on his cheek and grimaced. Time to face the music. He eased the trailer door open and squinted out into glare and heat, leaning against the doorframe while his fragile senses adjusted to the morning assault.

A cluster of silver trailers caught the light, shining star shapes in his brittle vision. The air sucked moisture from his skin, and he lifted a hand to shield his eyes. The bare, pink ground between the trailers, ground littered with small, jagged stones, appeared completely devoid of life. With a growl, he eased himself down the trailer stairs. Where the hell was everyone? There should have been activity all around the campsite by this time of day, but the only thing that moved was the heat shimmer.

Stein walked a few steps from his trailer and turned slowly, looking for any sign of the others. The only thing he got was that uneasy feeling deep in his guts. Everything shouted quietness.

Too still. Too damned still by far.

"Hey, Johnson," he yelled.

Nothing.

He yelled again, then cocked his head to listen. But he didn't want to hear the small, faint voice in the back of his head telling him something was wrong. Too many stims made you edgy. *Fuck it.* He was in no mood for games.

"Johnson! Mitch! Hey, where the hell are you?"

Still nothing. The heat-thick air sucked his words away and left him with beating silence in his ears. The small, quiet voice in the back of his head got louder.

Jack had learned to rely on that little voice, but it didn't mean he had to like what it was telling him. It was as if something were stalking him like a man in black cowboy boots riding the dreamsnake in his head.

You've blown your cover, Jack. They're on to you, it whispered.

He scanned the trailers and concentrated on the sounds outside his head. Still nothing. Logic started to overtake the internal voice. There was no way the rest of the crew could know why he was here. Or could they?

What the hell was he doing in this place anyway? He hated heat. Okay, it was money, but sometimes that just wasn't enough. He licked his lips and crunched over to Johnson's trailer. He lifted a fist and banged on the metal shell.

"Johnson, you in there?" He waited a moment, then banged again.

The voice was back again, telling him stuff he didn't want to hear. The sun was beating down on the back of his neck, slamming heat into his body. It was funny the way no matter what star you were under, you always thought of it as the Sun. It might be a different color, but it was still Sol. He could feel the slight trembling in the ends of his fingers and the hard-wire edgy feeling around his teeth that meant the stims were really starting to kick in. His heart was racing now, but this time it had nothing to do with the chemicals. What the hell was he going to do?

He tried Mitch's trailer, but the results were the same. He didn't dare risk any of the others. Johnson and Mitch were the only ones who had treated him halfway like human since his arrival. These far-flung mining crews tended to be a pretty unforgiving lot, didn't like outsiders much. The new boy always had to prove himself, to earn acceptance, and Jack Stein hadn't been around long enough to make the grade.

He leaned against the trailer door, trying to ease some of the weight dragging at his limbs. You had to question a person's motivation for winding up in a place like this. But you didn't pry into people's backgrounds. Not out here. He squinted into the sun, then cursed out loud. Stupid to stand out here in the full glare. Bloody stupid. He walked around the trailer and squatted in the pinkish dust on the other side, using the trailer's bulk to shield him from the heat. He rubbed his hands on his thighs, leaving pink smears on his legs like chalk-dust trails on the sides of his suit.

It was still another eight days before the rotation shuttle was due. He'd already been here for two local weeks and found nothing. When the company had sent him in, he'd expected to have some answers within the first week, but so far he'd drawn a blank. Most of the eighteen-strong crew was fairly tight-lipped, but there'd been nothing in any one of their actions to indicate anything suspicious. Jack was pretty good at picking up the signs, and nothing up to now had triggered his internal alarms.

He peered across at the jagged pink cliffs where the main shaft lay. The light sparkled in sharp traceries from the crystalline outcroppings, even at this distance. The problem was, he didn't really know what he was supposed to be looking for. They'd called him into the office and said, "We've had reports of unusual happenings on Dairil III. We want you to go in and find out what's going on." That was it. Fat lot of help they'd been.

"So what am I supposed to be looking for?" he'd asked.

"Anything unusual. Anything at all," they'd said.

Well, now it looked like he'd found something, even if it was nothing. The men were supposed to be here. The camp should be full of noise, the rough, burly mining crew preparing for their day inside the mountain, swearing and grumbling as they usually did.

He hitched himself to his feet and walked slowly back around the other side of the trailer. He was achieving absolutely nothing here. The vehicles they used to get back and forth from the mine were still parked around the campsite, so at least that was something. Next stop had to be the mine itself, see if they were there. Grab his kit and drive over to the mine. That was the answer. He'd find them all there, waiting for him to show up, wide grins on their stubbled, sweaty, dirt-smeared faces. The fact that the vehicles were still there worried at the back of his consciousness, but he pushed the thought aside.

Stein had been in Intelligence once, but he'd left when the service hadn't treated him the way he thought it ought to. Intelligence. Well, he didn't feel very intelligent right now. It was far too early in the morning, and all he had was his sense of wrongness to keep him going. Not a good way to start the day. Not good at all. He rubbed the back of his neck as he trudged back to his simple, utilitarian accommodation.

Back in the trailer, he toyed with having another coffee before heading out to the mine, but then rationality took hold, and knowing it would do him more harm than good, he dismissed the idea. He grabbed his items of kit from where they lay scattered around the small trailer, donned his hard hat, reflective jacket, and shades, and headed back out into the glare. If the others really were taking him for an idiot, then this time he'd have something to say. He didn't go much with all this bonding shit they played. But then again, Jack Stein didn't really bond. Many years ago he might have wanted to, but now he simply couldn't be bothered. Experience had taught him otherwise. Everything was transitory; everything faded. Loyalty counted for nothing. You didn't trust anyone but yourself, and that was the way life worked.

Four yellow flatbed half-tracks stood at the end of the cluster of trailers that lay closest to the mine. Stein picked one at random, headed for it, and clambered aboard. It would take him about fifteen minutes to make it to the mine entrance. On the opposite side of the trailers lay the landing field where the rotation shuttle would set down and offload the relief crew. He knew from his background research that the site for the trailers had been chosen on purpose—closer to the landing field and farther away from the mine. Somehow it gave the crew a feeling of closeness to home, and kept them away from the constant reminder of the vast, enclosing caverns and shafts they toiled in day after day. At the end of a relative twelve-hour shift, you just wanted to get away from the mine, banish it from your thoughts, but it was under your fingernails and all over your clothes and in the sweaty lines in your face. Nothing really took it away. He gunned the motor and headed out along the well-worn track, clearly ridged with the marks of their daily comings and goings.

He glanced back once at the clustered silver trailers, squinting against the glare even through his shades.

Something seemed to waver in the air above them, something gray and sinuous, but then it was gone. He swallowed back the feeling that rose in his throat and turned to face the track ahead, sweeping out through the featureless rose-colored scree. He hated the way the stims did that—caused flickers on the edges of his perception. He liked to be able to rely on his senses, not worry about every tiny visual aberration conjured by the dark places in his brain. One day they were going to invent a stimulant that didn't have side effects. With a conscious effort, he tried to banish the lingering thoughts of snakes from his head.

The constant whine and rumble of the half-track gave him some comfort. Machine noise was always good for pinning down reality. He sucked at the water bottle as he jolted along, scanning the cliff face for any signs of life as he rolled the warm, flat-tasting water over his tongue. Nothing. Well, he hoped they were getting some sort of perverse satisfaction from this little game. He sure as hell wasn't. He circled the half-track to a stop and sat staring at the mine entrance, contemplating his next move.

Equipment lay scattered haphazardly across the ground where the crew had left it the previous evening. Large pieces of yellow metal, scratched and scored from use. One of the advantages about working in a place like this, you only had to worry about yourself. It really didn't matter how you left things. Nobody was going to take them, because there was nobody here *to* take them. The mining team were the only people on this godforsaken ball of rock, apart from the occasional shuttle crew.

The pink cliffs loomed above him, covered in jagged protrusions made even more jagged by the intensity of the light casting crazy shadows across the surface. Jack's concern suddenly started to become touched with logic. Up until now he'd simply been running on his gut. If the rest of the crew had gone inside to start work, surely they would have moved the equipment. So what was it doing still lying about outside?

He stepped down from the half-track, shielded his eyes, and let his gaze rove across the piled angular boulders to either side of the mine entrance, then on and into the man-made hole in the rock. It disappeared rapidly into the cool, shadowed interior of the cliffs, fading into darkness. No lights. No stirring of life. High above lay the vast solar panels that drew power down into the mountain's heart, but nobody had bothered to flip the switch. Maybe that was part of their game. So where were they hiding?

He gave the side of the vehicle a frustrated kick, then searched inside himself for calm. If the crew had concealed themselves in the shadowed entranceway, watching him, then losing his temper would only give them more satisfaction. He reached into the half-track, retrieved the water bottle, and took a healthy swallow. He wiped his mouth with the back of his hand, and tossed the bottle back into the vehicle.

"Mitch, you in there?" he yelled. "Johnson?"

Vague echoes of his voice filtered back from the mine entrance. He listened for a response, but all was still.

Reluctantly he stepped away from the vehicle and headed toward the entrance. The switches were about ten paces inside the mouth, on the left-hand wall, if he remembered right. He'd never had to switch the lights on himself. That was the job of the crew boss.

It was marginally cooler inside the shadowed rock. He walked slowly, looking for the bank of switches along the wall, listening for a sound that might give the rest of the mine crew's presence away. Only the echo of his footfalls came back to him from the wall, sounding strange and hollow in this vast empty space. The squirming-snake feeling was back in his belly.

"Shit, Stein. Get a grip, will you?" he muttered under his breath. "Anybody'd think you were afraid of the dark." He was, slightly, but he wasn't going to let anyone else know that.

The rows of red switches lay above him, a panel, just higher than his head. Using both hands he flipped them all, in groups. There was a satisfying rush and *whoomph* as all along the tunnel powerful lights surged into life, casting his shadow on the rock wall in stark silhouette. He turned and peered down the tunnel, but all he saw was rock and the dusty pink floor, scattered with chips of stone and the marks of boots and vehicle treads. Maybe they were farther inside. He supposed he could go back, get the half-track, and drive in, but now that he was here, he might as well walk. Stein knew if they really were here, they were unlikely to be very far. And if they were already working, he'd hear the sound before he'd gone more than fifty meters.

He noticed the strange patterns on the floor when he was no more than twenty meters in. Long, sinuous swirls marked the dust, and large patches had been swept free of litter. Here and there along the walls, deep piles of rock chips and other waste had been swept into small mounds. Stein stopped walking and frowned. He was sure the tunnel hadn't looked like that last time he was here. He listened again, but only quiet stillness, marked by an occasional dripping from somewhere off in the distance, came to him. He looked back down at the marks on the floor. The patterns reminded him of something. Something animal, but he couldn't remember what. He'd remember what it was later, when he wasn't thinking about it. That was how it worked. He ignored the shapes and continued walking.

Everything was silent except for the sound of his footsteps, and the slight hum of the lights overhead, and that faint *drip, drip, drip* from farther down the passage. If the other crew members were here, he should have heard something by now. At least he could get to the face of the latest workings and see if they'd even been there. Then he noticed something lying on the tunnel floor ahead. It looked like someone had dropped a glove.

He was nearly on top of it, bending down to retrieve it when he saw what it really was—a hand. Perfectly formed. Perfectly severed at the wrist. Just lying there in the middle of the tunnel floor. No blood. No pool of anything. Just a hand. He swallowed and stood quickly upright, staring down at it.

A big, chunky ring sat on one of the fingers. It was some sort of shiny black stone, and on it was a device, picked out in silver. A snake eating its own tail. The top half of the snake was black, outlined with silver, but the bottom half was of solid silver, marked with a pattern of scales. Leaning down, he could see that words in some ancient script lay within the looped body. The hand was broad and meaty, well tanned. He could see the neat cross-section where it had been removed from its owner.

He took a deep breath, stood again, and looked around, suddenly nervous. What the hell could do that? And more important, where was the hand's owner? He peered farther down the passageway. This was not turning out at all well.

Stein considered his options. He looked down at the hand and prodded it gently with the toe of his boot. It seemed solid enough, real enough. He dug the edge of his boot under the thumb and flipped it over. The thick fingers were slightly curled in toward a palm with pink-brown dust ingrained into the lines. There were calluses on the palm, just below where the fingers joined. It was a miner's hand, but he couldn't remember having seen the ring on any of the crew he'd met.

If the hand was just lying there, it had other implications. If there'd been an accident, nobody would just leave it there, lying in the middle of the tunnel floor. Something had happened to the crew. Not just one of them—all of them. He sucked in his breath, feeling foolish. *Great powers of deduction, Stein.*

A noise came from behind him: a whirring, slithery sound that was somehow both wet and dry at the same time. Slowly Stein turned, his guts gone cold.

Something was sliding out from the tunnel walls, out of the smooth, bare rock. Sinuous gray shapes pushed straight out into the air, iridescence sliding along their length. They were probing the empty air, slipping along the tunnel floor, like multiple tentacles coated in a slick of very fine oil that glazed the questing forms with vaguely shifting rainbow colors.

Stein took a step backward.

"What the hell . . . ?"

Jack woke back in the Locality, sweat pooling in the hollow of his neck. His hair lay slick, plastered across his skull. He sat slowly upright, trying to quiet the

pounding in his chest. The dream still lay like the taste
of bile within his mouth, making him feel like he
wanted to scrape his tongue, making him reluctant to
swallow.

He passed a hand across his forehead, then gently
peeled back the inducer pads at his temples, working
his nail under the fine adhesive edge.

Damned dreams were getting worse. He couldn't
sustain it for much longer if he kept emerging feeling
like this. He worked his tongue around the inside of
his mouth in an attempt to banish some of the taste,
then swung his feet off the bed onto the cold, stonelike
floor. He sat there, hunched, arms resting on his thighs
for a few minutes, grasping at the knowledge of which
reality he really was in. Any moment he expected the
walls to extrude vast gray tentacles.

The dreams were like that; they imposed themselves on his waking consciousness for several minutes after he'd emerged. Just the same way his reality
imposed itself on the dreams. In that half-blurred
boundary of emergence, sometimes it was hard to dis-
tinguish exactly which was which.

A drop of sweat fell from the tip of his nose onto his
thigh and he reached up to wipe at his face again. The
sting of salt was in his eyes. He took a moment or two
to compose himself, breathing slowly and regularly in
an effort to steady his pulse. He used the time to look
around the familiar bare walls.

This was his working room, about a third of the
way along the Locality closer to Old than New. It
would be about ten full years before he'd have to find
another and relocate. Plenty of time. His apartment
was closer to Mid and should be safe for about another
fifteen years or so. Not that he planned on being in the

Locality for that long, but it suited him for now, at least until he worked out what the hell he was going to do.

The Locality was a haven, one of several self-perpetuating urban structures that crept across the landscape by millimeters every week. It took from the ground upon which it lay the components it needed to build itself, constantly renewing and adding new apartments, offices, and other dwelling spaces toward New in shapes that were programmed into it. As with everything, it suffered decay. Eventually the life span of the tiny pseudo-organic builders ran out, and the walls and streets broke down to be recycled back into the whole, eating up the tail of the Locality near Old, consuming itself at the end. The Locality and structures like it had grown out of the old gated communities. As life became more perilous, and the technology had become available, those with the resources had built the first experimental structures. More and more had flocked to the security of their contained existence, and the environments became larger, first towns, then whole cities. The Locality had been one of the first, its immense growth organic as its population grew.

Jack's working room lay in an office complex where the rents were cheaper because of their proximity to the far end of Old. To be honest, it was much more Old than Mid, but it was close enough to the boundary to force the lie. But the location suited him fine; he had no need for the extended permanence to be found toward New.

Stein looked around the simple room, slotting reality back into his head. The blank walls and midheight ceiling were a uniform off-white. He kept the room simple on purpose, so he wouldn't be sent off on iconic tangents when emerging from dream state. Paintings, statues, and the like had too much resonance, not that he could afford them. Rather, he wanted to define the dream images, note them down before they slipped away from his semiconscious mind. It could take mere minutes for them to fade. The blankness gave him a canvas on which to paint his dream realities and give them substance without having them confused by the clutter of possessions.

At least he had something to report to his client now. All he had to do was try to sort out the dream image from what had really been there. For a start, there was the hand. The way it had been apparently severed made him suspect a dream plant, something injected into the dream reality by his subconscious, disconnected from what was really going on, but he couldn't be sure. He worked his tongue around the inside of his mouth again and reached for the water bottle he kept handy by the sleep couch. As he sipped, he sorted and classified the images one by one. Then he reached for his handipad, thumbed it into life, and started making notes.

The ring was interesting. The Ouroboros had significance, he was sure. The snake eating its own tail was a classic archetypal symbol—something easily found inside dreams—but countless societies and organizations throughout the ages had used it. He wondered what it might mean in the true context of the dream. There was power there. Maybe too much. It would link to the snake shapes sliding out from the mine walls as well. It was a starting point. He picked up the rock shard from the mine on Dairil III and hefted it thoughtfully in one hand. Warburg had been right. He had been given just about all he needed with that little chip of stone.

Still, he hadn't learned much. The mining crew had disappeared, that much was clear, but he already knew that. That was why Warburg had hired him. The fact that Warburg had hired Jack Stein rather than some more mainstream investigator smacked of something less legitimate, though. He could understand their wanting to keep the disappearance quiet, but there was more going on here. He needed to work out why a large corporation like Outreach would approach a two-bit investigator like Jack Stein in the first place. He had no illusions about his status in the Locality's scheme of things. The call had come out of nowhere, and he hadn't really questioned it at the time. The whole deal was far too good to pass up.

He'd met Warburg at the plush offices up in New. The hard-faced corporate executive with his slick designer suit took him through what they needed. They'd had a mining crew out on Dairil III, somewhere out of the mainstream traffic lanes. Without explanation, the crew had disappeared. Travel to the planet would have taken months, but as Jack Stein was a psychic investigator, maybe they could cut through some of the time needed to solve the case. Time was of the essence, and there was pressure from on high to come up with an explanation soon.

Jack had taken him through his abilities, explained the dreams, the psychic clues. All throughout, Warburg had sat, fixing him with a flat, expressionless stare. When Jack had told him how physical prompts sometimes invoked clues, Warburg had merely nodded, slid the Dairil III rock shard across the desk, and asked about his rates. It didn't quite add up, but hey, he wasn't going to pass up a fat fee just because it didn't feel perfect.

The problem was that he was still no closer to understanding how or why the disappearance had happened in the first place. If his special intuition gave him nothing more concrete, he was going to lose everything but the small retainer Outreach Industries had paid directly into his account. He'd been running close to the edge for some time, and if he blew this one things were going to get really tight, and soon. Now he had less than a week to come up with something he could give Outreach.

Just perfect.

TWO

The traces of Jack's talent had originally appeared during his stint in the military. He had *known* things. And then the dreams had started. He hadn't confided in anyone, but people had started to pay attention. Stein was lucky. It was a good thing to be on assignment with Stein. Witchy Stein, they'd called him. It had made him popular, but that popularity was superficial. His knack for being in the right place at the right time eventually earned him his stint in Intelligence. After a while the regimentation and the shadow plays stuck in his throat and he'd sought a way out. He'd fought long and hard for his escape, but finally they'd let him go. It hadn't been easy.

His time in the shadow world had earned him a few contacts. Not everyone stayed in the game, and there were others, like him, who'd bought or bargained their way out. Most ended on the fringes of legitimate society—a population of spooks and ghouls, each carrying a dubious past. He was just another spook among the ghouls.

Jack sat at his desk, feet crossed before him, chewing over multiple possibilities. He'd been scanning lists for the last half hour, his handipad nestled on one thigh, seeking a trigger. Index after index scrolled past, heading after fruitless heading chipping away at his hope of finding something useful.

An hour spent studying his hastily sketched notes from the dream had failed to provide the link. Snakes. What did snakes have to do with anything? It made no sense. Nor did the severed hand. Usually he could rely on something more clear-cut from the dream state. He thumbed off the handipad and tossed it onto the desk. He needed to get out and freshen his head. The stark environment of his office was fine for work, but its emptiness was a constant reminder of the wasteland his life had become over the past couple of years. A trip up to New—a recreational excursion—would do him good. The clean, open spaces of New and the café society that made the district their own always managed to lighten his mood, even if it was only to laugh at the shallowness of the freaks and designer wannabes that hung out there.

He dragged his feet off the desk and pocketed the handipad.

Who was he to laugh at shallowness anyway?

Once outside his door, he muttered a command to lock up. Working in Old had its advantages, but there were disadvantages too, and he had some pretty expensive equipment in there—equipment he could ill afford to replace right now.

Down on the avenue, he peered at the shuttle schedule crawling up the marker pole. Five minutes. He'd have to change at Mid Central for the Newbound shuttle, but it would take much longer to walk. Connections were usually pretty good up at Mid Central. They seemed to coordinate the departures pretty well with the arrivals from Old. He gazed up at the far-above ceiling to kill time. The boys in Scenics were running a sunny day. Light, fluffy clouds scudded over the ceiling panels a hundred meters above him. It was just as well. Outside, through the scattered roof windows the day looked cloudy and dark.

Outside. He couldn't remember the last time he'd been outside. Away from the regulated protection of the Locality. Two, three years ago? It was just as easy to forget there *was* an outside sometimes.

An advertising drone bumped against the side of his leg and he pushed it away with his foot, frowning his annoyance. They weren't supposed to make physical contact. This one was covered in graffiti and bore a deep dent on the top of its domed head where someone had clearly taken a swipe at it. Probably screwed its guidance controls. It reoriented and skittered toward him again. He pushed it away. Even its slogans were unreadable. He shook his head and turned back to look for the shuttle.

Bump. The thing was pressed up against his leg again. Restraining an urge to kick it, Jack stooped and steered it into the gutter. It teetered on the edge for a moment, and then fell into the roadway, rolling around trying to right itself. Eventually it levered itself upright and homed in again. This time it collided with the gutter, once, twice, three times. Whatever guidance controls still remained finally alerted it that its way was blocked and it whirred away, scraping its sides against the gutter edge as it sought a way to remount the pavement.

Jack shook his head. You'd think the advertising sponsors would do something about it, take it in for repair or something. But this was Old. Everything in Old was disposable.

Darkness swept across the stop, and Jack glanced up. The ceiling panels were rapidly clouding over, echoing the dark sky outside. Jack grimaced. It looked like they were scheduled for rain after all. The shuttle was due any moment, but in Old you could never be sure. He was just as likely to get a soaking standing at the stop before the shuttle arrived. Sure, there were weather reports, but Jack didn't really pay attention to schedules, nor to the mindless bulletins that permeated the Locality's vid network. The people in Locality Operations liked to throw in a few surprises anyway, probably in an effort to simulate the outside world, make them all forget that they were living in an enclosed and programmed environment.

The first warm drops were just starting to spatter on the roadway when the shuttle hissed to a stop in front of him. The doors slid open and he ducked inside. Jack found himself a seat where he could watch the door and hunched himself into a corner. The car was empty. Graffiti covered the walls and seats. Wrappers and bits of food littered the floor. Nothing new there. He smiled wryly to himself. Yeah, nothing New at all. The car would be cleaned once it reached Mid Central and before it resumed the return journey to the tail end of Old, but by the time it returned, it would be in exactly the same state. The shuttles up at the other end of the Locality, in New, were completely different. They were untouched by any passage through the districts of decay.

The car lurched as the shuttle took off, and Jack settled himself back for the ride. He let his gaze rove over the advertising displays scrolling along the tops of the walls, reading but not reading them, letting them filter past his awareness. *Jack Stein, what the hell are you doing with your life?* No, he didn't want to think about that. He had other, more immediate questions to worry about. Snakes. Rings. Severed hands. What was the connection?

The shuttle slowed and the doors hissed open. A man stepped into the car, looked over at Jack warily, then sat in a seat diagonally opposite, right up against the other end of the car. The doors hissed shut and the shuttle started rolling again.

The suspicious look was not unusual this far down in Old. Crime was sporadic, but it existed all the same, and enforcement at the lesser ends of the Locality was less than efficient. But the man appeared to have decided Jack was no immediate threat and he relaxed, staring blankly at the opposite wall.

Jack studied him, taking care not to be seen looking. The man was short, stocky. His dark, receding hair was neatly sculpted and he wore it close to his head. His long coat had the shimmer of expensive fabric, augmented somehow. He perched awkwardly on the edge of his seat as if uncomfortable being there. He stared fixedly in front of him as if afraid of making the contact that a casual glance might provide. He was clearly not your usual denizen of Old or even lower Mid. Jack watched the man, wondering what he might have been doing down here. It could be anything. It could be anything slightly dubious. You could find all sorts of things in Old, if you were willing to pay for them, and this guy looked like he could afford it.

The shuttle slowed and the doors slid open. Jack's fellow passenger looked up with a start, then returned to looking at the opposite wall, but not before casting a lingering glance in Jack's direction. There was something sleazy, tainted, about the look, as if he were sharing a secret. Jack sniffed and looked away. The shuttle got under way again and Jack finally lost interest. He really didn't want to know, he decided. Instead he turned to half watching the passing buildings and people that wandered outside the window, and returned to playing with the connections in his head.

Five stops later the man got out. Jack watched him as he pulled the shimmering coat tight around himself and scurried off down the street, clearly eager to be away. They were about a couple of stops down from the true fringes of Mid, still more or less in Old. What business did a man like him really have down here?

A couple of other passengers came and went on the journey to Mid Central, and Jack huddled into his corner watching them, playing the game with himself he always did on the shuttle. Were there any special characteristics? Were there any clues to who they might be or what they might do? Observation was important, and it didn't hurt to keep in practice in his line of work. Besides, it helped to fill the time. When the shuttle reached his stop he stepped out with two others, looking across the stops to see if his connecting shuttle was due. The ceiling had returned to sunny day—a relief. He watched his shuttle curve off into the siding tunnel, then crossed to where he could board the shuttle for New.

He had only moments to wait. The connections really were good at Mid Central. Sometimes he wondered how they coordinated it without letting the New-bound timetable get out of synch. The Newbound shuttle he boarded was pristine in comparison to the one he'd just left, and he joined it with a number of commuters, heading up to offices or business meetings. Plenty to watch. He managed to snag himself a corner seat before anyone else and propped himself against the partition. Nobody gave him a second glance. He immersed himself in his thoughts, pretending to ignore the others.

The Outreach contract was a gem. It was important that he start to make some real progress. If he didn't get something for them soon, they'd start to get worried that he was wasting their time and money. Jobs like this one were few and far between, and if he played it right, it could make his reputation. He just couldn't afford to blow it. Screw something up for someone like Outreach and everyone who mattered would hear about it. Feeling eyes upon him, he glanced up. He made a face at the old woman across the aisle who was staring at him and she looked quickly away.

The shuttle pulled in to a stop. A few got out, but more piled in. They were standing in the aisle now, and Jack crept back further into his seat. He scanned the legs and shoes. Definitely better quality than what you'd see on Oldbound. The clothing was better, newer too. Two stops farther on and the crowd thinned a little. They'd just passed the stop for the Central Reservation, a vast open space covered in grass and trees, centered by a large lake. Families, kids, they'd all be there soaking up the greenery and the natural light from the transparent ceiling panels positioned above the recreational space. They could probably get the same thing if they ever took the trouble to go outside, but why should they bother? Here, inside their protected environment, everything was regulated, safe. They pretty much knew when it was going to rain or the exact wind speed, and there would be the occasional burst of entertainment from the fringe panels to keep the kids entertained. All just perfect.

Maybe it was a mistake coming up to New. Watching these people, seeing their regulated, ordered, safe lives, just put him in a bad mood. When it came down to it, he was escaping here in the Locality. Ultimately he was no different from any of them. He just played it a different way. Anyway, being up here was just a neat way of avoiding the inevitable set of answers he had to find—classic displacement.

Jack left the shuttle right in the heart of New. The sunny day had been replaced by an aerial display. Sleek fliers swooped and rolled on the ceiling panels above against a background of clear blue sky, leaving vapor trails in their wake, crisscrossing white against the immaculate pale blue glow. He stood at the shuttle stop watching the show with a few other passersby for several minutes before heading off.

Everything in New had the sharp-edged definition of recent construction. Office buildings rose shiny about him, with colored logos and messages climbing the walls and dancing across the surfaces. The buildings were decked in tasteful hues, one coordinated to the other, none of them clashing, designed to provide the optimal psychological environment. Advertising drones skimmed the groundspace, avoiding the legs and feet of passersby. One or two gave bursts of music as they passed, familiar catchy phrases meant to snag the attention. Jack just stood, soaking up the atmosphere. Everywhere was movement and activity. Maybe it hadn't been a mistake coming up here after all.

He picked a direction at random and headed down

a terra-cotta side street. The street led to a wide, open square. A tall sculpture stood at the square's center, flowing and realigning its surface, constantly reshaping itself with pleasing curves, painted in liquid gunmetal. Benches and seats lay at various points, some of them occupied by people talking to each other, or simply sitting back and watching the sculpture. Above, the clear ceiling panel, free of displays, allowed natural light to filter down. The place was empty of the ever-present drones. Such squares, scattered over the length of New, operated as an exclusion zone for advertising. Ambience, environment—that was what it was all about.

Jack spotted a café over on the other side and headed across. Finding a seat with a good view of the square's occupants, he watched the sculpture's soothing lines for a while, then turned to the people clustered in ones and twos around the open space. His attention fell on a young couple, absorbed in each other's company, and he felt a slight pang of something hollow. He'd never been good at relationships, but it didn't mean he didn't miss them—the comfort, the security.

He screwed up his face and shook the thought away. What did he want with comfort and security? He took a few moments keying in his order and waited for the drink to arrive before slipping out his handipad and placing it on the table before him. He prodded it with his finger, pushing it randomly across the table surface. A sip. A push. Another sip. Then he opened the device and thumbed it into life. He was supposed to be up here relaxing, clearing his head, but he knew he just couldn't leave it alone.

A few keys and there on the screen was the miniature image of the mine. Company investigators had gone in and taken vids, compiling the evidence. Jack watched the shaky images for a few minutes until they drew close to the mine entrance. This time the lights were on, and the familiar mine shaft opened up bathed in light. Crazy shadows stuttered across the shaft walls and Jack felt the postdream chill rising in his gorge. He flipped off the pad and shoved it deep into his pocket.

Jack finished his coffee in one swallow, stood, and left the square. He wanted a meeting with Outreach. He needed a meeting with Outreach. Warburg had to give him something else. The man wasn't telling him everything. Jack could feel it deep in his guts. The mine fragment, the vid, they were starting points, but if Warburg wanted results, he was just going to have to come up with something more.

Three

Jack sat back in a comfortable leather chair and watched the corporate executive across from him, waiting for him to speak. He wanted to see which way Warburg would take this. Try as he might, he couldn't get rid of the feeling that the man was playing him somehow.

"So, Stein. Have you got something for us?" Warburg sat comfortably in his chair, seemingly at ease, virtually in the same position, as if he simply hadn't moved since the last time they'd met.

William Warburg was approaching late middle age. He wore his corporate tan in the same way he wore his designer button-down suit: smoothly. Everything about the man was smooth: the office designed to maximize the positive energies; the comfortable chairs arrayed around the low circular table; the way he sat back in his chair, legs neatly crossed, without the hint of a wrinkle in the suit; the soothing subliminals flickering in the wall behind him. He tilted his head forward a fraction, waiting for Jack's reply.

"Mr. Warburg." Jack continued looking across at his client, observing the man's unreadable face before continuing. "I've made some headway. The sample you provided has yielded some results, but I'm afraid it's not enough."

A slight frown flickered across Warburg's brow, but he quickly regained his composure. "How so?"

"Well, it's provided me with some cues for the stuff I do, but I think that there's something you're not telling me. If I'm going to find out what happened to your crew, you need to tell me everything."

Warburg narrowed his eyes. "Look, Stein, if you want me to do your job for you—"

"No, wait." Jack lifted a hand to still the protest. "You don't have to tell me anything that might compromise your company security. I just want to ask you a couple of questions based on what I know so far. You want me to help you, you're going to have to help me."

Warburg pressed his lips together and sat back. "All right. Proceed."

"First, I need to know if there are any other interests involved on Dairil III."

"I thought that's what we'd employed you for, Stein. Is there a point to this?"

"Yes to both. If you suspect outside involvement, I need to know."

"Of *course* we suspect outside involvement."

"Well, then. Who else has interests on Dairil III?"

Warburg gave a long sigh. "If we knew that, what need would we have of your services?"

This was getting nowhere fast. Jack decided to try another tack. "What can you tell me about a design, a logo, a corporate symbol, anything like that—a snake biting its own tail? Does that mean anything to you?"

Warburg's frown got deeper, but Jack thought he detected the barest flicker in the man's eyes.

"Nothing," said Warburg. "Should it? Look, I don't see where this is leading. Why should some symbol, some archaic mystical sign, have anything to do with our crew's disappearance? We deal in hard facts and science, Stein. Our investigators turned up nothing at the site. That's why we brought you in."

"All right. You say your investigators turned up nothing. What about the structure of the mine itself? The walls. Had there been a breach of the mine walls?"

"No. Nothing like that. You've had access to the vids. If you're suggesting a cave-in or something similar, you're wasting my time. Don't you think we'd considered that possibility?"

Warburg's message was clear: He was rapidly losing patience. Warburg sighed again and then continued. "We've already looked at the logical solutions, Mr. Stein. We're left, therefore, with the illogical." He looked pointedly at Jack before continuing. "So is there anything else?"

"Okay, Mr. Warburg. No, there's nothing else. I won't take up any more of your time."

"Good," said Warburg, standing. "You can find your own way out. And I trust that we can expect something a little more concrete by the end of the week."

"Oh, there is one more thing. . . ."

"Yes. What is it?"

"Can you provide me with the personnel records of the missing crew?"

"Yes, I can't see why not. I'm a little surprised you didn't ask for them earlier. See my executive assistant on the way out. He'll arrange it."

Jack nodded, inwardly cursing himself as he left Warburg's office. The man was right. He hadn't done his groundwork properly. The name of Outreach had lured him in and he'd rushed into it, eager to be the first kid on the block with a contract from the big boys. First things first. He had to learn not to rely so much on things just falling into place.

Still, Warburg had told him more than he expected. His familiarity with the Ouroboros, the slight flicker of his eyes. There was something there. "Some symbol, some archaic mystical sign," had been the words that came so readily to the man's lips. It suggested more than just a passing familiarity. Jack's gut feelings were starting to work overtime.

He asked Warburg's assistant for the records, and the man led him down to another office, this time characterless and unadorned with the trappings of good corporate taste, then left him with a pudgy administrative clerk.

"The Dairil III crew? Certainly. No problem. If you can bear with me for a few minutes, I'll just upload them to a card for you, once I find them."

The man busied himself with a screen.

"Ah, here we are." He pulled out a card from a nearby stack and slotted it into a recess.

"You're investigating the disappearance. There's no point, you know," he said quietly, without lifting his gaze from the screen.

"What do you mean?" said Jack.

"There's no point. You won't find anything."

"Maybe. Maybe not."

"There's no 'maybe,'" said the clerk. "They don't expect you to find anything."

"What do you mean?"

The clerk glanced around behind Jack, then motioned him closer. "I can't talk here. Somewhere we can meet? Tonight?"

Jack fished in his pocket for his own card, but the clerk waved his hand. "No, no cards."

"All right," said Jack. He debated with himself for a moment, then dismissed his office. Somebody might be keeping tabs on it. "My apartment? Mid seventeen. Four-three-six-nine."

The clerk nodded, then spoke more loudly. "Here you are, Mr. Stein." He handed him the data card. "I think this contains everything you need."

"Thanks," said Jack, pocketing the card. He leaned closer. "But what—?"

The clerk frowned and shook his head. "Later," he whispered, then spoke in a normal voice. "If you just follow the corridor up to the right, that will take you to reception. Good-bye, Mr. Stein. If you need anything else, you can get in touch via Mr. Warburg's executive assistant. Just ask for Gleeson. That's me."

"Um, thanks," said Jack, waiting for something else, but Gleeson had already returned to whatever he was doing.

Jack fingered the data card in his pocket as he walked up the hallway, thinking. So it seemed that Outreach really was playing him. But why? Why would they want to do that? And yet somehow the clerk, Gleeson, had been almost too convenient. He chewed at the inside of his bottom lip.

He'd just have to wait until the evening to find out.

He boarded the shuttle along with a group of commuters, all leaving for home from one of the staggered shifts that operated throughout New. He shouldered his way past a group in conversation and settled into a corner seat in his usual favorite spot. He was only half watching the crowd; there was too much on his mind right now.

It had to be more than just luck that the particular clerk—Gleeson, he'd said his name was—should happen to be on duty at the very time Jack showed up to ask for the records. Just too convenient . . . for Jack. And yet Warburg had seemed to want to get rid of him as quickly as he could. But he hadn't missed a beat when Jack had asked for the personnel files. Normally companies were a little more sensitive about employee records. Maybe there was something to what the clerk had been saying. And the whole Ouroboros thing . . .

Just as the shuttle's doors were about to close, someone forced their way between the closing doors. Jack caught the movement from the corner of his eye. There was nothing unusual about it; people did it all the time, but something about the man seemed familiar in the brief glance he'd snatched between the crowded bodies—something that snagged at his memory, and from not too long ago. Well-cut clothes, finely sculpted hair. He strained, trying to catch a glimpse between rocking people as the shuttle passed stop after stop. People boarded. People left. Still he failed to catch proper sight of whoever it was. By the time the shuttle had cleared somewhat, there was no sign of whoever it had been.

"Get a grip, Jack," he muttered to himself. Now he was finding things where there was nothing to find. He settled back in his seat and closed his eyes, running the tips of his fingers over the smooth-edged data card that sat in his pocket.

"Jack! Jack Stein!"

Jack's eyes snapped open. The shuttle had just

drawn out from the stop and a tall, emaciated figure was loping down the car toward him. Hollow cheeks and a sallow expression heightened his corpselike appearance. A loose gray coat hung from his bony frame, and his big tombstone teeth were grinning as he bore down on Jack's corner seat. Others in the car frowned or looked away uncomfortably as the man passed them. It was no wonder; he bore an almost palpable aura of the unclean. Pinpin Dan—the last person Jack had expected to run into.

Pinpin Dan was another fringe dweller. He had talents for getting into places that people didn't want others to have access to. That made him popular in certain sectors of the Locality. They'd worked together once or twice when Jack had had need of the man's unique talents.

Jack nodded as Pinpin Dan collapsed into a heap of bones onto the seat next to him.

"So what are you doing up in New, Jack? Slumming it, eh?" Pinpin grinned a feral grin and gave a donkey's bray of a laugh.

It was not only Pinpin's profession that kept him on the fringes. His personal habits and predilections left a lot to be desired.

"Yeah, you could say that."

"Or are we up here wooorking?" He drew the last word out, loading it with special significance, and tapped the side of his nose, looking at Jack knowingly. Lank strands of graying hair plastered to the top of his head barely disguised his mottled scalp. He slumped back into the seat and scanned the other passengers. "So which one is it?" he whispered. "Who's the subject?"

"No, nothing like that, Pinpin. I just came up here to get a bit of headspace."

"Yes, yes, yes. All right. Be serious with me, dear Jack. You never did have much of a sense of humor. So *are* you wooorking?"

"I've got a couple of things happening."

"Good, good. Good to hear that you're gainfully employed. And before you ask, you know me—Pinpin Dan never wants for work. So, enough of that. I'm trying to remember when was the last time I had the pleasure of your company. How long has it been? It was . . ." He held up long spatulate fingers and started counting. "Ah, never mind. Too long, dear boy. Too long." He grinned.

He scratched at his bony chest and peered around the car, giving a sniff. Jack watched him sidelong. Not only had he forgotten about Pinpin Dan, he'd forgotten how much he disliked the man. Probably why he'd never thought to ask how and when he'd acquired his peculiar name. Also probably why he was reluctant to ask what he was doing here. He'd likely been cruising the park, looking for— No, Jack didn't want to know that. He narrowed his eyes, watching as Pinpin Dan unashamedly scrutinized their fellow passengers, each in turn.

Licking his lips, Pinpin Dan became bored with the car's occupants and turned his attention back to Jack.

"You must come and visit," he said. "Come and see my sumptuous new accommodations. I've moved on since last I had the pleasure of your company." He leered. "It really has been far too long, Jack. I have fond memories of the times we worked together. Now, wait just a minute. Here." He dug around in his coat and slipped Jack an iridescent card. Jack turned it in his fingers, watching the way the light sent shattered colors over the card's surface. "All the details are there. The card's readable too. No need to copy things down. So handy."

Jack slipped the card away. He'd noted the address as he did so—somewhere up in the midrange section of New. Pinpin Dan was moving up in the world. Somehow Jack found the idea distasteful. Pinpin leaned closer.

"So, really," he said into Jack's ear. "You can tell me what you're working on. I'm always *very* interested in what you're up to, Jack."

Jack drew back from the hot, fragrant breath in his ear and shook his head. "Not right now," he said.

"Ahhh. You always did keep things close to your chest, Jack." The shuttle slowed and Pinpin glanced up. "Here's my stop anyway."

Pinpin leaned over to grasp Jack's shoulder as he stood, then leaned close. "Now, you come and see me, Jack. Catch up on old times." He grinned again, all teeth, tainted breath whispering in Jack's face, then loped off down the car. Jack closed his eyes, waiting till the shuttle had pulled out of the stop before opening them again.

Pinpin Dan. Visit Pinpin Dan? Not bloody likely. He fingered the hard edges of the card in his pocket.

It was peculiar running into Pinpin Dan after so long. He did the sums himself. It was well over a year since the last time he'd seen him. He scratched his chin thoughtfully. Things didn't happen by chance to Jack Stein. Coincidence was always loaded. Events seemed to coalesce around Jack, pushing him in directions he hadn't expected. People, places, chance happenings, all worked together to keep him alive and lucky.

There'd been that time out on maneuvers when he'd twisted his ankle on a rock where no rock should be. The rest of the squad had gone on, leaving him sitting, cursing his own stupidity. Three minutes later the point man, the one who had taken over from Jack, stepped on a mine, taking out half of the squad. After that he'd been more aware of the sorts of coincidences that happened around Jack Stein. A chance meeting was invariably more than simple chance.

He'd be in a bar just at the right time to overhear a conversation. He'd run into someone who would point him to someone else who just happened to be the key to solving a particular set of problems. The thing was, it always happened to Jack, not anyone else. Then, as he became more aware, he started noticing patterns in his dreams. At first he thought he was imagining things, the old déjà vu syndrome, but slowly, somewhat reluctantly, he realized that it was more than that, that he was somehow different. He told no one about his dreams, but people started to notice his peculiar prescience. Of course he denied it, even to himself at first, until he could do so no longer, but things stacked up. Then he'd started to pay attention to the strange, uncomfortable feelings that worked deep in his guts, warning him that something wasn't right.

No, things didn't happen to Jack by chance. So why Pinpin Dan? He tugged at his bottom lip as he considered. None of the possibilities was very attractive. Not a single one of them.

Four

"I want your girlfriend," said the White-Haired Man.
Jack looked up at the escarpment where the figure stood. The man was tall, thin, angular, the long white hair forming a nimbus around his high-cheekboned face. Behind him sat a structure, like a hut, cobbled together from iron girders and bits of old railway track. It hunched like a brown-and-gray beetle, partially obscured by the man's body. Funny that there should be railway track. The railways didn't run anymore, hadn't for years.

"But I don't have a girlfriend," said Jack.

The wind stirred the man's long brown coat around his boot-sheathed calves. He narrowed his eyes. "Where is she?" he said.

Jack swallowed. "I've already told you. I don't have a girlfriend."

The man's eyes held a glint of hardness. There was something *wrong* about the eyes, but try as he might, Jack couldn't work out what it was. The man waved his hand and slowly the ground beneath Jack's feet trembled and rose. Jack thrust his arms out to retain balance.

The man was grinning now as Jack rose toward him, a slight, sinister grin.

"No!" said Jack, fighting against the chill in his chest.

He pushed himself away from the figure, willing himself awake. *This is a dream*, he told himself. *It has to be.*

He forced himself up through the layers of consciousness, floating. The White-Haired Man's face became less distinct, dissipating in the ether.

"I will find her," said the man.

And Jack woke, the last words echoing inside his head.

He'd dozed off after scanning the personnel records for what had seemed like hours. It was bad enough that he did this stuff for a living without his subconscious throwing things at him from a tangent. The dream had nothing to do with what he was working on. At least, he didn't think it did. He pressed his lips tightly together. He didn't need this.

He looked down at the handipad on the low table in front of him. The personnel records still sat open. He'd gotten maybe two-thirds of the way through them, and there was nothing to trigger a connection. Even the names Johnson and Mitch had been constructs of his mind, populating the second-sight dream with shreds of familiarity. Nothing to go on there. All he was left with were the snakes. He slotted the card back out of the handipad and, holding the small, flexible sliver up to the light, turned it around and around in his fingers, as if he could see through the mysteries it contained to some sort of truth buried deep within.

* * *

When his visitor arrived, Jack had progressed no further. He was still playing with data cards, sliding them one over the other and watching the colors while he thought. The two cards had been delivered in the space of a couple of hours, one Pinpin Dan's, the other containing the personnel records of the Dairil III mining crew. Separate, unconnected incidences. But nothing in Jack Stein's life was unconnected. There was always a trailing network of threads. All he had to do was tie them together.

The personnel records had told him little. Each of the missing crew had a good share of shady history, lists of trouble, and close scrapes with the company— just the sort to be attracted to a far-flung mining operation where the pay was reasonably good and they were out from under the watchful scrutiny of company authority. Not one of the crew had any past connection to underground organizations or fringe political groups, as far as he could see. Their past records of employment were a checkerboard of short-hop contracts and drifting from company to company. Jack wouldn't really have expected anything more. He slotted the data card back in and started scanning the records one more time.

"Visitor," said the wall, interrupting his concentration.

"Who?" said Jack, thumbing off the handipad and sliding the data cards back into his pocket and out of sight. He wasn't expecting anyone, apart from the little clerk from Outreach, but it paid to be sure. The wall lost its drab tones as colors bled onto its surface, painting a picture of a short, rotund man standing outside his door, shifting nervously and checking the corridors to either side. It was Gleeson, all right.

"Let him in," said Jack, then called out, "I'm through here."

Gleeson entered the room just as his simulacrum faded from the wall. Jack waved him in the direction of a chair.

"So what is it you have to tell me, Mr. Gleeson? And let's face it, I can't go on calling you Mr. Gleeson. Have you got another name?"

Gleeson took a seat and licked his lips nervously before speaking. "Um, Francis," he said.

"So, Frank," said Jack.

"No . . . *Francis*," said Gleeson. He scanned the walls, hesitating.

"Francis, then. Look, there's nothing to worry about. This place is as secure as anywhere else. You can talk. You seemed pretty sure you had some information for me when we last spoke. So let's stop playing games. What is it you were so eager to tell me?"

"Have you had a chance to look through the personnel records?"

Jack nodded, restraining the urge to lift his hand and feel for the card in his pocket.

"Gilbert Ronschke?"

The name had been one on the list. "Yes, what about him? I didn't see anything particularly interesting, anything particularly special about him. Should I have?"

Gleeson hesitated again. "But Gil was . . . is special. It was supposed to have been Gil's last contract. He had enough put away to start his own—"

Jack cut him off. "What are you saying, Francis?"

"You see, it's just that Gil is a friend of mine. A very close friend."

Jack looked across at the little man and considered. "I see."

Gleeson chewed at his lip and wrung his hands. Either he was hamming it up, or the little man really was worried. "Gil was supposed to be home by now. You see a lot in administration, Mr. Stein. Particularly at a company like Outreach. A lot you're not necessarily supposed to see. I asked my own questions, made my own inquiries, and found nothing. And I'm from *inside* the company. It's impossible. You've got to help me, Mr. Stein."

"But Francis, the company's employed me to do exactly that—to find out what's happened to the crew. Why would you need to come to me? I'm sure the results of my report will be made available to those who need to know."

"You don't understand. It's like a wall of silence has been drawn over the whole thing. There was a previous investigation, but whatever they found out has been hushed up. They're even trying to pretend that the investigators found absolutely nothing. Now there's pressure—pressure from outside and from inside the company to give a proper accounting, but I believe there are those within the company who don't want anyone to find out what really happened. I believe you've been hired to give such an accounting, one that won't lead anywhere, one that's inconclusive, but that will stand up to scrutiny. I also believe there are individuals within the company who know precisely what did happen out there and not only are behind it, but are behind the attempts to keep it quiet."

Jack sat back. Something uncomfortable was working in his guts again. If what Gleeson said was true, than his sense of being played by Warburg was closer than he had first suspected. But so far he had nothing tangible to support the feeling, nothing more than the squirming feeling and Gleeson's statement. Psychic investigation was fairly fringe, but it had earned itself some credibility over the last few years. They simply couldn't believe that Jack would fail to find anything.

"So," he said, "if there's been an investigation, what's happened to the report?"

Gleeson sighed. "Nothing. I've looked, but I've found nothing. And you have to understand . . . my position . . . if I were to ask too many questions . . ."

"Tell you what, Francis. If what you say is true about why I was hired, then I want to do some finding out of my own. I don't particularly like being taken for a fool."

"But what can *you* do that no one else can?"

"Let me worry about that. I'm going to help you, but first I'm going to have to ask you for a little bit of help too."

Gleeson gave him a puzzled look. "What can I do?"

"You say you and this Gilbert Ronschke are close friends."

Gleeson paused and looked back down at his hands. "More than friends," he said quietly.

"Then you might have something of his that you can lend me."

Gleeson looked up. "I don't see what—"

"Part of what I do is use the images prompted by physical objects to provide clues to whatever it is I'm investigating, but I need actual physical contact with these things. Things, objects, gather the energies of the people who own them or use them, kind of like a personal imprint. I can do things with those energies, use them to guide me. Sometimes it's a direct insight, or sometimes it will be a series of clues that appear in a dream. Sometimes it just prompts my instincts. All I need is something small. Something Gil felt an attachment to."

Gleeson thought for a moment. "Yes, perhaps there is something."

"It can be anything, a treasured article of clothing, a holo, a piece of jewelry, anything like that."

"Yes, I'm sure I can find something. And I should bring it here to you?"

"No. I'd rather come to your place, if that's where it is. It will help me get more of a feel. Those energies can be found in people's homes too." Unfortunately, Jack had little control over the way those impressions would manifest themselves. He waited for some sort of reaction. If Gleeson was prepared to play along, then there might be some legitimacy to his claims.

Gleeson stood and started to walk around the room, touching objects, peering into the shelves. "I still don't see what you can do," he said, almost inaudibly. There was a defeated slump to the man's shoulders. He was chewing at one thumbnail.

"I know some of it may be hard for you to believe, but you're just going to have to trust me for the time being," Jack said.

Gleeson just stood where he was.

Jack continued. "There's something else you can do for me as well."

Gleeson turned slowly. "Yes," he said, and sighed. "Anything. What is it you want? I have to know what happened."

"Answer a couple of questions."

He nodded, crossed back to the chair, and sat, still clearly ill at ease. "What do you want to know?"

Jack thumbed on his handipad and turned it so Gleeson could see. He keyed up the rough sketch of the ring symbol he'd made. "Does this mean anything to you?"

"No, nothing," said Gleeson with a quick shake of his head.

"Nothing you can remember in company records—a logo, something like that?" Another shake of the head. "Well, perhaps its name—Ouroboros. Does that mean anything to you?"

Gleeson thought for a moment. "Sorry. No, it doesn't mean anything. I could have a hunt through the records, though, see if I can come up with anything."

Jack grimaced. He'd been sure there was a link. If Gleeson was really involved and had been conducting his own investigation, then the little man would surely have come across it in his search through the records. He had one more idea.

"Yes, I think that would be useful, if you can do that. See if you can find anything in the records that's even marginally related. And, um, there's one more thing. Does the company have a research arm? Something secret they're working on?"

"Of course. Always. Doesn't every major corporation? I don't have anything to do with that area, but I can try to find out for you."

"Good, how long will you need?" Jack asked.

"Two or three days at most. I'll have to be careful about when and how I access certain records. They're fairly sensitive about those things. Usually, now, I'm pretty good at covering my tracks. It's natural for someone in my position to be accessing these records, but most of the high-level stuff is tagged. I have to be careful not to leave a pattern."

"Fine, do it. Meanwhile, can you leave me your address? I have one or two things I need to follow up in the morning, but if you can, meet me at your place about midday tomorrow."

Gleeson patted at his pockets. "I don't have a card."

Typical. A man who spent his days working with data and records had none of his own.

"That's okay. Just say your address. Record."

The round-faced administrator spoke his address in clear tones. Jack nodded. He would get his diary to parse and transfer it later.

"End record," said Jack. "Now, unless there's anything else you can remember . . ."

"There is one more thing." Gleeson was still fidgeting. He sat clasping and unclasping his hands and he looked around the room as if searching for some sort of trap.

"Well . . .?"

"It's just—" He reached inside his coat and pulled out a handipad. "—this."

"Yes? It's a handipad."

"I know what it is," Gleeson snapped at him.

Jack looked at the little man speculatively. He hadn't expected that. Everybody had his or her little surprises. Gleeson continued more calmly after taking a steadying breath. "This is Gil's, or rather, it's something he had put away. I found it in the bottom of a cupboard. He told me to look after it if anything should—"

"Was Gil involved in something?"

"I don't know. Maybe. I don't know. He just said I should take care of this."

Jack hesitated and then reached across and took the handipad. "You say this wasn't his."

"That's right. He had it shoved in the bottom of a cupboard under some old clothes. I knew it was there, though. He seemed to think it was important. Maybe you can use it to find some sort of clue as to what happened to him."

Jack flipped open the handipad and thumbed it on. Standard design. Nothing special about it. But then . . . nothing. A blank screen and then a message: *Enter password*. Who the hell passworded their handipad? Jack pursed his lips and thought. Gleeson said it wasn't Ronschke's and yet Ronschke had thought it important enough to hide, important enough to let Gleeson know about it in case something happened to him. What exactly was it that Gleeson's companion had been involved in?

"Can I hang on to this?"

"If it will help you find Gil, of course. I intended for you to have it."

"And you're sure he wasn't involved in anything, um, shall we say, suspect?"

"Look, I told you I don't know. He might have been. But if he was, I think he would have told me."

"Fine. I'll still need something personal of his, though. I really don't think this was his; I'm not feeling anything special from it."

There was always the risk that when he picked up any personal object his inner senses would be filled with impressions. What he'd told Gleeson was true. They seemed to accumulate the energies of those who owned or touched them. The longer something was in someone's possession, the stronger the images Jack received. The handipad was doing nothing, which was a little strange in itself. That blankness could happen with things that were new, or those that had been passed from owner to owner, never in one person's possession for very long.

"Yes, I already told you it wasn't his." The impatient tone was back again.

"All right, Francis. I heard you. That's all I need from you for now. I'll see you tomorrow."

Gleeson nodded and stood. As he reached the doorway, he turned. "You will find Gil, won't you, Mr. Stein?"

"I'll do what I can. Oh, there is one more thing, Francis. If I'm going to help you, you really *are* going to have to help me. The Outreach contract is about all that's keeping me going at the moment. This extra work is likely to start costing something pretty soon."

"We . . . I . . . have some funds put away." Gleeson looked as if he had swallowed something sour.

What did the man expect? That Jack was going to do this stuff for free?

"Good. I'll let you know how much I'm going to need."

Jack waited until Gleeson was well and truly out the door before settling down with the mystery handipad. He tried typing in a few logical combinations for the password, but every single one came up a blank. He thumbed it off and sat back staring at it. Why had Gleeson brought it with him? There was something not quite right about his story. One: Gleeson had said he'd always known about it, as if he'd discovered it where it was supposed to have been hidden and he was not supposed to have seen it. Two: Gilbert Ronschke had told him about it and said to look after it, yet Gleeson knew nothing more. If they were so close, surely his partner would have confided in him. Then there was the little man's aggressive tone when Jack had pushed him. And yet he'd barely pushed him at all. Clearly Gleeson wasn't quite everything he made himself out to be, but then people rarely were.

The White-Haired Man was back. Jack couldn't tell where they were; the surrounding images felt fogged, and slipped away from his perception as he reached for them. The light was blurred, as if distorted, slightly filtered, bending the surrounding images as if through smoky old glass.

"Take it," said the man.

Jack took a step back. The White-Haired Man was holding something out toward him.

"Take it," he said.

Jack stood where he was. The White-Haired Man tossed the object at Jack's feet. It was a handipad, solid, gray, standing out from the blankness around them. The man turned and strode off into the shadows.

Jack stooped and retrieved the object. He flipped it open.

"Enter password," it said in a chill voice. Swirling colors moved across the display.

"But I don't know the password."

"Enter password," it said again.

Jack's fingers wouldn't work. They were stiff, cold. He tried to key something, anything, but his fingers wouldn't obey.

The colors changed. Slowly an image formed. It was the symbol—the all-too-familiar symbol—a snake biting its own tail.

"Enter password," said the voice.

"Ouroboros," said Jack.

The colors disappeared. The symbol disappeared.

A deep vibration echoed through the landscape, and then the handipad grew. It grew larger and larger. The display expanded, swallowing his head, swallowing his body.

Jack was drawn down, down, down, inexorably into shimmering blackness.

Jack sat on the edge of his bed, rubbing his temples. Damn. That was all he needed. The White-Haired Man was clearly linked. He wouldn't keep appearing otherwise. Of course, he might not actually be a specific person, but the image was clear enough for Jack to suspect that he was. He was vaguely reminiscent of Pinpin Dan, but different. Very different. It couldn't be Pinpin Dan himself, could it? No. He didn't think so. The disparity was too evident, even in a dream.

He sat for a few moments, playing with the pictures, transposing himself as the various figures and components of the dream, an old technique he'd learned to search for hidden meaning. He saw himself as the White-Haired Man, but there was nothing there, then as the handipad itself. Neither revealed anything. No, Jack Stein was Jack Stein, in the dream and out of it.

This had never happened before, this dream overlap. His first dream about the White-Haired Man had taken place before meeting Gleeson. And this dream about the White-Haired Man was unprompted—no inducer pads, no physical object to act as a trigger. It had just occurred.

He pushed himself to his feet and went to retrieve his own handipad from the living area. Perhaps the clue was there in the vids he'd downloaded from the company records and he'd simply missed it.

His shin connected with the edge of something hard in the darkness and he crashed to the ground with a curse.

"Lights!" he spat out, massaging his leg. As he blinked against the glare, he gave the coffee table an accusing look. Stupid. In his half-awake state, he'd forgotten that he'd reprogrammed the living area during the night. Bored and frustrated, he'd rearranged the furniture, often a good displacement activity to help clear his head. The coffee table that used to live across the other side of the room had regrown itself halfway across the floor space, right in the way of where he was used to walking in the darkness of sleepless nights.

He struggled to his feet and hobbled across to the shelves. He was awake now. Pain was a good awakener. The handipad was where he'd left it, but so was the one Gleeson had left. He hesitated for a moment, then took the other one from the shelf, hobbled back to the couch, and sat. Handipad in one hand, he used the other to keep massaging his shin as he ran through last evening's meeting.

He'd told Gleeson that he had some things to attend to in the morning, but that wasn't strictly true. He'd just wanted some space to think. Too many threads were pulling from different directions. Leaving the rapidly forming bruise on his leg, he turned his attention back to the handipad. He flipped it open and thumbed it to life.

A blank screen, and then, just as before, the request to enter a password. It was too much to hope for, but he keyed in the word all the same. Nothing. Then he tried a few more—*snake, serpent*, other variants. Still nothing. He killed the handipad with a sigh and sat back. If he could locate the owner of the device, he might be able to work out how it was tied in.

There was only one sure way to get past the password without finding the owner that Jack knew, and he didn't like the thought one bit.

Pinpin Dan.

It always worked like that—a chance meeting, an unexpected occurrence—and suddenly significance attached itself to whatever had happened. Threads tying themselves one to the other, even without Jack's help. This time the web was already feeling a little too close for comfort. He just hoped Pinpin Dan wasn't the spider.

With another deep sigh and a shake of his head, Jack went to make himself some coffee, leaving the handipad where it lay.

Once he'd kick-started his brain—coffee was always good for that, high caffeine, rich and bitter, the waking ritual, rather than the stims he used for bursts of focused concentration when he was on a heavy case—he dressed hurriedly, retrieved his own handipad from where he'd left it the previous evening, and slotted Pinpin Dan's card in.

Of course, it meant that Pinpin Dan would be able to contact him on a whim at any time, but you had to take the good with the bad. As soon as the data was loaded, he flipped the card onto the coffee table, retrieved the other handipad from the couch, and shoved it deep into his pocket. He'd dispose of the card later. He keyed the sequence for contact.

Pinpin Dan's feral features floated onto the display.

"Jack. So soon, and so eeeearly? What an unexpected surprise. And of cooourse a pleasure, my boy."

Jack glanced at the wall display. It wasn't that early. "Hey, Pinpin. I need to come and see you."

"One would almost believe in the fates, dear boy. You're lucky you caught me. I have to go out for an hour or so, but I should be available after that. I see you have the address."

Jack looked at the wall display again: 8:45. An hour or so. That should give him time to get up there, maybe grab another coffee once he'd arrived, see Pinpin Dan, and still leave himself plenty of time to meet up with Gleeson.

"Yeah, fine. I'll see you at your apartment in about an hour and a half."

"I gather this is moooore than a social call, Jack."

"Uh-huh. I'll tell you about it when I see you."

"I look forward to it."

Jack killed the connection and looked around the room, trying to remember if he'd forgotten anything.

Yes, of course. He turned to the wall. "Download last recording," he said. Gleeson's address.

"Download complete."

He checked the display. Gleeson lived not too far from where Pinpin had his apartment, maybe three shuttle stops at most. That was handy. It was also another point worth noting. How come a modest Outreach clerk lived in a district like that? He filed the thought away for later.

He closed his handipad into his right pocket and patted it gently. Although the two were slightly different, he didn't want to confuse them, did he?

Five

Pinpin Dan really had come up in the world. The address led Jack to a tall, glossy apartment building at the Mid end of New. Last time he'd had cause to visit Pinpin Dan's place, he had been living in the demolition end of Old. Whatever the man was into, it was paying off. Jack looked up at the building, unable to help the sour expression that climbed across his face. There just wasn't any justice. The rainbow sky on the ceiling panels above the building did little to improve his mood.

On the tenth floor he checked the address. This was the place, all right. Thick-piled pseudo-floor had muffled his steps all along the corridor, and the place was clean, very clean. The building probably had its own still-functioning cleaning routines. This far beyond Mid, even in the New end of Mid, that wasn't a surprise. That Pinpin Dan would be in a place like this, that was the surprise. No justice. Definitely no justice.

He rang and waited.

The door opened and a youthful face peered out, short blond hair cut close around her ivory-skinned face. Wide blue eyes looked up at him. The girl must have been all of fifteen. Sweet face, but there was something hard about it too.

"Yes?"

"Jack Stein. I'm here to see Pinpin Dan."

The girl nodded and left him standing there. So Pinpin Dan's tastes had changed none. Jack pursed his lips. He could act as judge and jury, but for now, just right now, circumstance didn't permit him the luxury. One day Pinpin Dan would get what was coming to him, but it wasn't about to be today. Moments later the girl reappeared.

"This way." She stood back and let Jack enter, then walked lightly off down a wide hallway, beckoning him to follow.

Pinpin Dan's apartment was enormous. The walls were done out in plush purple, black edging at top and bottom. Thick pale gray carpet ran the length of the hall. At least six large doorways led off from the hallway, but the girl continued on, leading him all the way to the end, opened another door, and stood back, allowing Jack to enter.

Pinpin Dan sprawled across a large white couch in the room's center. Before him sat a wide, low table, two tall Oriental vases filled with ostentatious dried flower arrangements almost masking him from view. In the table's center stood a sculpture—two naked boys writhing together, their lean, muscled bodies slick and shiny, catching the light as they moved. Jack dragged his gaze away from the piece and back to Pinpin.

"So, Jack, dear boy. Welcome. Welcome. You found me all right. What do you think of the new accommodations?" he brayed as he waved his hand about the room.

"Yes, Pinpin. Very nice, I'm sure, but I'm really not here to discuss your decor."

"Oh, dear Jack. I'm hurt. Always sooo serious. Such a shame. Now, I see you've already met Wilhelmina, or Billie, as she prefers to be called. Can't stand abbreviated names myself, but there's no telling her." He sighed. "Nonetheless, Wilhelmina, will you see to some tea, please?" The girl nodded and slipped out of the room. "She shows promise, that one," said Pinpin, watching her lithe, slim frame as she disappeared up the hallway. "Bright, so very bright. And a real talent for the wooork."

Jack didn't really want to think about what other talents Wilhelmina might have.

"So, now. Find yourself a spot to sit and we can discuss what it is you've come to see me about."

Jack found a thick-padded armchair to one side, where he had an unobscured view of Pinpin and could avoid looking at the mobile sculpture. The damn thing was too distracting.

"This," he said, and slid the handipad across the table.

Pinpin leaned forward and retrieved the device, turning it over and over in his bony fingers. "What's the problem?" he said, suddenly all businesslike.

"Passworded. I need to get into it."

"Hmm. Not yours, I presume."

"No, but I need to find out whose."

Pinpin flipped it open and thumbed it into life. "Yes, I see." He poked at the keys, concentrating. "And how did you come by it? Or should I not ask?"

"Unimportant. How long will you need?"

"Oh, no more than an hour or so. Getting into it

won't be the problem. Finding out who it belongs to may be a little more difficult."

He was interrupted by the reappearance of Wilhelmina, carrying a tray with two steaming Oriental-designed cups. She placed one in front of each of them, then stood back holding the tray in front of her.

"Wilhelmina, thank you. Now go and find something to do." The girl nodded again and left them. Pinpin followed her longingly with his gaze. "Now where weeere we?" he said, half-distracted, finally returning his attention to the device. The scent of fragrant tea drifted up from the cups, almost too sweet.

"Yes, it may be a little more difficult to locate the owner, but normally I would expect the handipad to be linked to the home system. I can trace the connection, if one exists. Otherwise there may be some clue in the contents. Of course, I'm not promising anything, but I think I might be able to do something. You know me, Jack."

"I'd appreciate it."

"We'll work out exactly how much you appreciate it later," said Pinpin, glancing up, a calculating look in his eye.

"Oh, and about the contents . . . I'd appreciate not having them appear on the open market anytime soon, if there's anything there."

Pinpin sighed. "Yes. All right. Soooo untrusting, dear boy. But for now, tell me what this is all about, Jack. The fact that you've come across a locked handipad, however you happened to come by it, intrigues me slightly."

"You know better than that," said Jack flatly.

Pinpin grinned. "No harm in trying, Jack. Now, is

there?" He lifted his cup and sipped delicately before placing it down. "When do you want it?"

"I have something to do not far from here. Should take me no more than a couple of hours. I can call in on the way back. I'm in a bit of a hurry on this one."

"Fine, Jack. Fine. Leave it with me. I'm sure that how much of a hurry you're in will be reflected in our later discussions." Pinpin placed the handipad carefully back down on the table and looked at it thoughtfully. "Wilhelmina, my dear," he called. "Show Jack out for me; then come back in here. We have some wooork to do."

The girl reappeared and led Jack up the hallway, leaving Pinpin Dan poring over the device in front of him. Pinpin had gone into work mode. Jack had seen that look of concentration before.

"'Bye," said the girl at the doorway.

"Good-bye," said Jack. He thought about saying something else, wondered briefly about what words he might use, but decided against it. There was nothing he really could say.

Gleeson's apartment building was far more modest than Pinpin Dan's, but still in the good end of the district. There were no signs of the powdery, flaky look that buildings got as they crept toward the high end of Old, and the inside was still clean, untarnished. The nearer things got to the demolition end of Old, the place where the Locality's structure consumed them back into the never-ending cycle, the first traces of age and decay started showing. Smooth outer surfaces lost their color, faded. If you brushed against them, a fine dust adhered to your hands and clothes. Metallic surfaces grew smudged and stained. There was none of that here. Not like his own place. Jack made his way to the door, rang, and waited. Moments later the little clerk ushered him in nervously.

"I haven't got long," Gleeson said. "What can I show you?"

"Have you come up with anything yet?" Jack asked, standing just inside the doorway, trying to get an impression of the apartment. Usually he could sense something from a place, but this time the area was uncharacteristically devoid of any impressions. It was almost as if there hadn't really been anyone there for some length of time.

"No, no. Not yet. I told you it wasn't that easy. I have to be careful."

"Yes, of course." Jack would have thought Gleeson's eagerness to find out what had happened to his partner might prompt him into action by now. It appeared that Gleeson was more cautious than he'd thought. Either that, or the perceived danger was more real than Jack had suspected.

"Did you share this place with Gilbert?" he asked. "I mean, did Gilbert live here for any length of time?"

"Oh, yes. Between contracts. He'd always have several months back before he went out again. Would you like to see his room? He uses it as his office, or just when he wants some space."

"Lead the way."

Gleeson led him to a modestly appointed room, nothing out of the ordinary. A bed, furniture integral to the walls and floors. There were no bright colors, nothing obtrusive. If anything it felt unlived in, like the apartment. It could nearly be a room ready for someone to move in. That might make sense, though, if Ronschke was in residence only between assignments.

Jack had no idea how much time the miner might actually spend in here, even if he was back for months at a time.

A shelf unit held various objects laid out in neat lines. "What are those?" asked Jack, pointing to them.

"Souvenirs, mainly. Gil used to bring back something from each place he worked." He moved closer to the shelf and touched his finger to one or two of the objects, shards of rock, a crystal, a piece of pottery. "I can tell you about them, if you want."

"No, that won't be necessary. In fact, I'd prefer it if you didn't."

Jack moved to the room's center and closed his eyes, trying to *feel* what lay in the room. The impressions were vague, nothing defined. He used this approach rarely, but his current options were limited. Normally he didn't need to force the sensations. They'd just come to him.

He had to have something to work with. Finally something sparked in his abdomen—he felt a pull. He opened his eyes and moved toward the shelves. Gleeson was watching him curiously.

"What's this?" Jack asked him, reaching for a small, deep-blue bottle.

"I'm not sure. I think it came from somewhere nearby, a construction site near the Locality or something. Gil never said much about it."

So why should it be special? Jack had no doubt that the bottle was what had sparked the feeling in him. He picked it up and turned it over in his hands. It was something old: he could see that. The glass was pitted around the edge, and a patina of whiteness speckled one side at the lip. Yeah, it was old, or made to look old. The blue was deep, intense, a color he rarely saw.

"Do you mind if I borrow it?"

"No. Whatever you need."

"Good. I'll return it, of course. Can you take it out of here for the moment? I want to see if there's anything else."

He handed the bottle to Gleeson and moved back to the room's center as Gleeson left and then reappeared, minus the bottle. He wasn't concerned about Gleeson touching it. If the two were cohabiting, then Gleeson's own presence should be all over the place, including Ronschke's stuff. Eyes closed again, stilling himself, Jack reached out. There was still the pull from the bottle, but duller now, farther away. He tried to ignore it and work on the rest of the room's contents. Blank. There was nothing else. Usually there'd be at least some sign of a room's occupant, at least the barest trace, something to signify that someone lived here. It was a strange sensation, almost like a taste, but something that occurred deep in his guts and the back of his head.

Maybe it was because Ronschke only spent short spells here. It took time for a person's presence to build an impression. Eventually, even after a few months, that too decayed. Everything in the Locality decayed, Jack thought to himself, even those things that supposedly didn't really exist. He gave himself a wry smile.

"What is it?" said Gleeson from the doorway.

"Nothing. That's it. I'll need to take the bottle tonight. I'll return it early tomorrow evening. Hopefully we'll have both come up with something by then."

Gleeson nodded rapidly, slipped out of the room, and returned to hand him the bottle. The little man stood there, as if waiting for something, watching Jack expectantly. Finally he spoke.

"I'll try to get the information you need, Mr. Stein."

Somehow Jack was comfortable with Gleeson referring to him as Mr. Stein. Something about the guy made him feel edgy. There was nothing that prompted familiarity between them.

"Of course," said Jack. "I'll see you tomorrow, here. I'll see myself out."

He left Gleeson standing there, trailing his fingers over the objects on the shelves. Despite himself, despite the discomfort, he couldn't help feeling sorry for the little man. There was a real sense of distress about him. Jack was more concerned for himself, though. Jack Stein was the one with the problem. Barely closer to a real clue—Pinpin Dan and a small blue bottle. It wasn't a hell of a lot to show.

A short shuttle ride and he was back at Pinpin's. He waited outside on the street for a while, watching the ceiling panels and fingering the bottle inside his pocket. He wanted to be sure he wasn't being followed. Maybe it was just the old ingrained paranoia, but the sense he'd had on the shuttle was still there. Something was not quite right, something working deep in the pit of his stomach. People came and went, barely glancing in his direction and he stared after them suspiciously. *Come on, Stein. If they are following you, they're hardly going to walk right past and look at you.* No, they didn't have the slightest bit of interest in him. It was typical. The anonymous Jack Stein was making his impact on the world again.

He'd been standing there for about ten minutes, plucking up the will to return to Pinpin's apartment, when he was assailed by a sudden sense of wrongness. This wasn't his paranoia; this was something else. The uneasy feeling in the depths of his stomach grew to a chill deep in his guts and chest, then expanded, crawling like strung wire all along the length of his veins. His pulse started to race, his breath to become shallow. Frowning, he turned to the apartment building, trying to keep his breathing steady. It was there. Whatever it was, it was coming from the building. He knew he had to get up there, and fast.

He pushed past a pedestrian, ignored the shouted protest, and raced for the building, counting the seconds, the sense of urgency pounding in his chest. He punched the elevator controls, barely able to stand the eternity it took to arrive. Then he was inside. The elevator crawled up through the floors, some half-remembered tune, reworked, filtering through the sound system. He leaned against the doors, willing it faster. After what seemed like an eternity, an eternity bathed in the stark and surreal, it slid to a halt and the doors parted. He stepped out into the corridor and stopped. His senses were screaming, *Caution*. He stood listening, trying to hear any noise above the pounding in his ears, but everything was quiet.

Slowly, slowly, he edged down the corridor toward Pinpin Dan's apartment. The door was open. He stood outside, pressed flat against the wall. He'd learned too long ago to trust his senses to ignore what they were telling him now. Taking a deep breath, he took a cautious step inside.

A step at a time, he moved down the wide hallway, down along the plush purple walls, listening with every careful placement of his feet. The thick carpeting masked the noise of his footfalls. The apartment was silent, still—too still. He thought about calling out, but he didn't want to reveal himself. Not yet.

He reached the room at the end of the hall and found . . . Pinpin Dan.

Pinpin was lying sprawled across his sumptuous couch, a wide grin on his face, his head at a crazy angle. His eyes stared right through Jack, seeing nothing. Jack didn't have to check. He could tell the man was dead.

"Shit," he said under his breath. He hated dead people. He hated dead people he hated even more.

"Shit."

The large vases had been smashed across the low table, their contents strewn like twigs across the floor. The statuette of the two boys lay tumbled on its side, still writhing, pushing up and down on the table surface, the rhythmic sound of engineered ceramic against glass the only sound in the room. There was no sign of the handipad.

"Shit," he said again.

He crossed to the couch and gingerly patted Pinpin's pockets, but there was nothing there. Reluctantly he levered the bony frame to either side and peered under him, but still nothing. He stood and rubbed the back of his neck, avoiding looking directly at the corpse. He didn't want to really touch anything. He certainly didn't want to touch Pinpin's sallow, dead skin.

The girl. Where was the girl?

He looked around the room, behind the couch, but there was no sign of a body, apart from Pinpin's. Whoever had done this to Pinpin might have taken her with them. But now he was making assumptions, and he knew better than to assume.

He left Pinpin where he lay, gently closed the door, and walked slowly back up the hallway, listening. At each door he stopped, paused, then moved on. Halfway along the corridor, he sensed, rather than heard, a slight movement. He pressed himself back against the wall and, using one outstretched arm, swung the door wide. Slowly he eased his face around the frame and glanced inside. It was a bedroom. A broad bed dominated the room, draped with a plush pink silken cover in disarray. Along one wall hung a black-framed mirror. Keeping back against the wall, he checked the reflection, but nothing moved. The room looked safe enough, so he stepped inside.

Things had been thrown across the room, items of clothing; the bedcovers lay half-on, half-off, trailing pink satin across the floor. Somebody had been in here. He couldn't imagine Pinpin keeping the place like this. There was the faintest noise from the closet. Jack moved across and flung the door open and then pushed clothing out of the way. There, huddled tight into the corner, sat the girl, her head buried in her knees. Jack pulled the clothes roughly right back out of the way and she looked up, an expression of fear contorting her waiflike face.

"No!" she cried, pushing herself tighter into the corner. Jack swallowed and raised a placating hand.

It looked like she was okay after all—scared, but okay.

Six

She had screwed her eyes shut tight and she flinched away from his hand as he reached for her.

"Wilhelmina," he said. Then, "Billie," with a touch more authority. "It's Jack Stein. I was here before. You remember. I'm not going to hurt you."

She opened her eyes a fraction, then peered around him, looking for anyone else.

"It's just me, Billie. No one else. There's no one else here." He crouched in front of her, one palm still raised in front of him in gentle placation.

She looked at him uncertainly. "W-where are they?"

"Who? Who was here?"

"Two people, a man and a woman. They, they . . ."

Her voice faded off and she bit her lip. Her breath was coming in shallow gasps. He moved his hand toward her shoulder, trying to reassure her, but she flinched back from the contact.

"Try to stay calm, Billie. I know it's hard. Take a deep breath and tell me what happened.

"There was shouting. I didn't see them come in. I was working." She used the same emphasis on the word as Pinpin Dan. It gave Jack a chill.

"I heard the shouting and watched from behind the

door," she continued. "They were arguing. And then the woman did something to Uncle Pinpin and everything went quiet. I hid in here."

Jack held out a hand. "Come on. Let's get you out of there."

She nodded hesitantly, stepped out of the wardrobe, and sidled past, avoiding his hand. "Uncle Pinpin?" she asked, heading for the door.

Jack grabbed her shoulder. This time she let him. "No. There's nothing to see." He turned her to face him. "What did they look like?" he asked.

"Big. Both of them were big. The man had long black hair and dark skin and there was something funny about his eyes. The woman had short red hair. She was big too. The man was thin, though."

"What were they arguing about?"

"The handipad. That's what I was working on. Uncle Pinpin told me to go and see what else was on it while he made a call."

Jack crouched in front of her and looked into her face. "So he got into it?"

"*We* got into it," said Billie, squaring her shoulders, despite her obvious distress.

"Yes, of course," said Jack. "That's what I meant. Did they get it? Did they get the handipad?"

She shook her head. "No, I hid it when I heard them shouting." She reached over to a coat hanging in the wardrobe and dug out the handipad. "I didn't think they'd look here."

Clearly they hadn't. They hadn't thought to look inside the wardrobe either? He frowned.

"That was good thinking, Billie." He reached for the handipad, but she covered it with both hands, pressing it to her chest.

Jack stood again. "All right, you can hold on to it. But keep it out of sight."

She gave a self-satisfied half smile and slipped it into her back pocket.

"We need to get out of here," said Jack. "In case they come back." Her face acquired that look of fear all over again.

Just for a moment Jack was lost. Where could he take her? She had to have family somewhere. It didn't seem like they'd care where she was, though, if she'd been living with Pinpin Dan. He wondered how long it had been since she'd seen them. "I'll tell you what. You come with me now, back to my apartment, out of the way. Then we'll work out what we're going to do with you."

"But what about Uncle Pinpin?"

Jack shook his head. "There's nothing you can do, okay? Just forget it." He pushed her gently toward the doorway.

She barely resisted, and he herded her out of the apartment, making sure she wouldn't dart back and get a view of Pinpin Dan's grinning, sightless form.

They were in the elevator, halfway down to the street, before she spoke again. "I'm worried about him," she said.

He took her shoulders and looked into her eyes. "It's too late to worry about him. He's dead, Billie. They killed him." There was no other way of saying it.

Her bottom lip trembled slightly. She swallowed and looked away with a set jaw. He did too, waiting for their descent to take them to the street.

Jack's own apartment was the only logical choice. If Pinpin's assailants had made the connection between him and the handipad, they could locate his office easily enough. Whoever *they* were. It would be a little harder for them to find out where he lived. He'd made sure of that. He kept his business dealings primarily through his office. Whatever the handipad contained, it was clearly enough to have prompted Pinpin's demise. Not a good sign. So that left the girl. What the hell was he going to do with the girl? His apartment first, yes, but then? He didn't even have a spare bed. He could program the apartment to build one overnight, but that would take time, and it was already afternoon. And in the meantime . . .

Half a block's walk to the shuttle stop without another word; then they waited in silence for the shuttle while Jack turned over the options in his head, all the while keeping a careful watch on the passersby. Billie glanced nervously up and down the street, occasionally glancing up at his face. Damn, Pinpin had his number. That didn't mean he had Jack's address, but it wouldn't be too hard to track it down. If whoever these people were went through Pinpin's records . . .

"Why would they want to—"

"Shhh," he said. "Not here."

The shuttle hissed to a stop in front of them and he bundled her inside. With relief, he saw the car was empty. Waiting for the doors to close, he guided her to a seat and sat her down.

"Billie, how old are you really?" he asked.

"Twelve," she said with a frown. "Well, almost."

Shit, thought Jack. *That* young. It must have been the hardness in her face that had made him presume she was older. What did he know about the age of kids anyway?

"Haven't you got any family? Where are they?"

She chewed on her bottom lip, giving him an appraising look. Then she shook her head.

"Well, where are they? What happened to them?"

"I don't want to talk about that," she said.

"All right. Have it your own way." He sat beside her, staring across at the advertising.

"How long have you been with Pinpin Dan?"

"I forget."

"Well, what is it? Weeks, months?"

"Months, I guess. He was nice to me. He showed me how to do things."

Jack nodded, trying to chase away the possibilities of exactly what kind of things Pinpin Dan had shown a young girl of her age how to do.

"So did you find out who the handipad belonged to?" he said, glancing at her for her reaction.

"Maybe," she said, looking wary again.

He turned to face her. "Listen, Billie. You can tell me, or maybe you'd like the man and the woman who were in the apartment to ask you. *Maybe.*"

She stiffened. Her eyes grew wide for a second and then she regained her neutral expression.

"The Residence," she said grudgingly.

That was enough. The Residence was a broad living complex on the coast, immobile, unlike the Locality. The Residence was the rich and famous and security. The Residence was wealth.

"Ouch," said Jack under his breath. "And a name?"

"Van der Stegen," she said. "Joseph, or Joshua, or something."

Joseph or Joshua Van der Stegen, or maybe something like that. The name wasn't familiar at all. Pinpin's fate had already made Jack wary, but this Van der

Stegen might just be grateful for the return of his handipad, grateful enough to provide a few answers.

"Where are we going?" asked Billie.

"To my place. I already told you. You'll see when we get there."

This seemed to satisfy her for the time being, because she relaxed back into her seat.

The shuttle doors slid open and a few people boarded. Jack sat back in his own seat. More questions could wait until later.

Jack's apartment building was plain, unremarkable. Any decorations had faded long ago, slight discoloration marking where they may have once been. He had chosen this particular block purposely. He just didn't want to live anywhere that stood out. Sometimes, just sometimes, the work took him places where he made enemies, people who might be happy to find him without any trouble. Anyway, he didn't have any real friends, people who might visit. Jack was solitary, private. The dreams and visions drove the rest of the world away from him, even inside the safe environment of the Locality.

His apartment was on the sixth floor, halfway down a corridor leading the length of the building from the elevators, giving him a clear, uninterrupted view. No hidden alcoves or turns. No surprises. It was on the front side of the building, giving him a clear view of the street below, not that he had ever needed it. Not yet. The only time he ever really looked out was to give himself something to do while he was chasing thought patterns through his head. Most of the time he kept the windows opaqued, leaving the artificial distractions of the ceiling panel displays to the consuming masses.

He ushered Billie inside and she looked around, peering into rooms and shelves, poking here and there while he stood with his back against the door, watching her.

Finally she turned and looked at him. "It's not very big."

"Well, it's not meant to be big. I live here, that's all. I don't need it to be big."

"Uncle Pinpin's apartment was a lot bigger."

"Just forget about Pinpin Dan."

She seemed to accept that for the time being, and sat. "What do we do now?"

Jack rubbed his jaw. "First you answer a few more questions for me."

She made a face. "Haven't you got anything to eat?"

Jack sighed. "All right. I'll fix something for you. But I'm still going to ask you some more questions."

He wandered into the kitchen unit, looking for something he could feed her. He finally found old, self-heat spaghetti in one of the cupboards and popped the seal.

"So was there anything more on this Van der Stegen? Do you know where in the Residence he is?"

"No," said Billie from the other room. "It's easy to find out, though. Uncle Pinpin showed me how."

That was one good thing. He watched her through the hatch as he waited for the spaghetti. "And you said you'd been working on the handipad. Anything interesting on it?"

"There's a whole lot of science stuff," she said with a shrug. "I don't know."

"Science stuff?"

"Yeah, like numbers and letters and things. And just the normal stuff."

Jack wandered back into the living room and plonked down the spaghetti. Billie looked down and screwed up her face. She took the proffered fork and prodded at it dubiously.

"Haven't you got anything decent?" she said. He could hear Pinpin's intonation in the words and he bit back what he wanted to say.

"That's it," he said instead. "That's what you get."

She sighed and lifted a forkful to her mouth.

"Do you know who it was that Pinpin called?"

"Nuh-uh," she said around another mouthful.

"Could it have been those people who came, the man and the woman, or was it someone else?"

"I don't know. Maybe."

"Well, which one is it?"

"I don't know," she said, thrusting her jaw out.

"Okay. Eat your food."

He sat back and watched her as she ate. The threads weren't pulling any closer together. If anything, they were drifting apart, and new ones were being added with every turn. Billie herself was an unexpected complication that he didn't need, and one that had no place in the existing pattern, as far as he could tell.

Finally she tossed her fork on the table and sat back, her legs propped up before her. She looked a lot older than twelve. But what did Jack know about kids? How was he supposed to know what a twelve-year-old kid looked like? There was a hardness around her eyes, a shadowing, and a firm set to her mouth, but her face still had that childlike quality, the big eyes, the roundness and softness of the young. He had no idea what he was going to do with her. She pushed the spaghetti container out of the way with her foot and returned his gaze as if waiting for something. Finally she sighed, shook her head, and then got up to wander into the kitchen.

"What are you doing?"

"Looking for something to drink. You're not very good at simple stuff, are you?" He stared after her. She was like no kid he knew, not that he knew very many.

There was a disgusted noise from the kitchen. "Water and coffee, is that all you've got? Little, little. What a place to live. Nothing in it." She appeared in the doorway. "You need looking after, Jack Stein." The way she leaned in the doorway had a peculiarly adult stance to it.

"And I suppose you're the one to do it?" he said.

"Nuh-uh."

She disappeared, then reappeared a moment later with a glass of water and wandered back to the couch.

"So who looked after you? Before Pinpin, I mean," Jack asked her.

"Me. I looked after me. Uncle Pinpin didn't look after me. He just taught me stuff. It was me looked after him."

"So where did you live before?"

"Way down Old. That's where I met Uncle Pinpin."

"Hmm," said Jack, trying to keep the tone of disapproval from his voice. "What were you doing there? Who did you live with?"

"Others. That's all. No one you'd know. It's better when there's more of you." She shrugged again, and took a sip of her water. Jack didn't want to ask what was better, or how; he could guess. There was a contradiction here—the offhand, mature responses, the glass held between too-small hands.

Billie was clearly becoming bored with the conversation. She placed the glass down and was looking around the small living area and jiggling her legs up and down. It wasn't up to him to look after the kid, but he had a gut feeling that despite the lack of connection, she was here for some reason in the whole scheme of what was going on. He just had to work out what it was.

"Is there anywhere you can go? Someone, somewhere? Family maybe?"

"Nuh-uh." There was a resentful look on her face.

He'd forgotten. She didn't want to talk about family.

"Well, I guess you'd better stay here until we get all this sorted out and we can work out what we're going to do with you."

"I'll do what I want." Resentment in the voice.

Jack gave a sigh of exasperation. "All right. You do what you want. You can go back down to Old if you want. See if I care."

Billie narrowed her eyes at him, then shifted position so she was sitting on her hands. "Well, I *want* to stay *here*."

"Okay, then, you stay here," said Jack.

There was a long silence while Jack sat thinking of what else to say, while she continued to fidget and look around the room with a bored expression.

"Listen, Billie, I've got to go to my office and do some work. Are you going to be all right by yourself for a while?"

She swung her head around to face him. "Why can't I come?"

"Because you can't. I need to be alone when I'm working."

And he did. He didn't need the distraction the girl could give. Besides, he didn't want to advertise her presence to the world at large. He shoved his hands into his pockets, and his fingers met the small blue bottle he'd taken from Gleeson. The bottle would help him prioritize, sort things, establish his next move. If he could get some sort of lead on Gleeson's partner, he'd be able to work out what was going on with Outreach. He ignored her frown, the slight pout to her mouth.

"All right," he said. "You're going to stay here. I'm going to do some work. I won't be gone for too long. Let's set things up for you." He turned to face the wall. "New voice."

"Waiting," said the wall.

"Say something, Billie."

"Like what?"

"Anything. A bit more."

"How am I supposed to know what you want me to say?" She gave an exasperated sigh.

"That's fine. The system will recognize your voice now. If you have any trouble telling it to do things, try saying it a different way. It's matched to me, so some commands might be different, but it learns as you go along. I don't think you'll have any trouble with it if you've been working with Pinpin and you're as good as he says you are. If you get bored, it links into the entertainment network, but I hardly ever use it except for vids. You can watch some vids, or play some games or something. Will you be okay here? I'll only be a couple of hours."

She looked at him calculatingly, her eyes narrowed slightly. "Why wouldn't I be?"

"Fine," he said, and sighed. "I'll be back later. Oh, and one last thing."

He stood and crossed to the wall. The apartment had only one bedroom, and she was right, it was small, but there might be enough space for a bed over to one side of the living area. She wasn't very big.

"Command," he said to the wall. "Bed, by the left wall. Single. Start."

A small chime of acknowledgment came from the wall itself.

At least he could get that much started.

He left her there staring at the opposite wall.

He was probably stupid for leaving her with access to his system—a child with her attitude and one who'd been under the tutelage of Pinpin Dan. It was crazy. She could strip his system, screw it up somehow, and be gone before he got back. He had no idea how much Pinpin Dan had shown her, how much she could do, but if she was as good as Pinpin had said she was . . .

At this stage, he didn't see that there was any other choice. Maybe she'd be scared enough or sensible enough simply to stay put.

He was thinking about what he'd come back to find all the way down to the street.

Jack's office was still secure, despite his fears. His fail-safes told him that nobody had tried to enter since last he'd been there. Anybody trying to enter without his knowledge and a quick short message would be beamed to his handipad and a record made. Any tampering with the door at all would do the same thing. He closed the handipad and shoved it back into his pocket. It didn't hurt to be careful, particularly at the moment. The day's events had given him an uneasy feeling about security, about everything, really. He hoped to hell that Billie was going to be all right at the apartment. He had to find somewhere proper to take her. He slipped inside, locking the door behind him.

Taking his handipad back out, he thumbed it on and slotted in the data card containing the personnel records from Outreach, then went to sit on the edge of his sleep couch. Gilbert John Ronschke. Gleeson's partner. There. A big man, solid. Square features. Tanned and bearded. Jack imagined the man, tall, well muscled, spreading a little with the onset of middle age. Patches of white in the beard. He had no way of telling how recent the picture was, but Ronschke had been with Outreach for about seven years. So assume that he was seven years older than the picture on the record. Graying now. Perhaps losing his hair. He concentrated on the image, and then hit a sequence to age the features, going through a few variations so he'd have some options to carry around in his mind. He doubted that he'd get rid of the beard, but he tried it anyway. He thumbed the handipad off and placed it down on the table.

He dug out the small blue bottle from his pocket and placed it beside him on the sleep couch, then stripped off his coat, trousers, and shirt and hung them neatly from the rack beside the couch, there just for that purpose. He kept the offices at a temperature that was cool, but not too cool with his shirt removed. Too warm and it dulled his edge, even in sleep state. Too cold and it became uncomfortable, but he preferred it slightly chilly. Settling himself comfortably on the couch, he lay back, reached for the inducers, and placed the adhesive pads on his temples, pressing them in place with his thumbs. He reached for the bottle—thick glass, chunky and cold—and clutched it firmly in the center of his chest. Right, he was ready. Ronschke's image was still strong in his mind.

"Commence," he said.

Within seconds, the waves of sleep were pressing down on him, dragging him through alpha and lower. He concentrated on the bottle held firmly in his hands, linking it with the image of Ronschke that still floated sharply in his perception. Gentle curtains of darkness swept over him, folding him away from the outside world.

Jack stepped out into gray. No, it was more than gray. It shimmered, wreathed, mistlike, faint colors crawling across the surfaces. Yes, they were surfaces. They reminded him of something. Something long and sinuous, moving through walls. They pressed up against him and around him, and yet they did not touch. Where was he? The place was full of impossible geometries. There were surfaces that weren't surfaces. Shapes moved through and over each other. How could that be? His mind was trying to make sense of what he was seeing, but he was struggling.

He looked down at his hand. The blue bottle lay there, but it was larger than it had been before. He focused on the shape, trying to shut out the surrounds, guide the images. Focus on something solid. That was the way. Ronschke. Gilbert John Ronschke. Where was Ronschke?

And then he was somewhere else. The impossible shapes were gone. The shimmering rainbow gray was gone. A bare room. Clinical. The walls were blank. A slick, hard floor, dark, devoid of furniture, defined the room's boundaries. No, he was wrong; one wall was glass, thick glass from floor to ceiling. Shapes moved beyond it—indistinct, blurry forms—but he couldn't make them out properly. It looked like there were people behind it. A vague pinkish oval shape pressed up against the glass from the other side, dark smudges for eyes, and then it drifted away again into indistinctness. The movements continued beyond, gliding with ill-defined human movement. A large industrial chair sat in the room's center, bright lights glaring down upon it from above. There was no other furniture apart from a shiny metal trolley. On its top, something lay covered with a thin white cloth. In the chair sat a figure. A big man. A big man with a beard, flecked with white. He stared at Jack and spoke.

"That's mine," he said. It was Ronschke. "Will you give it back to me?"

Jack looked down at his hand, at the blue bottle he held. He looked back up at the chair. Ronschke strained, his face growing red with the effort. Jack suddenly saw why. Straps bound him to the chair—broad straps at arms and legs, and there was another across the man's forehead. They were dark gray, made of something he didn't recognize. The chair was thick, and seemed to have some sort of machinery built into it. It reminded him of one of those old dentist's chairs. The lights glared down on him, harsh and white. Ronschke fought against the restraints, then collapsed back.

"It's mine, not yours. Give it to me!" he growled.

Ronschke pushed against the straps, his eyes growing wider, his face growing livid and contorting with the effort. Cords stood out on his neck, and blue veins pulsed on his forehead.

"What are you doing here?" said Jack. He was suddenly close beside the chair, looking down at Ronschke.

The man looked up, naked aggression on his face.

"What are you doing here?" Jack repeated.

Ronschke's expression changed and his eyes filled with panic. "I don't know. I don't know. I don't know," he said. "The thing in the cloud place. The water place. The air place. The place of dark earth. The place of cold fire. I don't know."

"What thing? What place?"

"I don't know. I don't know," said Ronschke. "The stone," he said quietly. "The key to the door."

The panic trickled from his features, and he relaxed back into the chair. His voice took on a wheedling tone. "Will you give it to me? Please," he said. "It belongs with me. It's mine. It belongs in my home. Won't you take me home? Is that why you're here?"

Jack reached down and unstrapped one of Ronschke's wrists, meaning to give him the bottle. Ronschke lifted his arm and . . .

There was no hand. His wrist ended in a blank, meaty stump. Severed.

And Jack was awake.

Ronschke was alive. The dream image had been too clear, the interaction too real for it to mean anything else. Maybe not undamaged, but alive all the same. Jack could tell Gleeson that much.

Slowly he peeled off the pads, placed the small bottle down beside him, and reached for his handipad.

He'd spent more time than he'd thought at the office. Out on the street, starburst patterns were playing over the ceiling panels, filling the inside sky with colors. The smell of damp roadway floated up to him. It had been raining while he'd been locked away in his workroom. A slow creaking came from the buildings around as they divested themselves of the moisture, small beads of water gathering on the outside surfaces and forming shimmering trickles that ran down the flat walls.

Jack watched the displays above as he waited for the shuttle, thinking about what Ronschke had said. Sometimes the dream words meant nothing. Sometimes they explained everything. This time he just didn't know. Was Ronschke the owner of the severed hand? It could be just a blind, tying the two dreams together, something again planted by his subconscious mind, but there was too little to really go on at this stage. Bright starlight traceries fizzled away at the ceiling's edges, tracking into nothingness. Movement off to his right caught his attention. The lights of the approaching shuttle appeared out of the gloom in the far end of Old, growing nearer. The shuttle eased into his stop, and Jack clambered aboard, lost in thought.

By the time he got back to the apartment, Billie had apparently been busy. Jack stood at the door, waiting for it to open at his command. Nothing happened.

"Let me in," he said. No response. "Let me in, dammit!"

A voice came from the wall—he knew it was Billie's voice, but somehow disguised. "Who's there?"

"Billie! You know damn well who it is."

There was a moment's pause and then his door opened. *His* door. She'd locked him out of his own apartment.

He strode into the living area and glared at her.

"What the hell do you think you're playing at, Billie? How did you do that?"

She glared back at him, wariness in her stance. "It was easy. I was scared. What was I supposed to do?"

He took two steps across the intervening space and stood over her. "Don't try anything like that again, do you hear me?"

She cringed back, climbing quickly onto the couch and scuttling back from his anger.

"Oh, shit. I'm not going to hurt you, Billie. Just put it back the way it was. Okay?"

She looked up at him with wide, fearful eyes, but her jaw was set, teeth firmly clamped together. How did you calculate damage? The girl was scared, but she remained defiant. Jack slipped out his handipad and bottle and placed them down on the low table, then sat.

He sighed. "Can you put it back? *Please.*"

Whatever had happened to the girl over the course of her young life had left its marks. Jack bore his own scars, but how did he measure them against what he was seeing now? The way she had scrambled away from him was too quick a response, too automatic. The world changed. Things supposedly got better—modern technology, society, enlightened civilization—but still there were people. Always there were people. And where there were people there were the inevitable consequences. He didn't like to think about it, but faced with it like this . . .

She nodded slowly, watching him hesitantly, still wary of his already faded anger.

"All right," he said. "When you're ready. And when you've done that, I think there's something you might be able to help me with. Okay? If you're so good with systems, then we can put it to some good use. I need to research the Locality data banks. Do you think you can help me with that?"

"Yes," she said, relaxing a little, some of her belligerence and self-confidence returning. "Easy."

"Good. You can start on it in the morning. For the moment we have to work out the sleeping arrangements. I've started growing you a new bed, but it won't be ready till about halfway through the night. We need to work out where we're going to sleep in the meantime. I guess tonight you can sleep on the couch. We can work out what we're going to do with you over the next couple of days. I don't want you out there on the streets alone."

"I can look after myself."

"Yeah, sure you can." For all her bravado, he could still see the fear and tiredness in her face. "What about those two at Pinpin's, eh? Whoever sent them might have some idea that Pinpin Dan had someone staying with him. And what if they come looking?"

"I can look after myself." This time the tone was not so self-assured.

"Right."

He reached for the handipad, flipped it open, and started scanning his notes, letting her get on with whatever she was going to do. He watched her surreptitiously out of the corner of his eye as she stood close to the wall, giving his apartment's systems the commands that would restore his access, talking in low tones so he couldn't overhear. It was funny—she could have stood anywhere in the room to give the commands, but there she was, huddled secretively against the wall. He did the same thing. Well, let her have her little secrets for now. He wasn't going to press it.

He was drifting in that muzzy half-aware state, floating, warm. Soft, smooth skin, warm pressure across his abdomen, sliding across his belly. Fingers fumbled with his pajamas, loosening the ties. Fingers raking gently through the hair, tightly curled at his crotch. Fingers lightly encircling the base of his penis, gentle pressure, then motion. He felt himself responding, his penis growing hard within the touch. He made a low sound of pleasure deep in his throat, and shifted slightly to give better access. The fingers touching the underside of the shaft traced up, seeking the sensitive areas, lightly stroking—gentle touch of small fingers, small hand, arm circled around his hip, cool skin pressing against him from behind. Small hand, small arm—

"What the fuck!"

He spun, grabbing the wrist tight, thrusting it from him.

"Lights! Billie, what the hell are you doing!"

He held her wrist tightly at arm's length. She sat there staring at him, wincing with the pressure and looking at him with wide eyes, her lower lip trembling. Her slim body pale, naked, her budding breasts tipped with pale pink.

"B-but I thought . . ." Her voice trailed off and she bit her lip.

"I don't care what the hell you thought. You *don't* do that." He thrust her wrist away. She rubbed the wrist with her other hand, staring at him with wide eyes. Jack bunched the covers and threw them at her.

"Cover yourself."

His erection had faded. He pulled the remaining cover around himself and stared at the girl. There was fear in her face, and something else—lack of comprehension. Moisture welled in her eyes.

Shit. What was he going to do with her? His mind tumbled with the implications. Pinpin Dan? Maybe others. Who had taught her that? There had been nothing clumsy about her touch, as if she'd known exactly what she was doing.

"Listen, Billie, you don't do that." He tried to keep the feeling out of his voice. He had hurt her. She was still massaging her wrist. "Are you okay?"

She barely nodded, her look now one of accusation. Jack felt suddenly powerless. "Billie, I didn't mean to hurt you. But you don't do things . . . like that."

"Why not?"

"Because I'm nearly four times as old as you. Because you're a young girl. Because . . . shit . . . it's just not right, that's all. Damn it! I could be your father."

"So what?" she said, regaining some of that ever-present self-assurance. "You were the one who said it. You said we'd work out the sleeping arrangements."

So what? I could be your father. So what?

"I meant *sleep*. That's all I meant. I don't know what it means to you. Who told you it meant anything else?"

He stood, dragging the sheet behind him, wrapping it around himself. She watched him from the bed, her jaw set. It seemed to make no difference to her that he had said he could have been her father, and the implications of that were worse than the thought of Pinpin Dan. Something bottomless opened in the depths of his stomach.

"Was it Pinpin who taught you to do those things?"

"Nuh-uh," she said.

"Then who?"

"Don't remember," she said.

He looked away. When had it started? Maybe it had been in her time in Old, with the *others*. It didn't really matter—not now.

"Billie, I want you to listen to me. Please. You *never* do that again. Not with me, not with anyone else. You just don't."

Never was a long time, but he couldn't express it any other way. He couldn't tell her there was a time and a place and it was some years away yet. He couldn't express any of the conflicting thoughts running through his head in a way that made sense right now. He stared at her, temporarily lost for the words that would express what he was feeling. "I'm going to sleep out on the couch. You stay in here." She was still rubbing her wrist. He'd grabbed her hard. "Is your arm okay?"

She nodded and drew the covers more tightly around herself.

He left her there and moved out into the living area, shutting the door behind him. What had happened had been a shock, but there was another shock as he realized what he was feeling. Jack suddenly knew what it was. He was feeling *responsibility*. She was all of eleven years old. *Shit*. What could he do? He didn't know. How did you deal with something like that?

It was a long time before he reached the edges of sleep again. Her light was still on, a yellow crack beneath the bedroom door, his bedroom door, by the time he finally did.

Seven

An insistent chiming woke him from his fragile sleep. The sound was unusual. There was something about the tone, deeper, slower than normal. He growled and levered himself upright. Then he realized he was on the couch. What was he doing on the . . . *Oh, damn!* He remembered. Fragmented images of last night. He vainly tried to work the taste of them from his consciousness and the grit from his eyes.

"Lights," he muttered.

The wall blossomed into the police corporate logo. Police? What the hell did they want? He glanced at the bedroom door, making sure it was closed.

"Yeah, answer," he said, making clear that he didn't appreciate being disturbed.

A sallow face, dark, cropped hair and bright blue, slightly epicanthic eyes, replaced the logo.

"Jack Stein?"

"Yeah, what of it?"

"I'm Special Investigator Louis Ng. I need to ask you a few questions."

Jack shrugged and pulled the cover tighter about himself. It had been a long, unsettled time before he'd been able to catch a few fragments of sleep last night.

The memories of what had happened flooded his semiawake mind, and he curled his mouth in distaste. Half-awake was bad enough, but half-awake with things on his mind *and* police questions was almost too much.

"Well, make it quick."

"Are you familiar with one Heironymous Dan, also known as Pinpin?"

Heironymous? Heironymous? Shit, no wonder he'd called himself by another name.

"Yes, maybe, and . . .?"

"Heironymous Dan may be able to help us with certain inquiries."

Not bloody likely, thought Jack.

"Unfortunately it appears that Mr. Dan's exact location is currently unknown. It has become a question that we'd like some answers about. It seems he may have disappeared from the Locality. We would very much like to establish his whereabouts."

"I'm sorry to hear that, but what's it got to do with me?"

The police were awkward. The Locality had little need of law-enforcement services, and when they did, the police hung on to things. They had little enough to do most of the time, their actions directed by the higher-ups who managed them rather than any set of statutes. Every time they were pointed at something, it became like a personal mission. They were run by a privatized corporation, and that corporation answered only to their paymasters. Sometimes that meant things got ugly. True, there were emergency services, but that was hardly their first purpose in life. Jack, working on the fringes of what they did, was an obvious target. It was difficult to work out how much he should show them he knew. Probably the less the better.

Special Investigator Ng seemed to be waiting for something. His image frowned and continued.

"What would you know about that, Mr. Stein?"

"Sorry, about what?"

Ng gave a slightly exasperated look. "About the disappearance of Heironymous Dan."

"What should I know?"

Ng's frown deepened and he glanced off to one side before looking back. "The records show you in attendance at Mr. Dan's apartment yesterday. Does that prompt your memory?"

In his half-asleep state, Jack had forgotten there'd be records, that they'd know he was there. "Yeah, I visited Pinpin. What of it?"

Ng paused. It didn't seem like the answer he'd expected. "We're concerned, Mr. Stein, because apparently there were no other visitors during the day. Perhaps you can tell us what you do know."

That threw him. Billie had been very clear about Pinpin's other visitors. Somehow they must have tampered with the records—not an easy thing to do. The police weren't making any accusations yet, but it wouldn't be long.

"Listen," said Jack. "This is my statement, for the record, if you want a statement, and you can record it that way if you like. I visited Pinpin Dan. Went over to see his new apartment, that's all. I met him by chance on the shuttle and he invited me. I can show you his card if you want. It's around here somewhere." He made a show of shuffling around on the coffee table and looking. Ng glanced back down to one side and then at the screen again. They were definitely recording.

"New apartment?"

"Well, yeah. New as far as I was concerned. I hadn't seen him for a few months."

"So it was a social visit."

"Yes. I've already told you that."

"You don't seem very surprised that we're interested in finding him, that he seems to have disappeared."

"Shit happens. Pinpin wasn't one to make a lot of friends. Quite the opposite." That much was true.

There was a flash of interest in Ng's expression. "So you're saying that Mr. Dan had enemies, people who might want to harm him."

"Yeah, I suppose so."

"And what can you tell us about that, Mr. Stein?"

"Nothing. It's just the sort of guy he was."

Ng was now looking down at something in front of him, out of shot. "You're an investigator, aren't you, Mr. Stein? A *psychic* investigator." So they had his records out as well.

"Yeah, and . . .?"

"And before that, you spent some time in Intelligence."

"Where are you going with this, Ng?"

Ng looked up. "Just making sure of the facts, Mr. Stein."

Jack let a trace of annoyance slip into his tone. "Well, you've got them right, okay? I'm sure you can get what you need from whatever you've got there. It's early. If there's nothing else . . ."

Ng pursed his lips in disapproval. "I would have

thought you might be a little more cooperative, Mr. Stein . . . under the circumstances."

"What circumstances? You wake me up, throw a bunch of questions at me while I'm half-asleep. What circumstances?"

"I apologize for disturbing you, Mr. Stein, but I would have thought, considering the disappearance of your friend—"

"Hey, Ng, listen, he was an *acquaintance*. Get that right. An acquaintance. Nothing more. Now, unless there's anything else . . ."

"No, there's nothing else . . . for now. We'll be in touch." Ng paused before signing off. "Um, there is one thing, Mr. Stein."

"Yes?"

"You're working on some sort of—" He paused and cleared his throat. "—assignment currently . . .?"

So the police had some sort of interest in the Outreach case too. They wouldn't have brought it up otherwise.

This guy, Ng, clearly had a pretty low opinion of what Jack did. When Jack didn't answer, Ng continued. "Would you like to tell me what you're working on right at the moment? Perhaps there is something about that or your client that could assist us."

Jack snorted. "If you think I'm going to tell you that . . ."

Ng pursed his lips. "All right, Mr. Stein. As you don't seem to have anything useful to tell me for the moment, that will be all for now. We'll be in touch."

The image faded to blank wall.

Jack stared at the place where Ng's face had been, still seeing the curled lip and the hostile, knowing expression. Police. He didn't need police sniffing around him at the moment. If what Ng had said was true, then they were likely to start poking around his affairs with a little bit more energy than just a casual call. Ng's tone had been polite. Too polite. No accusations. No suspicion of direct involvement, at least not obviously. He didn't like the implications. It meant they considered him a suspect. Of that there was no doubt.

So what had happened to the records in Pinpin's place? More to the point, what had happened to Pinpin's body? Ng hadn't even mentioned the girl. That was strange. It was also a little strange that they had become involved so quickly. Who had tipped them off? Ng said that Pinpin had disappeared. No mention of why they wanted to talk to him. No mention of murder. No mention of a corpse. That was odd too. How much did they really know?

He scratched at the back of his head and stood, shrugging the sheets around himself. More questions than answers, and he hated that, but most of it would have to wait until later.

Now, what to do about the kid? He thought maybe it was best to just act normally. He could give her something to do, keep her occupied while he was busy himself. He thought for a while and recorded a set of names into the wall unit. When he was finished, he crossed to the bedroom door.

"Billie, you awake?" he called outside the door, hesitating to open it.

The door opened and Billie stood there, looking at him warily, already fully dressed.

"Listen," he said. "I've just had a call. Police. They wanted to know what I was doing at Pinpin's."

A quick look of panic flickered across her face, and she clutched the doorframe with one hand. The look disappeared as quickly as it had appeared. "What do *they* want?" she said, squaring her shoulders, a clear belligerent tone in her voice. She had the reactions rehearsed in a way that said she'd been existing on the wild side for some time—fight or flight. It was a pattern he was starting to see a lot.

"Did they say anything about me?" she said.

Okay, she'd clearly had experience with the police before. Or maybe it was just stuff that had rubbed off from Pinpin.

"No, nothing. And that's a bit strange, don't you think?"

"S'pose." She chewed it over for a second or two. "What about the two that came—the man and the woman?"

"No, nothing about them either. Anyway, it means I'm going to have to move a bit more quickly on this. I have to go and see someone and sort something out. You going to be all right here on your own again?"

She nodded.

"Good," he said. "You can do that research for me while I'm gone. Look up those things for me. I'm going to need my handipad with me, but we can download whatever you come up with when I get back. I've left you a list of topics in the system. Then I think I might need to go on a little trip."

"Where?"

"The Residence," said Jack, and Billie narrowed her eyes.

Out on the street, Billie's last admonition still rang in his ears. "And bring back something to eat."

What the hell did he know about looking after a kid?

A flicker above him drew his gaze. Fireworks. Fly-pasts. Head tilted back, chewing at his bottom lip, he watched the display. Of course! Foundation Day. They always played celebratory images on Foundation Day. He'd completely forgotten what day it was. It showed him how out of touch he was with the real world, how much he was bound up in this crap that kept happening inside his head. He wasn't only locking himself away in his apartment; he was hiding away in his own head. He really should have remembered something like that.

The only true public holiday in the Locality, Foundation Day marked the birth of the structure, the first opening of the enclosed urban environment and the influx of the first few families and office workers who were to make the Locality their permanent home. In those days the Locality had been small, more like a small suburb than a city, an experiment, but as the experiment became a success and the lure of safety and an improved standard of living had filtered out into the world, the Locality had grown. Other, similar structures grew up across the continental vastness. The Locality was not only the first; it was also the biggest.

Foundation Day meant other things. The Outreach offices would be closed for business. Most places would be closed, apart from the cafés, bars, and restaurants, and all of those would be heaving with bodies. And he'd given Gleeson no set time when they were going to meet. He couldn't call him—not now. It might raise too many suspicions if he put in a call to the Outreach offices on Foundation Day and asked for the guy. What was Jack Stein doing calling the offices on a public holiday, and why Gleeson? He'd just have to find him elsewhere, hopefully at his apartment. He had to assume the little man wasn't going to be out celebrating with the masses. He just didn't seem the type, and with everything else that was going on . . . The apartment was likely where Gleeson had assumed they would meet anyway.

Foundation Day. It had turned out that there was benefit after all, especially considering the sudden involvement of the police. He needed to keep his movements as low-profile as possible, and he didn't want the problem of inept idiots trailing him to Outreach or anywhere else. Yeah, lose himself in the masses. The Foundation Day crowds should see to that. If he was going to be followed, it wouldn't be easy for them. There was nothing outside the buildings to record his movements, as far as he knew.

Jack walked to the shuttle stop, turning the conversation with Ng over in his mind. So there was a record of him at Pinpin's apartment, but no trace of the others. That spoke of pretty sophisticated doctoring mechanisms. It was funny that Ng hadn't mentioned Billie either. There was definitely something weird going on there. Maybe they didn't have any records after all. Maybe Ng had just been spinning him a story. Fragments of the dream with the White-Haired Man floated up in his inner vision. What had he said? *I want your girlfriend.* The words echoed inside his head. The White-Haired Man couldn't have been referring to Billie. That just didn't make sense. Though considering last night's events . . .

No. Not possible. It couldn't be possible. He couldn't allow it to be possible.

Jack grimaced at the thought, at the understanding of what the whole episode meant as far as Billie was concerned. He remembered his own first fumblings, his first awkward experiments at the age of fourteen or fifteen. Billie was way ahead of him there. She was *practiced*. The thought did more than scare him.

As the shuttle slid to a halt in front of him and he climbed aboard, he was still thinking. He glanced around, looking for an empty seat. The shuttle was full, even this far down the Locality. Just what you'd expect on Foundation Day. Everyone was heading up to New for the celebrations. Kids, families, all heading for the wide-open spaces of parkland. It didn't matter where they came from, what they looked like. Everyone was the same on Foundation Day, even Jack Stein. He sank back against a door panel and suppressed a sigh. He'd gotten barely enough sleep, he'd missed his coffee, and there wasn't even a seat.

Gleeson was in.

"We need to talk," said Jack, as the small clerk looked at him nervously from the doorway and glanced up and down the corridor.

"Come inside," said Gleeson, beckoning him forward hurriedly, and Jack slipped past him into the apartment. Once he was inside, Gleeson shut the door and murmured, "Lock." He paused at the door, listening for a few seconds, then turned.

"What are you doing *here*?" he asked. "I didn't expect to see you today. I know you said today, but I just assumed you'd forgotten what day it was."

"You should never assume, Francis. Anyway, things are moving in ways I'm not too happy about," said Jack. "I said I might need some help from you. Well, now's the time." It was the time, all right—time to put the little man to the test.

"What is it?"

"Listen, do we have to stand here in the hallway?"

Gleeson seemed to remember himself. "Yes, of course. Sorry." He ushered Jack into the living area, a worried expression etched across his face. He perched on the edge of a couch and waved Jack to a chair facing him. Jack glanced around the room. Everything was precisely ordered. Edges lined up with edges. Neat arrangements. There was no flair or particular taste in any of the arrangements, but the place was neat, almost obsessively so. Austerity and neatness. Perhaps that was the little man's life. So how did Gil Ronschke fit into that? He couldn't see Ronschke fitting easily into such ordered neatness. The rough-and-ready exterior that Ronschke portrayed would surely be out of place in such pristine order. He could almost picture Ronschke blundering about the neat apartment, Gleeson fluttering after him, putting things back in order. Maybe it was the contrast that worked. Opposites and all that stuff.

"I had a call from the police this morning," said Jack.

The furrow in Gleeson's brow deepened. "Damn," he breathed. "Police? What did they want? How much do they know?"

"Nothing. Nothing important anyway. But I think I've got some news for you."

Gleeson's expression relaxed slightly. "Yes?"

"Yes, I'm pretty sure Gilbert's okay. I don't know where he is yet, but I think he's okay."

"You think?"

"Yes, I think. Remember, what I do isn't necessarily an exact science. It's too early to be certain, but I thought you'd want to know that there was something positive."

"He's all right? Where is he? Why hasn't he been in touch?"

"Wait just a minute. Slow down. I told you I can't tell you where he is yet."

"But he's all right?" Gleeson sat at the edge of the couch, eager to pounce on the merest shred of information. Maybe too eager. It was almost as if the little man were hamming it up.

"I think so," said Jack warily.

"You *think*?"

"Yes, I *think*. I have only so much to go on. I have to do some more work."

"Oh, I see," said Gleeson, the initial rush of eager anticipation trickling way.

"Let me ask you," said Jack. "Has Ronschke had any recent medical treatment of any kind?"

Gleeson frowned. "Gil. Call him Gil, or at least Gilbert," he said absently before continuing. "No, I don't think so. That would be unlike Gil. Most unlike Gil. He abhors medicine. Hates doctors. Wants to do everything himself. He wouldn't even submit to the enhancement options. He prefers to work out." He shook his head slowly.

"I see," said Jack.

"What?"

"Nothing. It doesn't matter, for now." There was no point in upsetting the man unnecessarily if he really was on the level. He tucked the information away for later.

Gleeson nodded.

"That bottle you gave me was quite useful," said Jack, changing tack.

"Have you got it?"

Jack shook his head. "Shit, no, sorry. It's back at my office."

Another frown flickered across Gleeson's features and remained there for a second or two. Despite everything, the fact that Jack had failed to bring the bottle with him had annoyed the little man. These sharp reactions were in total contrast to his soft, almost weak outer presence.

Jack continued. "But that's not important for now. This morning's police call tells me I have to move quickly. I need to take a short trip, and I need you to pay for it."

"Where?"

"The Residence," said Jack slowly.

"Why on earth do you need to go there?"

"That doesn't matter. All you need to know is that I have to go."

Gleeson sat back and folded his arms. "I'm not happy about this, Mr. Stein. You're not telling me very much."

Jack watched him for a moment or two before continuing. "I think it's better if you don't know at the moment. Better for all concerned. Listen, you can be sure as soon as I have anything solid I'll let you know. There's little point otherwise, is there?"

Gleeson peered across at him, assessing. "All right. Just tell me how much you need."

"Enough for a return flight out to the Residence and maybe a bit extra."

"What do you need extra—"

Jack stopped him. "You don't need to know that either. I've got expenses. Normally I'd be charging a daily rate as well, but circumstances are a little different this time."

Gleeson stood and started pacing. "I'm still not happy about this, Mr. Stein. Not at all happy. And I'm becoming less so by the minute."

"Do you want me to find out where your friend is or not?"

Gleeson seemed to remember himself with that little reminder, stopping in midstride. "Yes, of course I do, Mr. Stein. Of course I do."

"So what about you?" said Jack. "Have you found anything?"

"I don't—"

"Company records, Francis. You were going to do some digging for me."

Gleeson walked to the back of the couch. "You have to understand, it's not that easy. I have to be careful. And if I were in the office today, there would be questions. I can't risk that. And neither, I think, can you."

Jack pinched the bridge of his nose between thumb and forefinger and sighed. "All right. But you have to understand that we need to move more quickly than this. The urgency applies just as much to you as it does to me." He looked up at Gleeson, daring the little man to argue. He couldn't afford to pander to the clerk's seemingly fragile emotions. He had far better things to worry about. Nor could he hint at how large this thing was becoming, the sense of unease growing inside him. Gleeson was flighty, he might panic, and with Jack's information resources sitting at rock bottom, he couldn't afford to have him disappear. He really did need the man's help with Outreach. His access, his position, was invaluable.

"Yes, yes. I understand," Gleeson said resignedly after a pause.

"Good. So let's see about booking that flight. Return. Private charter."

"Private—what?"

"We need to be discreet. Besides, there's not many other ways to get out there. One. One in the name of Louis Warburg." That would do. It was anonymous enough not to draw questions, and he liked the amusement factor of throwing those two names together. He ignored the questioning look and sat back as Gleeson started issuing instructions to his wall unit.

Jack still had no idea what he was going to do about Billie. In his guts he was starting to know there was a reason she was there, part of the bigger picture, but it wasn't enough. Tangles and complications. And every time he thought about last night's events, a chill flowered inside. What sort of life must she have had? What had she been through? It wasn't his problem, but at the same time it was. It had become his problem. He wasn't responsible. He couldn't be responsible for what had happened to her, what she'd been through, and yet he *felt* responsibility, as strange as that was. He didn't *want* to feel it, and right now it was cluttering the spaces inside his head.

Gleeson finished the arrangements, pausing twice for instructions. Finally it was done, and Jack pulled out his handipad to download the details. He checked the booking, nodded to himself, then looked back up at Gleeson.

"Oh, and one last thing, remember?" said Jack. "As I said, a little something to cover those extra expenses wouldn't hurt."

Gleeson pursed his lips, nodded grudgingly, and

then issued further instructions to the wall unit. Jack held out the handipad and watched for the download, then nodded in satisfaction.

"Thank you, Francis," Jack said. "I know you can't do anything about Outreach today, but as soon as you can, sometime in the next couple of days, I could use that other information I'm after."

Gleeson nodded again slowly, pressing his lower lip with his teeth. He took a deep breath. "And Gil?" he said finally.

"As soon as I can," said Jack. "I don't know how long that will be, but I'll be in touch. I think it might be better at the moment if you didn't try to contact me—at least for a few days. If I need to talk to you, then I'll talk to you, okay? I'll see myself out."

He left Gleeson standing there, a trace of veiled hope buried in the desperation written across his face. Maybe the man was just fucked up, and maybe Jack was being too suspicious. It had happened in the past. Gleeson might be on the level after all.

By the time he got back, Billie had done the thing with the door lock again. Jack growled, feeling stupid, standing uselessly in the corridor, again denied access to his own place.

"Dammit, Billie, let me in."

A few seconds and the door finally opened. He stalked into the living room and glared at her.

"I thought you were supposed to have put things back the way they were."

She was sitting on the couch, her knees pulled up to her chest, her arms encircling them.

"Well?" he said.

She shrugged.

"Is that it? Shit, Billie, if you're going to stay here you'll have to stop making things difficult for me." He tossed his handipad onto a nearby armchair and waited. She shrugged again and looked away.

"Jesus, Billie. What is it now?"

"You said you'd bring something back."

"I don't—"

"I'm hungry," she said from between closed teeth, not looking at him.

Jack sighed. She was right. He'd forgotten all about it. He didn't eat breakfast; the stims he used so regularly suppressed his appetite anyway, so it was easy enough to forget. He rubbed his forehead and sat.

"Yeah, okay. I forgot. We'll grab something out and then I'll have to go to the port."

She turned her head to face him. "Anything I want?"

"Yes. Anything you want."

That seemed to satisfy her for the moment. She unfurled her limbs and leaned forward. "Can we go right now?"

"In a few minutes. First I want you to tell me what you've found out."

"It's all there," she said, gesturing to the wall with a tilt of her head.

"Look, I don't have time to read through it now. I'll download it just before we leave. For now, why don't you just tell me?"

"It's boring."

"I don't care if it's boring. The sooner you tell me what you've found, the sooner we go and get something to eat . . . whatever you want, like I said. Meanwhile, I want a coffee. You want one?"

"Nuh-uh," she said, wrinkling her nose.

"Okay," said Jack, and wandered to the kitchen. Billie started talking from the other room.

"There was too much stuff there," she said. "With those words you gave me, there were all sorts of, like, stories and history stuff."

"History stuff is good," said Jack as he waited for the coffee.

"But there's too much. I had to cut down the number of hits, and even then it was still too much."

"Uh-huh. But . . ."

"Well . . ." Billie's voice sounded doubtful.

"Go on."

"Well, there was all this history stuff about a snake eating itself, right? That was the first word you gave me. Ouroboros. Then there was more stuff on, like, chemistry."

"Chemistry?"

"They called it alchemy, but it was really chemistry. Just sort of weird. The way they talk about stuff is strange."

Jack wandered back into the living room carrying his coffee. He sat opposite her and sipped as he waited for her to continue. Her face was a mask of concentration.

She went on. "And the snake thing had other names too. Like Jormungandr. I don't know if I said that right. It was something to do with something called Yggdrasil or . . . I don't know."

Jack frowned. Even he would have difficulty dealing with those names, and he was used to strange research. They were tumbling from her lips as if she used them every day. Even remembering them . . .

"Yeah, okay, I don't know if that's useful. Anything else? What about 'stone' or 'key'?"

She nodded. "The alchemy stuff had things about that. What's a philosopher?"

"Um, why?"

"Because there was all this stuff about something called a philosophers' stone. And something else called an androgyne or something like that. Then there were other names like Para . . . celsus and Newton or somebody."

The first meant nothing to him, but the philosophers' stone was familiar, and Newton was easy enough. That was basic school stuff. He'd had occasion to deal with classic archetypes more than once, the way they cropped up in dreams repeatedly. So what the hell did alchemy have to do with what had happened on Dairil III? Something, clearly. Or at least the symbols from it. Gil Ronschke's dream image had talked about a stone for a reason. The dream images weren't random. Words spoken in dreams were particularly significant. Jack had learned that over the years.

"Hey!" Billie was looking at him accusingly.

Jack gave her a questioning frown.

"You going to tell me or just sit there like you're going to sleep?"

He bit back his reply, then answered more slowly. "A philosopher was someone who used to think about the world, what made things work, why everything was the way it was. They liked to find out the reasons things are the way they are. It's more complicated than that, but that's the idea."

Alchemy. What was the link?

"Okay, there might be something there, there might not, but you've given me an idea or two. I don't know who this Paracelsus guy was, but Newton had to do

with science, about things moving, right?" said Jack.
She shrugged.

"So what do you want to eat?" he said, changing the
subject. There was too much to think about in what
she'd told him already, and he needed time for it to filter through his subconscious. He tossed his handipad
over and she snatched it deftly out of the air.

"Anything I want?"

"That's what I said. You can download the research
while you make up your mind."

She started the download, then looked up. "I already know."

"What?"

"Molly's," she said.

"You're sure?" Jack ate a lot of crap, but there was a
limit. A Mollyburger was right at the edges of that
limit.

"Yep, Molly's," she said with certainty.

Great. Synth crap for breakfast—just what he
needed.

Billie tossed the handipad back and got to her feet.
He could scan the download on the way to the port
after he'd dealt with Molly's. There was a Molly's near
everything in New or Mid, and that was the way they
had to head.

Outside in the corridor, Jack grimaced as Billie
leaned over and locked the door. He had to do something about the way the girl was taking over his life
and his space. It just wasn't healthy. He watched her
all the way down from the apartment.

Out on the street, waiting for the shuttle, he remembered something.

"Billie."

"Yeah?" She was watching the Foundation Day displays above them—a rush and whirl of rainbow colors.

"No one called while I was out?"

"Dunno."

"What do you mean, you don't know?"

"I blocked all incomings. Took the system off the net." She said it completely matter-of-factly, as if it were the most normal thing in the world.

"You what?"

"Took it off the net." She shrugged. "It's back on now."

"Why did you do that?" Forget about *how* she'd managed to do it.

"I was busy." She shrugged again. "Don't worry. They can't tell."

Jack stared at her, but she went on watching the ceiling display, unconcerned.

Damn. If Ng had tried to contact him again, what would he have thought? It was bad enough that the police were interested. It didn't matter so much as far as work was concerned. Any new contacts would come through his office, and he'd be unlikely to get anything on Foundation Day anyway. He stood watching her askance, chewing at his bottom lip until the shuttle drew up in front of them.

They rode in silence, Jack absorbed in the downloaded information on the handipad. Occasionally he glanced up, but Billie was staring out the windows at the passing buildings and people. This time they'd been lucky enough to get seats. She'd been right. There was a lot of information, and most of it seemed next to useless. Page after page scrolled past his eyes and he barely absorbed a shred of it, relying on his intuition to draw him to key words or phrases. They pulled in to a stop. A couple of passengers boarded, and they were under way again. Midway to the next stop, something snagged his attention. He'd almost missed it in the casual scan. A sudden stab of awareness shot through him, and he backed up a few pages. It was a poem. A seventeenth-century poem.

> *Old Sages by the Figure of the Snake*
> *Encircled thus did oft expression make*
> *Of Annual-Revolutions; and of things,*
> *Which wheele about in everlasting-rings;*
> *There ending where they first of all begun.*
> *These Roundells help to shew the Mystery*
> *of that immense and blest Eternitie,*
> *From whence the CREATURE sprung, and into whom*
> *It shall again, with full perfection come.**

Jack stared at the words. He read them over again, looking for the thing that had caught his attention. Nothing there made any sense. He remembered the dream of the mining camp, the *thing* extruding from the wall, and felt a sudden, inexplicable chill. He snapped the handipad closed and stared out the window, feeling gray and iridescent multiple realities sliding away beneath him.

*Withers, George, *A Collection of Emblemes, Ancient and Moderne* (London, 1635), as cited in Harris.

Eight

Molly's was worse than he expected. Long lines of families and kids queued for the dispensing counters. A couple of the parents glanced at him as he took his place in line with Billie, taking in his scruffy appearance and long coat, disapproval clearly etched in their expressions. They could think what they liked. He was taking Billie to where she wanted to be, and just because it happened to be in the New end didn't mean he had to do anything special. Gradually the line moved on, people, families, kids grabbing their trays of crap and heading to find free tables. Finally their own turn came. Billie leaned forward and ordered, eagerness in her voice. The dispenser popped the food out in front of them, and Billie grabbed their own trayful of crap and headed to find a table. Once seated, Billie wolfed her burger, her legs swinging back and forth beneath her.

Jack watched her, toying with the stuff in front of him, not really interested. He didn't feel right here. This was not his place. What the hell was he doing here?

Off to one side, a young boy dropped part of his unfinished burger on the floor. He was leaning over sideways, reaching to pick it up, when the floor, sensing something it could use, swallowed the synthetic lump. That was the only way to describe it. Small ridges had extruded around the piece of burger, a depression had formed, and then the ridges had closed over the piece, making it disappear, as if some bizarre mouth had grown out of the floor and swallowed. Jack swallowed too, a sense of revulsion rising within him.

Seeing his piece of burger vanish, the kid started screaming. Jack narrowed his eyes and groaned under his breath. He didn't need this. He didn't need this at all. Struggling, he turned his attention back to Billie.

He was thankful it wasn't too long before she seemed satisfied and he could ferry her back to the apartment before heading back up to the port.

The port itself lay at the extreme New end of the Locality, right at the head. A large retractable panel formed part of the ceiling over a wide open-area, giving access to fliers coming and going to the major spaceport on the coast, the Residence, and other areas within easy striking distance of the structure. From time to time that meant other urban structures similar to the Locality, but transfers between the various mobile cities were few. The Locality was the most significant of all of them, dominating business and commerce on the continent. There were no roads—there was no need for roads. Since the development of mobility in urban living, fixed transport routes had become a thing of the past.

Jack left the shuttle at the last stop and headed the rest of the way by foot. After looking around the port area, he found the offices of the private shuttle company, his handipad out and ready. Once inside he simply keyed the booking information at a wall screen, and within moments a pilot was there to greet him.

"Mr. Warburg?" he said.

"Yeah, that's right," said Jack.

"This way, please. The Residence, right?"

Jack nodded and followed. He waited while the pilot clambered up, finished prepping, then opened the rear door for Jack to climb in. As soon as the pilot had checked that Jack was strapped in, he kicked the engines into life and slid the privacy screen shut. Jack smiled to himself. There was nothing quite like proper travel. He only wished he could afford to pay for it on his own. He looked up, marveling as always as the vast ceiling panel retracted, sliding back into the Locality's structure to disappear from view. The flier lifted slowly, then more rapidly, and Jack settled back into the plush, comfortable seat, watching as the newest of the Locality's structures, all hard edges, reaching and finding a newer architectural design regime—building fashions changed and these new ones were all glassy and metallic rather than the softer pastel shapes toward Old—slid past the windows, down and away below him, the noise of the rotors growing louder as the craft gained speed.

The flier banked and soared, the sound of its rotors beating over the cabin. The flier dipped and then headed out over the Locality's roof. Jack leaned over, his face pressed up against the window, peering down at the huge urban corridor crawling across the landscape beneath them. A vast swath, furrowed through the land, marked its progress, the track meandering back and forth as the Locality's preprogrammed sensors sought out the raw materials it needed. The structure's outside shone with slick iridescence, catching the light here and there and fragmenting it into star-shaped rainbows, sparking off the surface. The surrounding landscape denied the presence. Verdant, unsullied, it stared skyward, pretending that the mobile hive simply wasn't there. There was something wrong about it, thought Jack, as if it belonged to another place altogether. He wondered whether he too belonged to another place altogether, whether all of them belonged in another place, and then his thoughts turned to Billie.

It would be easy for him just to think of her as an ordinary kid—the experience at Molly's, her excitement as she'd thought she was going to be flying to the Residence with him, and then the disappointment—but then he'd remember. He'd remember the involuntary maturity, the damaged hostility, and he knew it was more complex than that. He absently fingered the top of the mystery handipad thrust deep into his pocket. If what Billie had said was true, and he had no reason to doubt it, whatever the handipad contained was beyond his reach. He was no scientist. Sure, he'd done his own research about archetypical images and the sort of mystical traditions that dealt with dreams and foreknowledge. In a way that was a science of its own, but formulae, equations, physics, all that stuff was really outside his knowledge or experience. What mattered was that the handipad's owner would want it back, and that other parties had an interest. Whether it would get him any closer to solving the Outreach problem remained to be seen, but he could force the connections in this case. Sometimes he just had to grab circumstance and shake it into some sort of shape that he could recognize.

Science stuff. What would one of the untouchable

wealthy of the Residence want with scientific formulae, with equations and the like, let alone material on philosophers and alchemy? Who even knew what they were into? The Residence folk kept pretty much to themselves. Their privacy could mask a multitude of diversions, a multitude of sins.

Again his thoughts drifted back to the kid he had somehow inherited.

"Billie," he'd said to her at Molly's.

"Uh-huh," she'd answered, preoccupied with demolishing her burger.

"Not that they're going to, but if anyone asks, I'm your uncle. I just brought you with me for a Foundation Day treat."

"Sure."

"Uncle Jack," he said thoughtfully.

"Okay. Just like Uncle Pinpin."

The chill struck deep through his spine. "No," he said. "Nothing like Pinpin. Just Uncle Jack."

"Uh-huh."

How could she have made that connection? No, he could see why. He shook his head, tasting the deeper implications and not liking them very much.

He looked out over his shoulder at the glittering snake of the Locality. Farther back, in the distance, the signs of regrowth marked the trail. The sunlight reflected across the roof panels, shimmering rainbows. Here, from this height, it was hard to imagine the enormity of the beast. Twenty-story walls had shrunk to the size of a finger's breadth. The districts were echoed by faint segments along the length of the beast. There were virtual borders, invisible from the inside, but defined by the outer shell and the patterns of the ceiling panels. Maybe it had something to do with programming and maintenance, a way to track where particular things were going on within the structure itself. The Locality trailed off, becoming smaller as the decaying materials were reabsorbed into the body. It left a long tail, just like the end of a snake. Jack had almost forgotten what it was like.

It had been years since he'd been outside. It was so easy to forget there even was an outside. Everything you might possibly need was there inside the Locality. Every single one of the inhabitants worked and lived and moved from day to day enclosed within their artificial womb, the umbilicus of the Locality itself feeding them at the touch of a button or a spoken command. What sort of life was it, really? They were like drones, characterless, devoid of real motivation or ambition. All they did was produce for the unseen corporation that owned the place. No, he had more important things to think about than the state of their collective life. They'd all chosen it, after all.

Going to Molly's had been a good idea. He'd been able to watch and check whether they'd been tailed on their way from the apartment. While Billie shoveled her face full of synthetic Mollyburger, he'd picked at fries, watching the door and trying to block out the noise of the Foundation Day families taking their kids for a treat. Family values, that was what Molly's was all about, or at least what they fed the consumers and their kids. Synthesized media crap along with the synthesized crap they stuck between buns. He'd examined the fry as he held it aloft in front of his eyes, wondering if it was real potato or some vegetable simulacrum made to resemble potato. Now, that would have been a real irony—making vegetables up to look like other vegetables. Jack had his own inbuilt cynicism working overtime, but Billie had seemed to enjoy the food.

Jack had had another thought while they were eating, remembering the way she had seized and distilled the information she'd researched for him.

"How much of that science stuff on the handipad do you remember?" he'd asked.

"Some," she answered with a shrug. Perhaps he could use that. It was better to pretend that he hadn't been through it himself. Safer that way, if it came to it. Nobody would suspect her.

"Doesn't matter anyway," she'd said. "I uploaded it to your system while you were out."

He slapped at his forehead with the tips of his fingers and gave a wordless growl between his teeth.

"You did *what*?"

"Uploaded it. After I finished looking at that snake stuff, I got bored. Had to do something."

"But wasn't it protected?"

"Sure." Another shrug.

"If you were bored, why didn't you watch a vid or something?"

"Didn't want to."

And that was that. Jack ran the possibilities over in his head. His home system now held the contents of the handipad. If the incident at Pinpin's place was anything to go by, that could be dangerous. There was no way he could claim lack of knowledge now. What if Pinpin's visitors came looking? He chewed it over as they sat there, but there were no other options.

"I'm worried about having that stuff there, Billie."

She paused midbite and looked at him. "What for?"

"What if that pair come looking?"

"Who?"

"That pair at Pinpin's."

She shrugged again. "Oh, those two. They can't find it. Not if I don't want them to. Nobody can find it."

Her matter-of-fact certainty was unsettling, but he let it be. What was done was done, for now. There was nothing to tie the pair at Pinpin's to his apartment, as far as he knew, and he'd just have to let it rest at that.

He stared out the side window as the land whipped by beneath. The terrain was passing him by just like the chain of events, and he felt as though he were powerless to stop the tide.

Before long the flier approached the environs of the Residence. Jack had had cause to be out this way only once before, but it looked pretty much the same as he remembered it. He watched the low, squat shapes overlooking the bay, the terraced gardens, the gravel drives. These were *houses*. And they were houses built the old way, brick upon brick, stone upon stone. No automatic-build program here, no technology to do the work for you. Craftsmen, people, stuff done the way it had been done years before build programs even existed. It reeked of money. It was funny how the more wealth people accumulated, the older were the things they collected and did. Antiques, houses built the old way, gardens, open air—the irreplaceable. How exactly did you value the marks of privilege?

He wasn't used to seeing living spaces like this. Nothing like the apartment buildings back in the Locality. These huge structures were built for one family, or even one person. What for? So they could keep private. So they could be selective about what they saw. Just like the way they all looked out over the ocean. One fixed view, seeing only what they wanted to see.

The flier started descending, heading for a landing

pad atop one of the nearby hills. They settled gently to the ground and the pilot opened the privacy screen. Blank insect eyes, reflective shades. No expression.

"Take this," he said, holding out a card. "It's auto call, for when you need to leave."

Jack palmed the card and frowned. "I'm not sure how long I'll be. Can't you wait?"

The pilot shook his head. "They don't like us hanging around. Strict rules."

He grunted his understanding. It wasn't ideal, but it would have to do. The door slid open and he climbed down to a flat expanse of grass. He backed away as the door slid shut and the flier took off again, quickly fading to an indistinct speck against the cloud-smudged sky.

"Hunh," said Jack. He'd forgotten. Last time he'd been out here, it was a prearranged visit. There'd been someone to meet him, to ferry him to where he was going in a slow-moving electric transport. This time it was walk.

Jack turned and looked for a way down, but the hilltop was an unbroken expanse of undisturbed grass, apart from the twin indentations marking where the flier had stood. Green, gray, and blue sky above. He felt disconnected, as if he were part of a dream sequence that had no relevance to anything he was working on. A slight breeze rippled his coat.

He flipped open his handipad and called up the map. Where was he going?

He reoriented the handipad, getting his bearings. He could see the house from here. It was a wide, stone affair. Columns ran along a porch around the outside. Broad windows reflected the ocean meeting the line of sky over the valley. Walls of glass. It sat high up on the opposite hill overlooking the bay, peeking over the tops of a stand of neatly arrayed and pruned trees. He chose his direction, plotting a path through the wide estates and headed on down.

Jack felt out of place. He *looked* out of place with his old coat, scruffy clothes and stubbled chin. Well, he had a reason for being here, and if the Van der Stegen name meant anything, it should mean something out here, not that he expected to run into anyone asking questions.

He reached the edge of the estate where the buildings started, and scanned the area warily. There was not a sign of life. No doubt he was already being scanned and monitored by various security systems, but there was no sign of people. The stillness, the silence was uncomfortable, especially after the crowded avenues of the Locality. He shrugged, a halfhearted attempt to shake off the feeling, and headed up toward his destination, his hands shoved into his pockets. Absentmindedly he fingered the mystery handipad. He wondered how many tourists they got out here. Probably not that many. Too expensive. He imagined how many actual people were tracking him now as he walked slowly up the hill to the big house that was his destination.

He'd just entered the grounds of the Van der Stegen residence when there were signs of movement from the building itself.

"Shit," muttered Jack. One of the electric transports he'd seen on his last visit was whirring down the drive toward him. It drew to a stop long after Jack had had time to study its occupant.

She was stunning. That was the only word for it. A shimmering robe hung about her, barely disguising the shape of her slim, well-proportioned body. Long chestnut hair was swept up in twin wings on either side of her face, a long, finely sculpted face with a wide, full mouth and dark, slightly almond-shaped eyes. Probably enhanced, but he could forget that for now. He could forget all of it. He could dream of a woman like this.

She took her time looking back at him, returning his gaze unconcernedly. "Yes?" she said finally. A deep, rich voice.

Jack finally remembered himself. "Hello," he said.

Good opening, Stein. She looked at him blankly.

"Um, I'm Jack Stein. I wanted to see Mr. Van der Stegen. Mr. Joshua Van der Stegen. This is the place, right?"

She took a moment before answering, considering. "Hmm. Well, Daddy's not here at the moment. I guess you don't have an appointment, or if you have, he's probably forgotten it. He does that all the time. People get used to it. Perhaps I can help you. If you'd like to tell me the nature of your business."

"Daddy?"

"Yes, Joshua Van der Stegen is my father. I'm Anastasia Van der Stegen."

"I have something that I believe belongs to him, Miss Van der Stegen. I wanted to return it to him in person."

Another pause and a coolness in the voice. "Right. Well, he's not here. You can give it to me. What is it?"

"I believe it's his handipad."

"I see." She seemed to consider for a moment, and then the frostiness rapidly left her voice. "You'd better come up to the house. Climb on."

He nodded and clambered up behind her. This

close, he caught a rich floral scent. Something like roses, but different. She swung the transport in a wide arc, then headed back up to the house itself.

"The house alerted me, and I saw you coming up the hill," she said over her shoulder. "I didn't think I recognized you, though Daddy has some pretty strange visitors. Apart from that, we don't get many people out here."

"So, Miss Van der Stegen, is it just you and your father here?"

He looked around at the grounds as she replied. Neatly tended hedges bordered the wide, lightly graveled drive. Beyond them lay flower beds, and farther back he thought he caught a glimpse of a tennis court.

"Tasha. Most people call me Tasha. Yes, just us, except for the people who work here, of course."

She eased the transport to a stop in front of tall, thick, paneled front doors, slid down from the front seat, and beckoned him to follow. A wide stone roof covered the parking spot, supported by neatly sculpted white columns. And speaking of neatly sculpted, Jack watched the movement of Tasha's back and legs beneath the sheer opalescent fabric appreciatively. The robe clung to her shape as she moved, delineating her body in vaguely pearly shimmers. She flung the door wide and waltzed inside. A moment later her voice came from inside.

"Well, come on, Jack Stein."

He grunted, jumped from the transport, and followed. This wouldn't do. He had to get a grip.

They entered a vast, echoing hallway. A tiled floor stretched before them, *real* tiles, black and white in a checkerboard pattern. A wide staircase circled to an upper level, a staircase looking like it was made of marble with a wooden banister, rich, dark, and deeply polished. Other doorways led off the entrance hall. Anastasia Van der Stegen stood leaning back against a wall, her position only enhancing the fall of the fabric about her body. She let her gaze rove languidly, slowly, up and down Jack's frame, taking in the coat, his boots, and moving back to his face. She pushed herself from the wall, crossed the intervening space, and stood close to him, too close. One hand reached up to finger the fabric of his coat. He could feel her breath on his cheek. It was sweet, fresh, and added to the heady floral scent that surrounded her.

"So, Jack Stein, let's see what you have to show me." Her voice was smooth, suggestive.

He fumbled in his coat pocket and pulled out the handipad, the right one, and held it out. She barely glanced at it, instead holding his gaze with her big, dark eyes.

"Daddy will be pleased," she said. She took the handipad and tossed it casually onto a nearby hall table. "Can't abide the things myself." Letting her fingers linger for just a moment, she turned and walked to the wall. Jack glanced around the sumptuous trappings. Above them hung a chandelier, multifaceted glass drops catching the light in rainbows.

"How did you come by it, Jack Stein?" she said without turning around.

"What?" he asked, momentarily confused.

"The handipad, of course."

"It doesn't really matter, does it?"

She looked at him over her shoulder, and before she could mask it he caught a brief look of calculation in the gaze.

"No, I suppose not."

He cleared his throat. "Um, Miss Van der Stegen—"

"Tasha." She turned to face him, leaning back against the wall again.

"All right, Tasha." He was having difficulty concentrating on why he was here. "Did your father mention that he'd lost his handipad?"

She shrugged.

"Or maybe that it was important?"

She gave a slight shake of her head. The movement caused a ripple to run through the robe's fabric, and Jack tracked it and swallowed involuntarily.

"So how do you know it's his?" she said. "Usually he's pretty careful with his things."

"Oh, let's just say I have my own ways of knowing."

Again the flutter of calculation in her glance, again the quick dropping of the shutters of naïveté. This girl was more than she wanted to let on.

She pushed herself from the wall and smoothed the dress against her thighs. "You said you thought it might be important."

"I just wondered. I thought it might have had something to do with his business. I've had a bit of trouble since I, um, acquired it."

Another shrug, and Jack found his attention wandering again.

"I wouldn't know anything about that. Daddy doesn't talk to me about business. I overhear things from time to time, but all that science and space doesn't really interest me."

Science and space. Those words brought his attention quickly back to the immediate.

Anastasia continued. "I am so sorry it's caused you problems. You must let me give you *something* to make up for your trouble." She let the statement hang between them. Jack tried to ignore the implications.

"It must have cost you to bring it all the way out here," she said finally.

Jack thought of a number and doubled it. Sometimes he hated bringing things down to money, but not this time. Anything she might give him would be a mere drop in the ocean to people like the Van der Stegens. After all, her family, the other people who lived around here, had an entire hive of worker drones to satisfy their needs and whims.

Anastasia turned back to the wall and spoke a command. "Have you got your own handipad with you?"

"Sure," said Jack, and dug it out and flipped it open, ready.

She spoke another couple of commands. The number was more than what he'd told her. Jack closed the handipad, feeling pleased at the unexpected bonus. He wouldn't be so reliant upon Gleeson and the Outreach contract now.

Thoughts of Gleeson suddenly reminded him why he was here.

"Listen, I would still like to talk to your father about this," he said. "Here's my card. I'm a PI, Miss Van der Stegen. Your father might have links to a case I'm working on at the moment, and I'd like to ask him a few questions."

She took the card and ran her finger slowly back and forth along the edge, watching him all the while. She barely glanced at the card, then slipped it inside some concealed pocket inside the robe. Jack struggled to think where there might be space for a pocket in the garment.

"Sure," said Anastasia. "I'll let him know. A PI?"

"Yeah. Psychic investigator."

"How interesting." He'd expected condescension in the reaction, but if it was there, there was no trace of it.

"Do you expect your father back?"

Another shrug. "He might be back. He might not."

"Well, it is important that I talk to him."

"I'll let him know when I see him," she said again with a shrug.

"Thanks," said Jack. "I'll find my own way out."

She said nothing. He left Anastasia Van der Stegen standing there, leaning against the wall, watching.

Once outside on the broad gravel drive, Jack muttered to himself, "Get a hold of yourself, Jack. You know better than to think with your dick instead of your head. Stupid."

He walked back down the hill, thinking about the Van der Stegen girl's behavior and his own response. There was too much going on there that didn't add up. Not only the feigned innocence, but other little things. She'd said she hated handipads, and yet she had loaded his without a blink. She was obviously aware of the effect she had on the male thought processes. What would she want to play with someone like him for anyway? He assumed it had to be play. Maybe it gave her a sense of power or something. And the casual dropping of the stuff about science and space—all innocence, but was it? Science and space. He shook his head and, as he walked back up the hill to the landing field, slipped the card into his handipad to call the flier that would take him back to the Locality.

By the time he got back, Billie was hungry again. Another visit to Molly's and another fight against the

Foundation Day crowds squeezed into the shuttle, and they finally made it back to the apartment. The synth food sat heavily in his stomach, and he felt the acid rising in his throat. He couldn't go on eating like this. Once upon a time he'd sworn to himself that he'd never eat that crap, but sometimes, just sometimes, easy was better. He resigned himself to getting some supplies. It wouldn't have mattered so much if Billie didn't get hungry so quickly. Jack could go without food for hours, sometimes days. Recently he often simply forgot to eat.

He didn't have time for this. He needed to think, to try to put the pieces together.

"Billie, I need to do some work. Then we can talk about what we're going to do with you."

"What am I going to do?"

"I don't know. Watch a vid or something."

He left her there in the living room and shut himself in the bedroom, lay back on the bed, and flipped open his handipad. There was a lot of stuff to go through.

Two hours later and he'd read all he could. Billie had left him undisturbed and he'd been able to piece together a few points.

The Ouroboros had been a recurring symbol throughout Earth culture from ancient times, not only in myth and legend, but in dream images as well. Even down to that chemist who had dreamed about the snake biting its own tail, which had led to the structure of benzene.

Archetypes. Dream images. Symbols.

And alchemy.

Big questions, one after the other.

What was the significance? How was it linked to the happenings on Dairil III?

He remembered the ring in the dream. Black and silver. It might as well be black and white. Positive and negative. Yin and yang. And inside the snake, the writing. It was Greek. It meant, "The all is one." He knew that much now, but it made no more sense to him than any of the rest.

So what did the symbol mean? From what he could glean, its primary meaning was a representation of the cyclic nature of the universe: creation out of destruction; life out of death.

The death part made sense, but it was a tenuous link at best. It had to be deeper than that. Then there was Ronschke's mention of the stone, whatever stone that might be. Linking the snake to alchemy, it could only be the fabled philosophers' stone, the catalyst to transformation. Change. The end is the beginning. As above so below.

The mystic rubrics tumbled through his head, fogging the thought process rather than clearing it.

He was wasting his time.

But somehow Outreach was linked to Joshua Van der Stegen and whatever lay coded on his handipad. And in turn that was linked to whatever had happened to Gil Ronschke and the rest of the mining crew.

If Van der Stegen was involved, it was big. Bigger maybe than just Outreach. Jack didn't know what Van der Stegen did yet, but he clearly had immense resources at his disposal. Science and space. Exactly the same sort of background that Outreach had in its Dairil III operations. Somebody clearly cared very much about what was going on. Pinpin's visitors had shown him that far more clearly than he would have liked.

And then there was Billie. What exactly was her role

in all of this? Sure, maybe it was just coincidence that she'd been there when he'd visited Pinpin, but he was reluctant to accept that. He had a feeling about it.

His thoughts strayed back to the ring in the mine. There was just too much there, too many symbols to tease apart. The black and white. The severed hand, cut off from . . . what? If the last Dairil III dream had told him anything, then the link was Ronschke, but he seriously doubted that such a ring would have belonged to the burly miner. Just not his style. And the ring was more than just a ring. The snake biting its own tail was a ring in itself. So it was a ring on a ring. It had dimensionality.

And then there was the thing coming out of the wall. Was it something alive? Was it the "creature" in that old poem?

His head hurt. He needed a drink, but he didn't have time anymore. He let the handipad drop to the bed beside him and sighed with frustration. Knowing what he had to do, he reached over, pulled open the drawer by the bed, and retrieved a stim patch. At least the drugs might give him some focus. Keeping his energy levels going and his concentration focused was what he needed now. With a look of distaste, recalling the sensations from the first Dairil III dream, he smoothed it on.

He still had work to do. Lots of work. Time to look at the material from Joshua Van der Stegen's handipad. Running his fingers back through his hair, he moved his head from side to side to ease the tension in his neck, and wandered out into the living room to talk to Billie and get her to give him access to the downloaded material.

Jack glanced at the wall as he wandered in. The material was already open, and Billie was scanning through it.

"I might have found some things," she said, looking up.

Nine

"Call waiting," said the wall.

"Who?" said Jack, barely able to contain the trace of annoyance in his voice. He'd made no further progress with the Van der Stegen material, and his frustration was growing. The pointers Billie had given him had been starting points, but nothing more. He didn't know why he'd expected anything else. She was currently in the other room fixing herself something to eat. Just as well. Whoever the caller was, he didn't want her seen.

"Identity withheld," said the wall.

He debated for a moment, then killed the notes display and said, "Answer." He'd been making limited progress anyway. Lots of fragments and passages about containment fields, bridges, exotic matter, riddled with formulae and theoretical assumptions. Way beyond him, even with the extra edge provided by the stim patch.

The face that swam into view was not one he recognized—a severe face, high browed, thinning white hair, dark, thick eyebrows.

"Jack Stein?"

"Yeah, and you are . . .?"

"Joshua Van der Stegen, Mr. Stein."

His daughter must have gotten her looks from her mother.

Van der Stegen continued. "I believe I owe you a debt of gratitude, Mr. Stein, for returning my, uh . . . property." He licked his lips and narrowed his eyes. Just for a moment Jack thought about the millions of little nonliving creatures scuttling around inside the wall to make the image change. "May I ask you how you came by it?"

At that moment Billie appeared in the doorway, carrying a tray of ready-cooked. The expression on Van der Stegen's face changed. "Ah, and this would be . . ."

Jack cursed inwardly. "My niece, Mr. Van der Stegen."

A frown flickered, and he glanced toward her pointedly.

"No, it's fine," said Jack, taking his meaning immediately. "We can talk in front of Billie."

"Ah, I see. All right then . . ."

Jack had already crafted what he was going to say in case of just such a conversation. He recounted the story about finding the handipad on a shuttle, dropped by someone whom he didn't know. When he was finished, Van der Stegen looked thoughtful.

"I see," he said. "I don't suppose you know who this person on the shuttle might have been?" He rubbed at his top lip with one finger.

"I don't mind telling you," said Jack. "Our friend on the shuttle isn't the only one who has expressed an interest in your 'property,' as you call it."

"How so?"

"Considering the exact nature of that interest, I'd prefer not to go into it right here and now."

"I see." Van der Stegen gave a quick nod, then paused, clearly considering. "I understand you're an investigator, Mr. Stein."

"Yeah, PI—psychic investigations. What of it?"

"And I don't suppose your current work would have anything to do with the object coming into your possession."

"Not exactly, no."

"Fine, then I'd like to make use of your services."

"I don't do business over a wall screen."

"I see."

"It's the nature of my work, Mr. Van der Stegen." He paused, spreading his hands. "It's not only a question of security. It has to do with the impressions I get from direct contact. It's important to what I do."

Van der Stegen looked troubled, but he nodded his understanding.

Jack clasped his hands and leaned forward. "Okay, you're interested in hiring me. So, let me guess . . . it has to do with the subject of our discussion."

"You don't need to be a psychic to work that out, Stein."

"Of course. Okay . . . if you still want to talk about it, you'll have to come to my office. We can discuss rates and other considerations there."

Van der Stegen stared out from the wallscreen. "Perhaps you could come here."

"No," said Jack. "I'd prefer to meet you at my office. Neutral ground. I need to make sure that the impressions are not contaminated by anything."

Van der Stegen continued to look troubled. "All right. If I must. But I have one or two things to take care of first. I can't get there straightaway."

"You have the address. How soon can you get there?"

"Give me three and a half hours."

"Fine," said Jack. "Off," he said, cutting the connection and glancing at the wall display to mark the time. Three and a half hours. Maybe he was out at the Residence, maybe he wasn't, but Van der Stegen didn't believe in wasting time.

He sat back again, feeling moderately pleased with himself. There was more than one reason he wanted to use the office. The systems there were rudimentary, making it harder for anyone to break in and monitor their discussions. Plus, what he'd said to the man was true. He wanted to get close to Joshua Van der Stegen, somewhere on truly neutral ground, where he could get a real feel for the guy. The clinical sparseness of his office would help with that. Van der Stegen was linked to the Outreach stuff somehow, and he needed to find out how. The fact that he had called just when Jack had been scanning the uploaded notes from the handipad didn't escape him either. Things worked like that—always. Always the strangely timed connections driving things forward. Coincidence was more than mere coincidence—always.

"So what are you going to do now?" said Billie from the doorway around a mouthful of ready-cooked. He'd almost forgotten she was there.

"Going to meet with this Van der Stegen guy and find out why everyone's so interested in this handipad of his."

"And what am I supposed to do?"

"Damn it, Billie. I don't know. Stay here. Amuse yourself."

She narrowed her eyes and mouthed the words back at him, silently, chin thrust forward.

Shit. "Okay, what do you suggest?" he said resignedly.

She said nothing, just stood there pouting.

"Well?"

"Can't I come with you?"

"No, you can't come with me. I don't want you involved."

"But he's already seen me. He knows I'm with you."

"Sure, but he thinks you're my niece. And that's the way I want it to stay. If I drag you along to the meeting, he's bound to have questions."

She picked at the ready-cooked, refusing to meet his eyes.

"Listen, Billie. Later, when I get back, we're going to sit down together and have a long talk. There are things I want to know about you, things we have to work out."

She glanced up at him suspiciously.

Jack suddenly had an idea. If she were as good with information as she seemed . . .

"But, all right, there is something you can do while I'm gone. The upload from the handipad. I've looked through it and can't make much sense out of it. Maybe you can go through it one more time and see if there's anything more useful."

"Like what?"

"See if it means anything, if you can tie it to the other stuff you were looking up for me. I want you to see if you can find a way the science stuff links to the history. Can you do that?"

"Uh-huh," she said slowly.

"Oh, and one other thing. Is there a way you can block incoming calls unless they're from me? I might need to get in touch with you quickly." He didn't know why he said that, but his gut feeling told him it was right.

"Easy," said Billie.

"Good. And while you're at it, see if you can find out anything about this Joshua Van der Stegen. Who he's involved with. Where he got his money. Stuff like that. Can you do that?"

She nodded. She seemed satisfied, so he grabbed his handipad and moved to get ready. She really did seem as if the challenge he'd set were something that would keep her absorbed. *Good.* Billie's presence was turning out to be a bonus, and with the way his mind appeared to be fogging any connections he could come up with, he could use a fresh viewpoint right now.

He arrived early, giving himself a good half hour before he expected Van der Stegen to arrive. It gave him the space to become attuned to the office, the surrounds, so they'd appear as nothing more than background noise to his sensitivity. He looked around at the blank walls, the spartan furnishings, the trails of equipment, and sucked air through his teeth. Impersonal and functional, just like most of his life. He'd ripped off the stim patches before leaving, but he still felt the chemical coursing through his bloodstream. It would be a couple of hours before the traces of it left. It meant he'd be a little on edge for the meeting. Not good, but there was little choice. The sooner he met with Van der Stegen the better.

He sat on the edge of the couch and stared at the wall. What was he really doing? He felt as if he were losing control, as if events were pushing him in directions he was powerless to shape, but there was nothing particularly new about that. It was about time he started to get hold of his life. The sheltered environment of the Locality did little to help.

Mentally he ticked off the people involved, trying to trace the connecting threads. William Warburg, the executive from Outreach. Francis Gleeson, an Outreach clerk. Gil Ronschke, an Outreach miner. Joshua Van der Stegen, connected how? Pinpin Dan—dead, but still connected in some way. And then there was Billie. Somehow she was tied into all of this, but damned if he knew how. The names just wouldn't come together. The only common thread was Outreach Industries.

And on top of everything, there was the dream. The White-Haired Man. Who or what was he supposed to represent? Something sinister, that much was clear. But what girlfriend? It couldn't mean Billie. There was just no way he could allow himself to accept that as a possibility, unless his subconscious mind was trying to tell him something that he really didn't want to hear. No, there was no way. Even Jack Stein's head was not that fucked up.

The door announced an arrival, interrupting the random chain of thoughts.

Jack called up the image and pursed his lips. It was Van der Stegen, right on cue, but he wasn't alone. He had another person with him, a woman. A big woman. The sight of her sparked something uncomfortable in his chest, but he let it pass. It was probably just the stims making him edgy again. It wouldn't do to let paranoia creep into the equation. He let them in.

Van der Stegen strode into the office and looked about imperiously, distaste clearly etched on his severe, dark-browed face. The woman entered behind him and took up a position by the door, her hands crossed behind her back. She was large-framed, solid. Reddish, short-cropped hair sat tightly above a squared face. She was dressed in dark, loose, nondescript clothes, giving her freedom of movement. She looked around the room first, then at Jack. There was a momentary flash of interest in her eyes; then she looked away. Okay, so this was Van der Stegen's hired muscle.

"Mr. Stein," said Van der Stegen, looking around for somewhere to plant himself. Jack gestured to one of the chairs, and perched himself on the edge of his couch, half standing.

"Jack. Just call me Jack, Mr. Van der Stegen."

Van der Stegen grunted and sat back on the chair, adjusting his clothing, still taking in his surroundings. Jack's gaze flitted from him to the big woman by the door and back again. The woman seemed content simply to stand there, watching, but there was nothing relaxed about her pose. He got the impression of tautness, tightly flexed steel.

"So, Mr. Van der Stegen," said Jack. "Glad you could make it, you and your friend . . ." He let the statement hang meaningfully between them.

Van der Stegen waved his hand dismissively. "This is one of my personal security staff. One can't be too careful."

"Right," said Jack. He watched her for a moment or two before turning his attention back. "So what can I do for you, Mr. Van der Stegen?"

Van der Stegen was staring at the simple desk. Jack followed his gaze. The small blue bottle belonging to

Gil Ronschke sat at one corner. Damn, he'd forgotten he'd left it there.

"As we discussed, Jack, I am interested in determining who removed my handipad and why. It's important that this remains quiet."

"That's understood. I'll want a thousand a day and, of course, expenses."

"Yes, yes," said Van der Stegen, as if he could barely be bothered with such trivialities. Jack suddenly wished he'd said a bigger number. "You mentioned other interests."

"Yes, that's right. But first, do you have any idea who this person who left my handipad on the shuttle might have been?"

Reaching for someone convenient he could slot into the story, Jack remembered the man in the out-of-place clothes whom he'd seen on his shuttle ride to New. Using what he could recall, he described the man.

Van der Stegen glanced at the woman by the door, who gave a quick, almost imperceptible shake of her head. Van der Stegen turned his head slowly to face Jack. "That's one of the reasons why I'm engaging you, Stein. The person you describe is like no one I know. It doesn't seem as if he's familiar to Marianna either." He looked down at his coat and brushed an invisible something from the lapel. "Now, what of these other things you mentioned?"

"Before we get to that, I need to know more. Who might be interested in the contents of your handipad? Who would have access to it?"

Van der Stegen fixed him with a hard look. "And what precisely do you know of the contents?"

"Nothing at all," said Jack evenly. "But clearly

they're important to someone; otherwise why would they bother to take it?"

Van der Stegen rubbed his top lip with one finger, the same gesture he'd used in the earlier call, and looked at him appraisingly. After a moment's consideration, he continued.

"Yes, all right. I suppose that's a possibility. It could have been sheer opportunism, but you're probably right. Some of the companies I'm involved with have high-level research projects. I like to keep myself abreast of their progress, and so I carry around detailed notes. Perhaps you might think it a little foolish, but that's the way I work. We all have our own ways of doing things. I'm simply a creature of habit. Suffice it to say that the content of those notes is of no real interest to you, Mr. Stein."

"Perhaps not," said Jack. "But we have to make certain assumptions. Why would someone want to take it?"

Van der Stegen sighed. "I suppose industrial espionage is always a possibility, but I doubt it. There is more than one type of opportunism, after all. There's simple opportunism and there's opportunism with intent. More likely it was the former, not knowing what they might find."

"So," said Jack. "Did you notice it was missing?"

Van der Stegen looked uncomfortable. "No. No, I didn't. I've been busy with a couple of other things lately."

"All right. It can't have been missing for long, though." Jack filed that away for later, nodding to himself. Apparently his gut feelings were right again. Gleeson had not been telling him the entire truth about how he'd come by the device. It was just all too con-

venient. If Van der Stegen carried the thing around
with him, making notes, he was likely to miss it pretty
quickly. The fact that he hadn't pointed to a relatively
small time window. "And who would have had access
to the handipad?"

"No one I can think of. There's the household staff,
of course, but they go through rigorous screening, and
I know most of them personally."

So Van der Stegen could afford the luxury of actual
staff, but Jack knew that already. He'd seen the house.
Nothing new or surprising there.

"And visitors?"

"We have very few." Van der Stegen shook his head.
"No, most of my business dealings occur away from
the Residence. Very occasionally I hold a meeting at
the house. Apart from that there's not much call for
visitors."

"What about your daughter?"

"What about her?" he snapped, narrowing his eyes.

"As you already know, I've met your daughter. I
just think we should consider—"

"What? That Tasha took it? I resent that suggestion.
Perhaps you should concentrate your energies elsewhere, Mr. Stein." Again, the motion with finger and
upper lip; then he rubbed his thumb and forefinger together and made to stand, but Jack waved him down.

"I'm not suggesting *she* took it, Mr. Van der Stegen."
Though Van der Stegen's reaction had definitely
pushed it up on the list of Jack's possibilities now.
"Rather, perhaps she might have had a visitor, someone who might just be such an opportunist."

"I suppose it's a possibility, but I don't believe it's
likely. And I would prefer it if Tasha were left out of
this."

"Fine." He'd deal with that line of inquiry his own way, and his own way would definitely involve asking Tasha a couple of pointed questions, but Van der Stegen didn't have to know that at this stage.

Van der Stegen stood and crossed to the desk. He reached for the bottle.

"Mr. Van der Stegen, I'd rather you didn't—"

Too late. Van der Stegen had picked up the bottle and was turning it over in his fingers.

"Nice little piece." Then he turned and saw the expression on Jack's face. "Is there a problem?"

"Nothing. It belongs to a client, that's all."

"Humph," said Van der Stegen, and returned the bottle to the desk. He stared down at it for a moment, then traced his fingers up one side again, oblivious to Jack's grimace. "All right, that's settled. How long before I expect to hear something from you?" he asked without turning around.

"I may need to contact you, perhaps talk to some of your people."

"That shouldn't be a problem." Van der Stegen withdrew a card from inside his coat and placed it carefully on the desk beside the bottle. "Is there anything else?"

"What do you know about Outreach Industries, Mr. Van der Stegen?"

The slight stiffening of the man's shoulders and the flicker of movement from by the door did not go unnoticed.

"Why do you ask?"

"Well, you mentioned industrial espionage. It's just a name that came up recently."

Van der Stegen turned slowly, glancing around the walls. "Is this place secure?"

Jack nodded.

Van der Stegen hesitated. "This information is to be kept strictly to yourself. It's not too widely known, but I have quite a sizable interest in Outreach. It's more as what you'd call a silent partner. I suppose it doesn't hurt that you know that, but how you came by that information—"

"—is my business for now, Mr. Van der Stegen. It's just useful to know my sources are reliable."

Van der Stegen shoved his hands in his pockets, but not before rubbing at his lips again, now firmly pursed. He gave Jack a long, hard stare, but apparently was satisfied, because he nodded.

"I'd prefer that knowledge didn't become public either. I have other concerns in the Locality that might see that involvement as a conflict of interests. I can trust your discretion?"

"Hey, you're the client, Mr. Van der Stegen," said Jack. "Client privilege and all that."

He nodded. "All right. Is that it?"

"Yes, Mr. Van der Stegen, that's it for now. I'll be in touch."

Van der Stegen and the woman left him sitting there, watching the door as it shut behind them.

Something about the woman was nagging at him, but he couldn't put his finger on it. It was more than the sense of unease she invoked in him. There was the barely disguised movement when he'd mentioned Outreach and . . . something else. That flicker of almost recognition as she'd entered. That could easily be explained, he supposed. If she was on Van der Stegen's security staff, then she could easily have remembered him from the household security monitors. Van der Stegen was sure to have had him checked out before coming. He didn't recognize her from anywhere else, he was almost certain. He remembered faces, and hers just didn't trigger anything.

Later. He could worry about that later.

He'd received nothing in particular from Van der Stegen himself. There were just the normal impressions that anybody could work out for themselves. No need for extra abilities. The man was used to command and power. He liked to be in control, and he expected people to fall into line with his wishes. Jack didn't particularly like the man from his first assessment, but then, he didn't have to. The guy was paying him, and he might just help to get him closer to the Outreach problem.

He wondered if Billie had made any progress with the Van der Stegen notes. He put in a call. As he waited, he wandered over to the desk and slid Van der Stegen's card around and around with one finger. He looked at the bottle that Van der Stegen had so thoughtlessly handled, and frowned. Van der Stegen was not to know the potential impact of that casual touch, he supposed. Just as well he'd finished with the bottle anyway.

There was no response from his apartment.

"Dammit, Billie. Answer," he breathed. He tried again.

Still nothing.

Where the hell was she? Something slithered past the depths of his abdomen.

He'd told her he might need to get through to her. Either she wasn't there or . . . she wasn't answering. For some reason, she wasn't answering.

He slipped the bottle into one pocket and Van der

Stegen's card into another. There was nothing left for him to do in the office anyway.

The door to his apartment was unlocked. A quick scan quickly told him Billie was well and truly gone. There was no sign of her. Either she'd been scared away by someone, or she'd been taken. A quick, guilt-filled chill raced through his chest, making it feel hollow and empty. *Okay, Stein, you're overreacting.* Maybe she'd gone off somewhere on her own.

No. Remembering the way she'd fiddled with the locking program to block his access, Jack doubted she'd simply have wandered off. So where the hell was she?

He walked warily through the rooms, one after the other, looking for some sort of sign. The place looked undisturbed, as if there'd been nobody there at all, let alone Billie. It was too ordered. Somebody had definitely been there, somebody who'd taken a lot of trouble to make sure things looked as if no one had been. If they'd been able to get past Billie's security, then what else had they been into? He suddenly felt violated. This was his place. No one came here. He continued scanning the rooms to see if he could tell what had been touched.

"Messages," he said, standing in the center of the living room with his fingers laced behind his neck, taking long, deep breaths.

Billie's voice floated out of the wall. "Uncle Jack. Got bored with that stuff. Too easy. Had to leave. Gone to see some old friends."

Smart girl. Maybe too smart to be Billie. He played the message again, but it was Billie's voice, all right. The way she emphasized certain words was all too familiar. Anybody could fake a voice, but it was harder to get the nuances just right. So he was right; something had scared her away.

Gone to see some old friends. But Billie didn't have any old friends, as far as he knew. Unless . . . *Old* friends.

Perhaps she'd left him something else.

"Next," he said. Nothing. He didn't even know how to access the stuff she'd been working on, but he didn't really have time for that now. He just needed her back.

"Clear messages," he said. Without even bothering to check the accesses to the system—whoever had been there wouldn't have left traces anyway—he headed out the door.

There was only one place to look. The far end of Old. The seedy end. The place where everything fell apart.

He had no idea exactly where to look, and that meant once more trusting his instincts. He already knew enough about Billie's past, and there were events from his own experiences to point to potential dangers at the far end of Old. Jack wasn't sure whether he should be more concerned about what might be down there waiting for her, or what had made her head that way in the first place, what had made her seek refuge in Old. Barely bothering to take the time to lock his door, he headed out to the shuttle stop.

It was getting late, and when the shuttle finally arrived it was nearly empty. The other pair who rode toward Old didn't seem in the mood for conversation, or for anything, really. They huddled in opposite corners of the car and avoided each other's gaze. That suited Jack just fine. He tried to remember the last time he'd been right down to the bottom end of the Locality, but it was long ago. There was just no good reason to go down there.

He alighted and stood watching as the shuttle crawled away from him, shuddering as it dealt with the intermittent flow of power. He'd forgotten what it was really like down here. Darkness swept across the rising walls in stuttering waves. This was darkness unlike the muted tones to be found in newer areas. Here the ceiling panels flickered, half capturing the displays, flashes of partial images strobing across the surface, then just as rapidly fading or blinking out altogether. The colors illuminated crumbling walls, a fractured shadow play that worked deep in his unease. The pop and creak of buildings nearing the end of their useful life came from all around. His fellow passengers had left him several stops back, and he stood alone in the middle of the street. From every direction came noise and movement—for in the midst of death was life.

Jack listened, scanning for any sign of actual real life, hidden somewhere in the midst of the sound of the dying buildings. He reoriented himself, seeking a direction that felt right, but couldn't find one. He'd let his instinct guide him. *Let's see just how lucky you are, Stein*, he thought. At random, he picked a building and headed toward it.

Ten

Jack stepped warily within the creaking walls. This was his third attempt, and he didn't know how many more likely buildings there were. Inwardly he knew, rationally, that a random chunk of the building's structure wasn't about to come crashing down on his head, but it didn't feel *right*. The whole building seemed to protest with every step he took. Not residential—this one had been an office complex. The whole layout was wrong for habitation. No longer offices—now gloom and shadows inhabited the empty spaces instead.

A flicker of movement off to one side and he stopped in midstep, holding his breath, listening. *Come on, Jack, get a grip.* Ever since that time in the military when he'd been captured, locked away in a subterranean cell with nothing but his imagination to paint bizarre pictures on the insides of his eyes, he'd developed a thing about dark places that had stayed with him. He still didn't like dark places, but thoughts of Billie were spurring him on. Perhaps somewhere in this maze of sad decay lay the pointer to where she might be.

Another slight movement, and this time the sound

of something scraping on the floor. He whirled as a figure materialized in the vast doorway off to his right.

"What do you want here, New man?"

As Jack's eyes adjusted, he could make out a figure leaning nonchalantly against one of the pillars flanking the entranceway. Details slipped into place. It was a kid. He wore a dark suit in the old style. Old, old style. Fashion usually ran in cycles of about twenty years, but that style of clothing was decades old.

"You look like a New man," said the boy. "What do you want down here in Old, New man?"

Jack hesitated. There was something slightly strange about the kid's speech, as if blurred by the barely disguised traces of an accent. Now that Jack could see better, more details were falling into place. The kid's hair was cut old-style too, close, cropped to the lines of his skull. What was he worried about? This was just a kid, after all. Wasn't it?

"I'm looking for a friend," said Jack.

The kid pushed himself from the pillar and strolled across the intervening floor space, his hands clasped behind his back.

"A friend, eh?" he said as he neared, looking Jack up and down. He did a circuit, walking right around the spot where Jack stood, all the time subjecting him to scrutiny.

Finally he stopped in front of Jack and stood, hands still clasped behind his back like an old man.

"And what sort of friend are you looking for?" he said quietly. "A boy friend or a girl friend?"

Snatches of a dream voice floated in Jack's inner ear. *I want your girlfriend.* The kid started walking again.

"Hmmm, New man? What is your fancy? A boy friend or a girl friend?"

"Neither. Just a friend. A *particular* friend. Maybe you know her."

The kid stopped his circuit and peered up into Jack's face. He subjected Jack to a look that bored right through him.

"And why would you think that?" he asked, his eyes never wavering. And then he started pacing again. Around and around. It was starting to get on Jack's nerves.

"She said she had some friends in Old."

The voice came from behind him this time. "Maybe we could arrange something. It depends."

Jack had had enough. He spun and grabbed the kid by his jacket and drew him close so they were face-to-face. "It depends on what?"

"Nuh-uh," said the kid, pulling his jacket free with a wrench and smoothing it down with his hands. He looked up and gave a shake of his head and a knowing smile. "You won't get anything that way."

Too much familiarity there and the familiarity hurt. However old this kid was, he'd seen too much for his years. It immediately put him in mind of Billie.

"Dammit," spat Jack from between closed teeth, feeling slightly ashamed for trying to monster the kid. "I'm looking for a friend, that's all. Either you can help me or you can't. Perhaps I can persuade you." He reached into a pocket to retrieve his handipad, and the kid took a hasty step backward, glancing warily from side to side, making sure of his escape route.

"I wouldn't do that if I were you, New man," he said quietly, and followed it with a long, low whistle through his teeth.

"But I was just . . ."

There were other noises from beyond the shadowed

gloom. Then Jack could see figures clustered in the archway, and others back behind the kid.

"Daman, you okay?" said a voice from the doorway—young, like the kid's, but somehow hard. There was the sound of metal scraping along a wall or floor; he couldn't tell.

"It's okay," Jack said, holding his hands out, and slowly, carefully he reached in and withdrew the handipad from his pocket. "I was just going to see if I could make it worth your while to help me out." He thumbed the handipad on, looking for the kid's reaction.

The kid lifted a hand, palm toward the vast doorway. "Cold, hard credits. We like numbers, New man. Now you're talking our language," he said. His face was still hard. "Who's your friend? Perhaps we can work something out after all . . . or, even better, find someone who might be even more to your taste. Sometimes you make discoveries down here in Old—discoveries that might surprise you."

"No, listen, kid—Daman, if that's what you call yourself—you've got it wrong. This really is about a friend. Her name's Billie."

Daman looked thoughtful and then suspicious. "Billie, eh? And what's she to you? You a relative or something? We sometimes get relatives down here, or people who *say* they're relatives."

"No, not a relative. Nothing like that. She's staying with me." Jack was aware of the shadowy forms lurking in the doorway just out of his sight. He didn't want to let on about the trouble. "Do you know her?"

Daman was silent for a long time. Finally he seemed to make up his mind. He gestured for Jack to follow, turned his back without a care, and headed toward the vast doorway. "No," he said over his shoulder. "But there's someone here who might."

Jack set his mouth in a grim line and followed. He didn't like the implications of what he was seeing at all. The connection Billie had to this place was painfully obvious, and he didn't need his gut feeling to tell him it was something uncomfortable. He watched Daman as he led the way. The kid's step was confident, relaxed, as if he owned the building. There was still something about him, though, that felt out of place. The kid just didn't belong. Sometimes there were people like that, but Jack had come across them only rarely.

As he moved beyond the doorway, the lurking shadows resolved themselves into shapes. About a dozen more kids eyed him warily. Their ages ranged from . . . After Billie, Jack couldn't be sure, but they were young, all of them. Most were boys, and a couple of the older ones held lengths of metal either hefted in two hands or dangling from one hand, resting casually against the floor. That had been the scraping sound. All the kids had one thing in common: a haunted, pinched look and eyes that seemed to go on forever. It was the look Billie had worn the first time that he'd seen her. Jack suddenly felt very exposed. But that was stupid; they were only kids. Sometimes, though, kids were more than kids. He should have learned that much.

Daman gestured, and the shadowy figures slipped away with barely a sound, melting back into the darkness.

"This way," said the kid, motioning Jack to follow. Across the broad expanse of floor, a large staircase swept up to the levels above, and Daman headed toward it.

"Be very sure you know why you're here," he dropped casually over his shoulder with no further explanation. Biting back a response, Jack followed.

The staircase didn't look like it belonged in the original building design, but it was hard to tell in the dim light. Jack couldn't imagine that it would be functional in an office block. Perhaps in its earlier incarnation in New, it would have made more sense. It was somehow grand, but wrong. There was a lot about this place that was wrong.

The stairs wound on and up, and he mounted them one after the other, trailing Daman's steps. After what seemed like three floors, but with no breaks in between, no landings or entranceways, they came to a stop. Daman stood above him, waiting. Another vast doorway and within, a pale glow.

"Are you sure, New man?" said Daman quietly as Jack reached the landing and stood beside him, waiting for the next move. When Jack said nothing, Daman nodded briefly and motioned him to follow.

An archway gaped in front of him, leading off into darkness. A faint light emanated from beyond the pillared entrance. Daman stepped through and said, "Lights," then gestured for Jack to follow. "It's kind of like that," he said, "when you first step through. When you come into somewhere new. All new places are full of wonder, New man, and there are wonders to be found here, if you make the right choices."

Huh? Jack said nothing, though he was wondering what the hell the kid was talking about. *Wait and see.*

On the archway's other side lay a vast room—grander than a ballroom—and Jack let out a low whis-

tle despite himself. Somebody had screwed with the
building's programming. Shapes, figures, parts of figures flowed over every wall—well, not exactly flowed,
but they moved with a kind of sinuous life of their
own. The light, now illuminating the space, came from
within and above and behind them. Even the floor
sparkled with a native fluorescence. As Jack watched,
slowly the figures changed, shaping and reshaping
themselves as he stood there transfixed, his mouth
hanging stupidly open. He'd never seen anything like
it. Not on such a scale.

"Who did this?" he asked. It was hard to focus on
one place. Flickers of movement squirmed in the periphery of his vision, a constant distraction.

Daman grinned. "Impressive, isn't it? Just one of
our little family. Like nothing you've seen, New man.
Like nothing you've seen. Pablo amuses himself when
he's not wooorking. Sometimes we call him Artist."

Jack clamped his jaw shut. *When he's not wooorking.*
The words sent a chill up his spine, but it gave him an
idea. He fumbled in his coat, then cursed. He'd left
Pinpin's card back at his apartment.

"You have a problem?" said Daman. "All problems
can be solved here."

"What is it, Diamantis?" Another voice, this time
coming from behind a clustered shape at the far end of
the room. The voice was distorted, muffled by the
sculpted shapes that lay around them.

"Someone to see you," said Daman/Diamantis, and
motioned Jack to follow. As they neared the blocky
shape toward the room's end, a figure stepped from
behind the shielding form.

"Who is it?" The speaker wore a cap turned back to
front, baggy, loose-fitting clothing in nondescript col-

ors, his hands shoved deep into his pockets. He leaned casually against a piece of sculpted flooring that had taken on a life of its own and risen spiraling into the air, and he looked Jack over. The lean features belied the native intelligence sparking in the eyes that now observed him.

"New man here is looking for a friend, someone he knows."

"So what's he doing here?"

"Shit, Pablo, you ask him."

"So what's your name?" said the boy called Pablo.

"Jack. Jack Stein."

"Well, Jack, Jack Stein, what brings you here?"

Jack looked the new kid over before speaking. This Pablo seemed to speak with some authority, and Daman had clearly deferred to him.

"A friend of mine left a message for me, saying I should meet up with her here."

"A friend, huh?"

"Yes, a friend. Do I have to go through this crap again?"

Pablo looked at Daman, who shrugged, and then spoke without making eye contact with Jack.

"Why would this friend ask you to meet her here?" He stood where he was, not looking at Jack, but rather at the animate floor, waiting for the answer.

Jack hesitated, but then realized there was no point trying to make up some tale. "I don't know. She said something about having spent some time down here. Maybe she knows some of you. I don't know. You tell me. Her name's Billie."

Pablo narrowed his eyes. "Hmm, I might just know a Billie. She's not here, though. She hasn't been here for a long time."

Jack suppressed a frustrated sigh. He could spend the rest of the night standing here going around in circles with these two.

"Okay. She's not here. She hasn't been here. Maybe you might be able to tell me where she might be . . . where she might go. I don't care what the hell you do down here. All I'm interested in is Billie."

The kid called Pablo pursed his lips, let his gaze rove over Jack's face, then looked away. The silence dragged on, punctuated only by the moans and creaks of the building itself. Finally Pablo slowly shook his head. "No, Jack, Jack Stein. I don't think we can help you."

Jack spoke from between closed teeth. "But there are other people you can help, right? People like Pinpin Dan. People like his friends. Is that right?"

It had the desired effect. Pablo gave a barely disguised intake of breath. His eyes were narrowed.

"What exactly is it you want with Billie?" he asked slowly. His gaze flickered to Daman and back again.

Round and round. Jack bunched his fists in his coat pockets and, in doing so, his hand came into contact with the bottle, which in his rush from the apartment, he'd forgotten to remove. The touch was electric. His spine stiffened. An image of Pinpin Dan floated up in his head, his long face looming close as they sat together on the shuttle. Then just as quickly it was gone. Jack felt the blood drain from his face. The sensation had been too strong. And then he was back in the vast room, the ever-changing shapes moving around him.

"Are you okay?" asked the boy, Pablo. He was peering at Jack's face.

"Yeah, yeah. I'm fine." He paused for breath. "Listen, Pablo. Maybe you don't want to tell me about Billie, but tell me about Pinpin Dan."

"Who are you, Jack Stein? What are you looking for?"

Daman, who up until this point had been maintaining his position outside of Jack's direct line of sight, stepped forward to stand beside his companion. There was hostility on his face, and he looked suddenly older. Much older. Jack could sense movement behind him, and it was more than the walls and ceiling. Jack slowly drew his hands from his pockets.

"Look," he said. "I'm a PI—I'm working on something, that's all. I know Pinpin Dan from way back. We used to work together a long time ago. That's how I know Billie."

There was a curl on Daman's lips speaking of something deeper. "And . . . ?"

"And nothing. That's it. Billie was staying with me. She left me a message. That's why I'm here."

There was a definite sneer on Daman's face now.

"She was *staying* with you."

Jack was already telling the kid too much, and he was clearly racing to conclusions Jack didn't want him to reach. Some of Daman's companions were a lot bigger.

"Look, you've got it wrong. It's not like that." Suddenly he knew he didn't have a choice. Quickly he gave them a summary of the events leading up to his journey to Old. Sometimes it paid off, acting the tough guy, but he wasn't stupid. These kids were hard enough, world-weary enough, that it'd just roll right off them.

Pablo moved back behind the sculpted shape he'd appeared from and sat, leaving Jack standing there with Daman staring at him with cold, hard eyes, and who knew how many others behind. Daman took a step forward and then started a slow circuit, his gaze fixed on Jack's face. Again, he clasped his hands behind him as he walked. Around and around, and then finally he spoke. "It's a nice story, New man. So you're telling me this Pinpin Dan's dead. That somebody killed him. What do you think, Pablo?"

Jack started to protest. "It's not a—"

"Sssst!" Diamantis stopped his circuit and lifted one finger to silence him. "Pablo?"

"Could be, Daman. You?"

"Nuh-uh. I don't like it. You must think we're fools, New man." Jack bit the inside of his lip and decided he'd wait. He didn't have long. Daman shook his head, a disappointed look on his face, and circled one finger in the air.

The first blow caught Jack across the back and drove him to his knees. While he was still trying to work out what was happening, there was a second, and then . . . dark pain flew down to cover his awareness.

"Fresh-ground coff—" *Bump.*
"Fresh-ground coff—" *Bump.*
"Fresh-ground coff—" *Bump.*

Jack struggled upward through the fog of hurt thumping in his head. Something was nudging his leg with annoying repetitiveness. He winced as he levered open his eyes. Light wasn't good. Not right now.

"Fresh-ground coff—" *Bump.*

It was the damaged advertising drone, or one just like it. Jack kicked out at it futilely and clamped his teeth together as the sudden motion pushed more thumping pain into the back of his head. He struggled to his feet and stood there wavering for a moment. The drone, without a leg to impede its progress, skittered off down the street, making contact with a wall, bouncing off, then continuing on its way. Still the upbeat voice went on: "Fresh-ground coff—" Jack leaned against the wall for support as the drone's voice faded cheerfully into the shadows at the dark end of Old.

He hurt. He hurt all over. They must have dragged him out onto the street after they'd finished with him. Maybe putting in a few extra kicks for good measure. *Not a good result, Stein. Not good at all.* What was he coming to? They'd only been kids. He supposed it could have been worse. He ran his tongue around the inside of his mouth, checking for further damage, but they seemed to have left his face intact. Gingerly probing the back of his head with his fingers, he found their attention there had not been quite so gentle. A large lump had already formed. He prodded at it and winced. So now it was more than painfully clear he'd reached a dead end. He didn't think it would be a particularly good idea to go back in and start asking more questions.

Still leaning on the nearest wall for support, he felt in his pocket. His handipad was still there. He could be thankful for that much, at least. He needed to get back to his apartment and slap on a couple of Rapiheals. Let the patches work on putting his body back together while he tried to collect his thoughts. Somehow he'd thrown away an opportunity, and he didn't quite know how he'd managed it. Something he'd said in there had triggered the reaction, and he didn't know what. Maybe it had been as simple as the mention of Pinpin Dan, but why that in particular would prompt the sudden aggression, he couldn't fathom. These kids had to know Pinpin Dan, or at least know of him, but that didn't help. He was no closer to finding out what had happened to Billie.

There was something else that had happened in there. He closed his eyes and willed the thought past the pounding in his head. He remembered. His fingers had fleetingly brushed the small blue bottle while he'd been inside. That simple touch had conjured the image of Pinpin Dan: stark, clear, and funereal as ever. But Pinpin Dan was dead. Pinpin could have no connection with the bottle, or could he? It seemed that the elusive Heironymous Dan had his long, disgusting fingers everywhere. He needed to figure out exactly how and where.

Later. Billie was still missing.

As he shuffled painfully toward the nearest shuttle stop, he ran the connections over in his head. Pinpin Dan. Billie. The bottle. Pinpin Dan. Diamantis/ Daman. Pinpin—dead. Billie—missing, maybe dead too. She couldn't be. He gripped the bottle inside his pocket, pressing it firmly inside his fist, but it gave him nothing more. No new image floated up inside his head, only more pounding. He gritted his teeth, swaying slightly as he waited for the shuttle to slide to a stop, then staggered inside to huddle in a corner, folded away in a cloud of frustration and bruises. The few passengers who joined him glanced at him and quickly looked away. Better not to become involved. Well, that suited Jack just fine.

By the time the shuttle reached Mid, the nausea had started, waves that swept over him in time to the regular throbbing in his skull.

Eleven

Two days he spent waiting for the Rapiheals to do their work. Two days he could have spent trying to hunt down the leads he didn't have. It seemed like about half of that time he spent hunched over the toilet trying to purge himself of his insides. Concussion. Definitely concussion. *Beautiful.* He knew it was stupid, but he tried to find solace in sleep, letting the patches act on him while he was unconscious, but there was no rest there. The snatches of sleep were populated with pictures of Billie and the White-Haired Man. They were trying to tell him something, but each time he reached for it, the voices and the images slipped from memory, scuttling away into confusing fog.

As an exercise to try to clear his head, he dragged himself out of the bedroom and collapsed on the couch. At least the nausea had passed, though the muscles in his abdomen and chest ached from the effort, and every time he coughed pain lanced across his ribs. They weren't broken, he knew, but they hurt like hell. Probably just bruised. He had to gain some focus, make up for lost time, and a big picture sometimes helped to shuffle disconnected parts into a meaningful whole. "Chart," he said, and the wall crawled into a series of motile colors. First the connections.

"Joshua Van der Stegen." The name appeared in a small oval in the middle of the wall. "Top right." The name slipped into position.

"William Warburg." He positioned that one top left.

"Anastasia Van der Stegen."

One by one, he positioned the names on the wall, including Billie, Pinpin Dan, Gil Ronschke, and Francis Gleeson. A few other ovals were left holding descriptions rather than names.

"Connect Joshua Van der Stegen, Anastasia Van der Stegen." A line sprang into place between the ovals. He nodded, wished he hadn't, and then lay back staring at the names. Gleeson he connected to Ronschke, Billie to Pinpin Dan, Gleeson also to Warburg. By the end he was left with three clear streams of people. On the right lay those connected to Joshua Van der Stegen, and on the left those connected to William Warburg and Outreach. Running down the center was a series of connections to Pinpin Dan, seemingly unconnected to either of the lateral lines. But just because Pinpin Dan was dead, that didn't snuff out the stream. Daman, Pablo, the kids in Old, Billie: They all sat firmly connected. He understood the obvious link, but underneath, there had to be something else. He grimaced. There was still one name that he'd forgotten.

"Jack Stein." One by one he traced the connections. He seemed to be the only thing tying the streams together. There was no way he was the nexus. There had to be more.

Half an hour later he was no closer to the answer. Two bubbles remained unconnected: The White-Haired Man and the pair who had been at Pinpin's place. The White-Haired Man was connected to him, but the other pair . . . obviously they were linked to Pinpin in some way, but that wasn't enough.

As an afterthought he added one more name: Louis Ng. The policeman had to have a connection somehow to this mess, even if it was only through Pinpin Dan. The police must have been tipped off by someone. They knew too much. Why else would they be investigating? No, there was definitely a connection there. So who had given them the information? Why had Investigator Ng been so quick to contact Jack Stein? It was more than just a security image of him in attendance at Pinpin's apartment—had to be.

"Keep," he said. "And stick it together with the stuff from the handipad. Also the Outreach files."

His head was starting to hurt again. He needed another Rapiheal and some painkillers as well. The Rapiheals had some analgesic properties, but not enough for the way his head was feeling right now. He could work with the chart again later. He stared at it for a few moments more before clearing down the wall and hobbling off to the bathroom to apply the appropriate patches. A few minutes later his head was starting to feel a little better.

He called up the files that Billie had been working on: the stuff about snakes, the science stuff. He scrolled through it at random, reading a passage here, a snippet there, just letting his subconscious do the work. It seemed like there were thousands of seemingly unconnected references. Most of the references to snakes related to the alchemical mythos he was already partly familiar with—philosophers' stone, gateways—but then something new snagged his attention.

*The serpent is the centripetal force, ever seeking to penetrate into Paradise (the Sephiroth), and to tempt the Supernal Eve (the bride), so that in her turn she may tempt the Supernal Adam (Microprosopus).**

Huh? What did that mean? And what was "Sephiroth"? The second part didn't mean much; it was the first part that had caught him.

Jack scratched at the back of his neck, nearly disturbed the patch, then carefully smoothed it back into place. He read a little further.

*This is the kabalistic Tree of Life, on which all things depend. There is considerable analogy between this and the tree Yggdrasil of the Scandinavians.***

Jack would have given up right there, but he'd heard Billie say that name: Yggdrasil. Another link. More old stuff that seemed to have no relationship to anything he was working on, but it was being put in front of him for a reason. He knew better than to believe it wasn't. Too many times seemingly random events had tied themselves together, shaping the elements of his life, and it projected into every single case he'd ever worked on.

Now the text was talking about triangles. Not circles—triangles. But somehow the triangles were supposed to be made up of spheres, or circles. That just didn't make sense. He tried to visualize a triangle made up of spheres and it just didn't come. He needed

*Harris, John N. *Spra Solaris Archytas-Mirablis*, Internet Publication, 1997.

***ibid*

someone to talk to, someone to use as a sounding board. He grimaced. If Billie had been here . . .

He shook his head and kept reading. Not only was a snake associated with this tree, but it traced paths through the branches. At the top of the so-called tree there was a circle. It had a name: Kether. He scanned, looking for the name, not knowing where this was taking him. He found it in another passage, and again there was something in it that he knew was relevant:

> Thus, then, the limitless ocean of negative light does not proceed from a center, for it is centerless, but it concentrates a center, which is the number one of the manifested Sephiroth, Kether, the Crown, the First Sephira, which therefore may be said to be the Malkuth or number ten of the hidden Sephiroth. Thus, "Kether is in Malkuth, and Malkuth is in Kether." Or, as an alchemical author of great repute (Thomas Vaughan, better known as Eugenius Philalethes) says, [Euphrates, or, The Waters of the East] apparently quoting from Proclus: "That the heaven is in the earth, but after an earthly manner; and that the earth is in the heaven, but after a heavenly manner."*

There. There was the alchemy connection. So what was this Kether, and what did it have to do with snakes, gateways, and circles? Farther down, he found a partial answer. It was the place of perfect unity. Kether was the place of perfect unity. Okay, that made it as clear as . . . And what was all that stuff about heaven being in earth and earth in heaven? Space, maybe? No, that didn't make sense either. Kabala, ca-

*ibid

bala, whatever they called it, he could see no reason for the connection.

Then he remembered what Billie had said about the science stuff. Numbers and letters. From what he could determine in the passages he had read so far, this kabala thing was all about numbers and letters, about some sort of secret code that would unlock the place of enlightenment—something that would . . . what? Unlock the door. Yeah, that was it. Numbers and letters. Scientific formulae. Maybe. Just maybe.

He leaned back on the couch and closed his eyes, letting the connections tumble into place.

The buildings of Old creaked and stirred all around him. He stood in semidarkness in the center of the street. He pulled out his handipad and thumbed it on. There was the chart, the names, almost too small to read. Three lines of ovals, one on either side and one down the center. The names shimmered, and then one grew large. It was his own name, Jack Stein, and it glowed, pulsing red like blood.

"Jack Stein," called a voice from a nearby doorway. The voice was familiar. "Sitra Akhar, Jack Stein. Sitra Akhar."

The words meant nothing. He keyed the words into his pad, wiping his chart from view.

"Save," he said.

"Who do you want to save, Jack?"

Jack glanced over to the doorway. Long white hair flowed around the doorway as if stirred by an oily breeze. He looked back at the handipad. Another name glowed on its surface: Billie. It pulsed in time to the creaks and groans around him. Jack felt the bottom drop from his guts. Cold. Cold inside.

"Save," said the voice.

He looked back to the doorway. The long strands of hair were changing, transforming themselves into long, sinuous bodies—snakes, climbing up the side of the wall. They left shimmering rainbow trails. He tore his gaze away, turned it back to the handipad. Billie's name was gone. The chart he'd been working on had replaced it. But wait, it wasn't the chart. It was some kind of diagram, circles interconnected with lines. Ten circles, each with a name in them, but he couldn't read the names; they were in some sort of unfamiliar script. The lines crossed and crossed again, back and forth between the circles.

"Sitra Akhar." The White-Haired Man, talking to him from the shadows in the doorway. Snakes surrounded his head. He was joined by another figure—short, dressed strangely.

"That's it, Jack, Jack Stein. Go and wooork," said Daman. Jack's heart was pounding. His breath came in short, shallow gasps. Daman took one step toward him, then another. "Come on, Jack, Jack Stein. What are you waiting for?"

The face changed. It wasn't Daman anymore. It was the kid, Pablo. The technical wizard down from Old. And then it was Daman. The faces merged into each other, fading in and out.

Then both of them were chanting: Daman/Pablo and the White-Haired Man, chanting in unison: "Sitra Akhar. Sitra Akhar."

A huge shudder ran through the Locality's surface, undulating along its length in dark waves. The ceiling panels at the far end of Old started to fall, tumbling in slow motion as the next wave slid along the outside walls. Buildings, streets crumbled and more ceiling panels fell, crashing in tinkling shards all around him. The whole structure was falling apart, piece by piece.

And he was awake again.

At least his head was no longer pounding. He passed his hand across his forehead, feeling the sweat-dampness of the dream. Strange, strange dream. He could see himself writing the words spoken by the White-Haired Man. Sitra Akhar. What had prompted that? Probably something he'd read while scanning the passages that Billie had pulled together for him. His unconscious mind was trying to tell him something.

He glanced at the display. He'd been asleep for maybe an hour, but the wall was still live. Line after line of text ran across it. He had to pin down the words before he lost them.

"Search. Sitra Akhar."

A couple of moments passed, words blurring into moving lines, and then a highlighted passage: *Sitra Akhar, refers to the left hand path of the tree. It also refers to those things associated with darkness and corruption.* The left-hand side of the tree. Why? He called up the chart again. William Warburg. That much was clear. Francis Gleeson? Darkness and corruption? He didn't think so. Joshua Van der Stegen was on the wrong side. Van der Stegen was on the right. And Pinpin Dan and the rest were in the center. Maybe he had the connections wrong. Perhaps the names were in the wrong places. It was worth considering. But he had no way to connect them any other way. He had to find the link. The White-Haired Man. The pair from Pinpin's apartment. That was where the clues lay. Then he could join the missing lines.

Just for a second he thought he'd try something.

"Connect all." A tracery of lines sprang up between the various ovals. It was strangely reminiscent of the kabala diagram—the tree of life. No, too many lines there, too many circles, but there *were* similarities.

He needed coffee. He cleared down the chart to its original form and shut down the display. He needed to work on it more. Threads, circles, lines—he wasn't dealing with possibilities; he was dealing with geometries and mathematics now, and if he didn't watch out he'd become ensnared in an artificial pattern of his own making. He had no grounding in this material at all.

Coffee was better. It would help him think straight. He was almost feeling well enough to venture out again, and the dream Daman had been right. What had he been waiting for? He had to find Billie, and find her soon.

He finished the coffee and had another. He needed the kick-start. He was already wearing too many patches, what with the Rapiheals and the painkillers. He didn't want to overdo it. As he stood there sipping, leaning back against the kitchen units, he had another thought. Sure, Billie was a priority, but he was supposed to be working on the Outreach stuff. He'd almost completely forgotten what had started it all. Almost. And if Billie was tied in, as he suspected, then solving the Outreach problem was partway along the path to determining Billie's location.

If he were going to get any sense out of this stuff, he had to talk to someone, but whom? He could hardly approach anyone else from Outreach. Not having Billie around was more difficult than he thought. He could have used her as a sounding board. Sometimes if he had only himself to bounce things off, the echoes became too distorted. He could wallow in the network for days without making any headway. There had to be a more sensible means of finding what he needed. Okay, all this stuff was freely available to the Locality's populace, but somebody had to maintain it. He called up the wall screen again.

"Services," he said.

A Locality site map faded into view, series of colored icons denoting the various facilities. Tiny wording appeared beside each, explaining what the graphics meant. He peered closer at the screen.

"Information services," he said.

A pink icon unfolded into a list, and he scanned the options. There. Library.

"Give me a map of where the library is."

It was about halfway up New, right next to one of the exterior walls. It was a shuttle ride and then a walk, about seven blocks west of the transit. The exercise would do him good.

First a shower and a shave. Try to recapture some shred of normality, at least pretend he was something resembling human. As he moved to the bathroom, he took a good whiff of his shirt. He stank. Humanity was long overdue.

He stood on the opposite side of the road from the library building. The only thing distinguishing it from its companions was the lack of logos or advertising crawling up the walls. Apart from that, it was new glass/metal, if perhaps a little more squat than the surrounding offices. There weren't many people around. Jack smoothed his hair, still slightly damp from the shower, and took a breath. *Okay, nothing for it.* He headed across the street.

He climbed the stairs and stood before two large glass doors. Inside there was a blank lobby, marble-effect floors and walls, but nothing else. There was no reception, no lobby furniture, merely a single double door on the other side. He pushed through the glass doors and crossed the empty floor, his footsteps echoing off the flat, shiny walls, floor, and ceiling. *Strange.* He stood for a couple of seconds outside the double doors, wondering whether he should knock. There seemed little point, so he pushed against the rightmost door, half expecting it to be locked. It wasn't, and it swung effortlessly inward, no sound apart from the sudden increase in volume of some sort of underlying ambient hum. Jack stepped inside.

The hum was louder here, and there was the smell of . . . he couldn't quite put his finger on it. It was sort of like machinery, but different, with a sharp tang about it. Jack stood just inside, his mouth open. Ranks and ranks of colored walls disappeared into the background, but they weren't just colors; they were iridescent. Bright glowing blues, reds, oranges, all colors imaginable were stacked in tiny cubes, one on top of the other. They filled the vast room from floor to ceiling. Jack let his gaze rove, tracking the lines, seeking some pattern in the ranks of softly glowing color.

"Can I help you? Hello?"

The voice came from over to the right, and he narrowed his eyes, seeking its source.

"Um, yeah. Hello?" he said.

A woman stepped from behind some sort of pedestal over to the side. He hadn't noticed it before in the rainbow confusion.

"Can I help you?"

She was short, slim, her midlength dark hair tied

back behind her head. She wore a plain white coat. Dark eyes, pale skin. But most people had pale skin in the Locality. She was quite good-looking in a formal, proper way. Jack cleared his throat.

"Um, yeah. Is this the library?"

She crossed the intervening space and stood just in front of him. "Yes, this is the place. What can I do for you?"

"I guess I expected something else," he said, scanning the stacks of cubes.

She gave a little smile. "It's quite a sight. Takes a bit of getting used to, Mr. . . ."

"Stein. Jack Stein."

He felt himself warming to her straightaway.

"Well, I'm Alice," she said. "I'm the librarian, whatever that means in this place. What is it I can do for you? We don't get many visitors."

He glanced around again, then back at her face, looking at him expectantly, a strange little wry smile on her face now.

"Well, I thought maybe you could help me. I'm doing some research, or trying to, and I keep getting lost. There's just too much stuff, and I can't find the links I need."

Her expression suddenly became interested. She studied his face for a moment. Her eyes narrowed slightly as she noticed the slight bruising still evident around one eye, but she moved on.

"And what are you doing this research for, Mr. Stein?"

"Alice, is it?" She nodded. "Well, you can call me Jack, Alice. I'm an investigator." Could he trust this woman? "It has to do with a case I'm working on at the moment."

She turned away and crossed back to the podium, beckoning for him to follow. "Interesting. So where do you need help?"

Behind the podium sat a comfortable swivel chair and a series of flat screens set above a rounded, kidney-shaped desk. She took the seat and gestured that he should stand beside her. She reached forward and touched one of the screens with her index finger.

He pulled out his handipad and opened it to his notes. "Well, it's a combination of things," he said. "There's a list of alchemical stuff, some other things to do with the kabala and . . . well, physics and other things."

She turned to look at him with a curious expression, her finger still poised near the screen. Slowly she withdrew it. "Interesting. There's not much call for that sort of thing."

"No, I guess not."

"What sort of investigator are you, Jack?"

Ah, here it comes, he thought. "Well, funny you should ask. I'm a PI, psychic investigator, if that means anything to you."

She nodded slowly, resting her hand on the desk in front of her. "So what do alchemy and kabalistic theory have to do with your case?"

He rubbed his hand over the bottom half of his face and grimaced. "Quite a bit, actually, but I can't work out how. I keep on getting these pointers to this stuff, but I can't make sense of it all."

Alice folded her hands in her lap. "Perhaps I can help you make some sense of it," she said. "That's why they employ an actual librarian in this place. They started out with an AI construct, but human beings can do things that AIs still can't. We can tie tangents together, make illogical links. Not that there's much call for it, as I say. Everything's there for people to get themselves." She shrugged.

"Maybe if I gave you some of my notes . . . ," he said.

"Sure. Look, I'd love to do it. That stuff fascinates me, and God knows, it would give me something to do."

"But I'm not quite sure—"

Alice stood. "Look, what I can do for you is compile the references you already have, strip out some of the dross, try to identify some sort of pattern in the information. I can also see what sorts of access we've been having in similar areas. Perhaps that might help, perhaps it won't, but it will give you some sort of coherence. I don't mind. Really, I don't. It might just ease the tedium of my little wonderland here."

Jack smiled.

It couldn't hurt. He scanned his notes, looking to see if there was anything overly incriminating. He nodded then, looking back up at her eager expression.

"Yeah, okay. Is this set up for . . .?"

She nodded and tapped the screen. "Go ahead."

He thumbed the handipad to send, then shut it down and slipped it away.

"Thanks, Alice. Look, I have to go and see someone now. Can I leave this stuff with you?"

She nodded. He reached into his pocket and fished out a card. "Call me if you need anything from me."

She smiled again. "I will."

Jack turned to leave, giving the strange multicolored walls one more look. He guessed they weren't really walls after all. As he slipped out the front door, he felt strangely light, almost happy.

Alice.

Right. The first stop was back to Gleeson. Gleeson was his primary link in Outreach now. If he followed that path, he'd eventually stumble on something that would lead him to Billie, because somehow she was tied up in this. He had to cut down on the number of paths and focus his concentration. It was like the diagram. There were too many lines. Francis Gleeson seemed like an unlikely source of anything more, but if the little man had managed to find out what Jack had asked him for, then it would be a start.

He was feeling more than vaguely alive by the time he reached Gleeson's apartment. His ribs still felt sore from the unwelcome exertions of the last couple of days, but he was close to functional. The long, hot shower had washed some of the past few days away, and Alice had been a breath of fresh air. He smoothed his coat and waited for the apartment's systems to announce him. It didn't take long. A breathless Gleeson opened the door a crack, glanced up and down the corridor, then ushered him inside.

"Where have you been, Stein? I've been trying to contact you, but I couldn't get through. I thought something had happened."

"Yeah, well, something did happen, but you don't have to worry about it," Jack said in a clipped tone.

"Well . . . ?"

"Well, what, Francis?"

"I called you several times. It said your system was off."

Damn. He'd forgotten about the screening that he'd asked Billie to put on his system. And now he had no way of getting rid of it. "I'm sorry about that. Technical problem."

Gleeson shepherded him into the living area. "Look," he said. "I don't care about that. I'm paying you to find Gil. So far you appear to have done nothing. I want to start seeing some results." The tone was distinctly churlish.

"Had you forgotten, Francis? I was waiting for some information from you."

"Yes, yes. Why do you think I called you? I don't see how any of this is going to help find Gil."

"Whatever you can provide, Francis, will get us closer to locating your friend."

"All right." Gleeson sighed and walked over to a set of shelves molded into one wall. After a moment of shifting things around, he turned, holding out a card. "I took no inconsiderable risk finding this for you. I hope it prompts some tangible results. I'm sick of being handed nothing more than shadows."

"I appreciate it, Francis. Do you know what's there?"

"Of course I know what's on it. Outreach has been pumping a steady stream of funds into a facility based offworld somewhere. There's been significant purchase of equipment and quite a large security allocation with it. I would guess this is what you're looking for."

Jack took the proffered card. "It might not be exactly what we're looking for, but I think it will help. Is there any indication where this facility is based?"

"No. Security's too tight on this. I couldn't access it. The only thing I know is that they call it Project Flatland."

"Flatland? What the hell's that supposed to mean?"

"That's all I know."

"That's too bad. But I guess it'll have to do."

"There is one thing. . . ." Gleeson paused, seemed to consider, as if the thought had just come to him, then continued. "It doesn't seem as if there are any new transport costs. Wherever they have these facilities, they must be on one of the existing outposts."

"And how many of those are there?"

"Oh, only about three, as far as I know."

"Is it conceivable that they could be on Dairil III."

"Well, yes. I suppose so."

"But if that were the case, why would Warburg allow investigations of a site near something he wanted kept secret?"

"Unless he thought there was no risk," said Gleeson, looking pointedly at Jack.

"Hmmm. I see." Jack fingered the card while Gleeson looked at him expectantly. "All the same, I just think it's a bit of a gamble on Warburg's part, don't you?"

"Perhaps," said Gleeson. "But anything offworld is less of a risk. It's easier to cover your tracks. How many people are actually going to go out there and take a look? The costs. Getting it arranged. The time it takes to get there. It's beyond the means of most people, surely?"

It was too easy—the connection to the mine, Ronschke's disappearance, but then again, Gleeson could be right. You could get away with anything if it wasn't under direct scrutiny, and who was there to scrutinize? Most of the miners were the sort who didn't leave tracks, or who didn't have anyone waiting for them to question where they were. If the two were connected, it still didn't explain how the miners were involved. What would be the connection between a research facility and a group of miners? Maybe they'd stumbled onto something that they weren't supposed to see.

"Listen, Francis. I know this is old ground, but was Gil involved with anything beyond his direct line of work? I mean outside of his mining contracts?"

"Haven't we already been over this, Stein? What about the handipad? I told you that he sometimes got involved in things, stuff that he wouldn't talk about. I must say, you don't seem to be taking this very seriously."

Jack returned the annoyed look with a flat stare. "I can assure you I'm taking this extremely seriously. I just want to be sure of things. I need to look over this stuff and then decide where it's going to lead us. I may need some more help from you, Francis. As you say, if someone wanted to get offworld, out to the scene, then it's not that easy, right? If I wanted to get out to Dairil III, how would I go about it?"

Gleeson looked vaguely alarmed. "There's only one way I know. You'd have to go on a company ship, and that would take forever."

"And could you arrange that?"

"I . . . I . . . suppose I could. But it's too risky. There's no justification."

"There's every justification, Francis. You forget, I'm working for Warburg. I'm on contract to Outreach investigating the very same thing—the disappearance of the mining crew. Warburg's paying me to find out what happened to the miners on Dairil III. Warburg himself told me that if I needed anything, I was just to ask. Well, now I'm asking. We don't have to advertise the fact, do we? Get me the schedule. Get me some sort of authority. I don't know. Official investigator, work-

ing for Outreach. Permission to travel and have access
to the site. Can you do that?"

"You don't know what you're asking. You don't
know what you're doing."

"Do you want me to find Ronschke for you?"

Gleeson chewed at his bottom lip. Finally, reluctantly, he nodded.

"How long will it take?"

"Not that long, but I'll have to be extremely careful."

"You be as careful as you need to, Francis. I'll need
some time to make a few inquiries based on what
you've given me here, but how long?"

"It will depend on the transport schedules, and I
have no idea what they're like. It will take a few
months to get out there. The link to the station, then
there's the shuttle down to the surface. Then there's
the expense. I suppose we can find a way to hide the
costs."

"Yes, of course." Jack was clear now. There was no
question that he needed to get to Dairil III somehow,
but that amount of time just didn't seem to make
sense. How could it be worth it? He still didn't understand how the miners were involved, but everything
else made sense. Where better to carry on secret research than out from under the eye of anyone, out on
some remote outpost where no one could check up on
what was going on? And plainly Warburg didn't expect him to turn up, didn't expect anyone to turn up
there. Sometimes power made people complacent. If
Warburg thought that the entirety of Jack's job con-
sisted of sitting around and having dreams, then he
had a surprise coming. Whatever he thought, it was

obvious that he didn't really take what Jack did seriously.

"But what if it's not Dairil III?" said Gleeson.

Jack gave Gleeson a hard look. "We'll deal with that when and if we come to it."

Gleeson shook his head. "This doesn't make sense," he said. "To spend so much time, to go all the way out there on a mere hunch. I cannot believe that that's the right decision."

"Listen, Francis," said Jack. "It's more than a mere hunch, okay? This is what I do. At least part of the answer is out on that mining world, and there's no other way I can see to getting close to what's happened to Gil—or anyone else, for that matter. Take it or leave it."

Gleeson was still looking troubled. "Yes, yes, I suppose you're right. I'm not convinced, though."

The trouble was, neither was Jack.

"So how do I contact you?" said Gleeson finally.

"Dammit. You don't at the moment. I'll be in touch."

"I'm not happy about that, Mr. Stein."

"You're not very happy about a lot of things, are you? Take it or leave it, Francis. It's the best you've got."

At the door, he turned. "Listen, Francis, one more thing. Who exactly *do* you work for?"

Gleeson blanched slightly, then flushed. "What sort of question is that, Stein? You know who I work for."

"Right," said Jack.

As he walked back down toward the elevator, Jack filed the little man's reaction away. He had a couple of days now to pursue his other inquiries, and that particular little revelation might just help. Gleeson was trying to play him too. If what he expected was right, then Gleeson was working for some other third party at the same time. There was still a nagging doubt working at the back of his mind that he was jumping to conclusions, but he had to be right. Gleeson's reaction had been enough to tell him that.

Twelve

Jack made his way back to his own apartment, wasting no time. He had thought he was over the worst of it, but he still felt weak, the patches only masking what was really going on with his body. The excursion to the library and to Gleeson's had taxed his reserves. Every step was becoming an effort. It wouldn't do to overdo it on his first day out. Back on the shuttle, he couldn't even be bothered watching his fellow passengers; he had other things on his mind.

He'd always been a little suspicious of Gleeson, but now that suspicion had more fodder. Gleeson, an unassuming clerk at Outreach, someone who would fade into the background easily, someone who had easy access to the sort of administrative data that kept a company running. It was just too easy. He'd been so casually forthcoming about his suspicions during their first meeting, so conveniently there. And then there was the handipad. Gleeson was the only source of that particular key piece in the puzzle. There was nothing to say it had any other origin. Oh, sure, Gleeson had some connection to Gilbert Ronschke, but it didn't have anything to do with the handipad, did it? There was nothing to say the handipad had anything to do with Ronschke at all. Van der Stegen had confirmed the timing was wrong. Something was definitely not right with Gleeson, and knowing that, Jack would have to be more careful from now on not to give his suspicions away. Gleeson was useful, no matter where his allegiances lay, and he could exploit that usefulness any number of ways. Besides, he needed Gleeson to arrange his trip to Dairil III, and he *was* going to Dairil III now. He was pretty sure of that much, at least. He couldn't see any other way he could get close enough to find out what he needed to.

Going to Dairil III. The thought left an uneasy feeling in his guts. Maybe it was just a hangover from the dream. Maybe it was something else. Time would tell.

By the time he reached his own section of Mid, parts of his body were starting to hurt again. He slipped out of the shuttle, trying to ignore the discomfort and keep his thoughts organized. As soon as he got into his apartment, he'd call up the chart and start shuffling the names again. But first another Rapiheal and some more painkiller. He couldn't think like this, and if he couldn't think, he couldn't work. With his body on low, his perceptions were less accurate.

"Come on, Stein, pull yourself together. You've had worse than this."

He was getting soft. Too much of the protected life inside the Locality. Petty jobs. Encapsulated reality. He could barely remember the times before the Locality anymore. After his escape from Intelligence—and it was more of an escape than a release—he'd drifted for a while. He had enough savings to last for some time. There wasn't much to spend money on when you were living like a spook. Acquisition required some sort of permanence. He'd drifted into a succession of the smaller fixed towns, never really clicking with anything. There was a string of inevitable sameness, and nothing had really felt right. He worked on a farm for a while, laboring, but physical work, good honest sweat, wasn't really Jack's thing. After a couple of months he'd made his apologies and moved on. Finally he'd happened on the Locality. Something about it, from the first time he'd seen its vast, shimmering bulk across the landscape, had fascinated him. He visited a couple of times, enjoying the slick modernity, the facilities, the entertainment factor, and there was something about the place that felt right. He'd felt good there. After the third visit he'd decided to stay, not really sure what he was going to do, but comfortable enough not to have to worry about it.

Almost by chance—as if that would ever happen—he had run into an old friend from the military. He was working in security for one of the major corporations that ran the Locality. He put Jack in touch with a couple of other people, and from there things had more or less fallen into place.

And it had led him to . . . where?

In the bathroom he peered at his face in the mirror as he smoothed the Rapiheal and painkiller patches into place. A touch of graying stubble, face losing its definition, sagging around the jawline, shadowy puffiness beneath the eyes, fading colors at the temples. His once-dark hair was touched by silver. He'd always been thin, angular, but there were hollows there around his deep-set, dark, and slightly haunted eyes. The thin nose, the slightly curved brows giving him an almost surprised look. All was familiar, but now the familiarity was going away. He almost didn't recognize the man he had been.

For a long time he just stood there; then he sighed. Okay, so he was getting older. So what? The patches, the drugs, they'd keep him going for a while yet, but there had to come a point, right? And then what? It didn't really matter. He spent too much time putting pieces of the past together to even think about the future. The future was little more than random possibility, and the shreds of fake reality he dealt with in his dream state were nothing more than a vague fog. His whole life was turning into a string of maybes.

He tore himself away from his reflection and headed back into the living room. Calling the wall display to life, and settling back onto the couch, he scratched at the back of his head. An empty ready-cooked lay on the low table—evidence of Billie's presence. He really should clear it away, but there was more than that. He could *feel* her, feel she'd been here. He closed his eyes and shook his head, then looked back up at the display. And there was her name, writ large in one of the circles on the wall.

Sitra Akhar. Darkness and corruption. Seek the darkness. Seek the corruption. He let his gaze wander over the diagram. Darkness and corruption. Everything was darkness and corruption in this place. It had taken him long enough to realize it, but the Locality was nothing more than a hive of poisonous decay. It just manifested itself in Old, the place where everything fell apart. That was the visible end of what lay beneath. He'd known it all along, but had chosen to ignore it. He could sense it now. How was he supposed to find anything that fit the description spelled out in the ancient words, anything that held that taint, when everything was the same? How the hell else had creatures like Pinpin Dan survived for so long? Jack was as guilty as the rest of them, filled with a grudging tolerance, but at the same time fully aware of everything that went on. It was just too easy to let everything happen, to let events slide past him without doing anything about it, merely coasting along. His abilities had made him lazy. His luck shouldn't make him lose his humanity, but here, somehow, insidiously, that was what it was doing.

So what about Billie? Was she any different? Of course she was. She'd just been stained by it all. That was a part of living—no, make that existing—here. You couldn't call it living, really. You got touched by the taint.

God, he really was getting maudlin—too many patches, not enough sleep, blind alleys one after the other. It all added up, but he couldn't afford to let the mood overtake him. There was work to do. Maybe he could put some of the pieces together before embarking on a voyage out to the edges of the system. That would put him out of circulation for too long. He had to find some clue to Billie's presence before that happened. Somehow the shapes on the wall in front of him held his key. He grunted at the irony. Here he was trying to unlock a key. It made about as much sense as everything else.

His thoughts flitted back to the last dream he'd had. The tree diagram had been as clear as day. Ten circles. Ten names. But what he had on the wall had more than that. Perhaps he had too many. And why was Pinpin in the primary place at the top of the tree? Was Pinpin the key? No, it didn't make sense. He might be integral to the connections that had been drawn, but there was no way a dead guy could be the key to the current problem.

Okay, he had a separate circle for Daman and one for Pablo. They were both kids from Old, so completely linked; he needed only one spot for both of them. He could get rid of Pablo's name altogether. On a whim, he removed Louis Ng's name as well. That felt right. So now he was left with eleven circles containing eleven names.

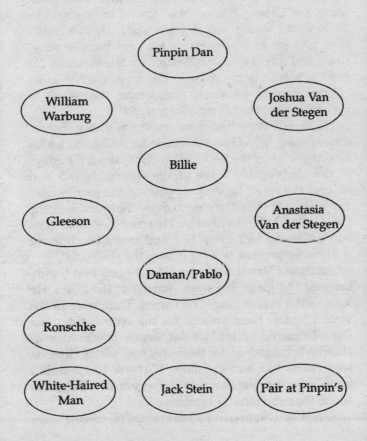

It still didn't work. One too many names, and besides, the picture was unbalanced. Normally he
wouldn't worry about it, but the dream image had
been so insistent. The pattern was an icon in his subconscious that was trying to tell him something. Sitra
Akhar. A clue—but what? He looked at the left-hand
names again. Warburg, Gleeson, Ronschke. The White-
Haired Man was on the left-hand side too. That made
sense. But Gleeson? Ronschke? Any of them could be
the key that would unlock this puzzle. He just didn't
have enough to go on. He let his gaze become unfo-
cused and stared at the wall. After a while he shook his
head. It wasn't going to come this time. There was no
epiphany, no revelation to spring from the depths of
his sensitivity into his conscious mind.

He stood, stretched, and started walking. Sometimes pacing helped him think. As he walked he let his
fingers trail over the back of the couch, along the edges
of the shelves, the edge of the chair. Around and
around the room he drifted, passing the names over
and over in his head, trying to draw the links. Seek the
left. Look for the corruption. He spied the small blue
bottle Gleeson had given him and crossed to retrieve
it. He stretched out to snag it from the shelf and . . .

Anastasia Van der Stegen. His fingers had barely
brushed the glass. He spun, staring at the chart. He
knew what was wrong. The names. They were in the
wrong boxes. Gleeson was on the wrong side. His
name belonged under Van der Stegen. It was Anastasia who belonged under Warburg. And where Gleeson
went, Ronschke had to follow. That was it! He didn't
know why yet, but that was the way it should be. He
spoke the command to rearrange it.

Stupid, Jack. Taken in by how things seemed. Things

were never really as they seemed. And if those connections made sense . . . yes! Gleeson worked for Joshua Van der Stegen—he had to. He was some sort of plant inside Warburg's organization. That would explain the easy convenience of his presence, the way he had fed the information to Jack. So that left Anastasia Van der Stegen. What was her connection to Warburg? He stared at the new configuration. Seek the left. Everything that tied these energies together belonged on the left. The two at Pinpin's were a minor part of the configuration, compared to some of the others. The only other major player, at least in his dreams, was the White-Haired Man. There had to be another link there.

Then he saw it. The White-Haired Man belonged beneath Anastasia Van der Stegen and on the left-hand side. Somehow they were connected too. Or were they? It could just as easily be the pair at Pinpin's apartment. For the moment the two were interchangeable, but if the dream clues were pointing him in the right direction, then it made more sense for it to be the White-Haired Man. Whatever the case, one of those two named boxes was surplus to requirements, and probably in the wrong position.

He'd leave the extra position for the time being, until he worked out the pathways, but took a moment to adjust the diagram so that the oval containing the White-Haired man now lay on the left beneath Anastasia.

Okay. Likely fact: Anastasia Van der Stegen was linked to Warburg.

Second: Gleeson, although on the surface working for Warburg, probably worked for Van der Stegen.

So where did that leave him? He had to explore the missing links somehow. Pinpin Dan was an obvious candidate, but he was out of the picture—completely. That left Billie, and she was gone too. Gleeson he already knew about.

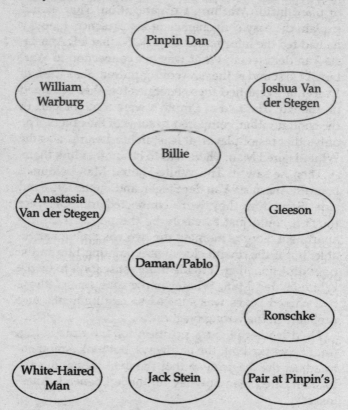

He stared at the chart and chewed at his bottom lip. Not enough. If he could find the pair that had been at Pinpin's apartment, then he might be able to find out what had happened to Pinpin. Apart from that, his only other option was Anastasia Van der Stegen.

The Van der Stegen girl was a problem. Everything he'd seen told him she was a spoiled little rich girl used to getting her own way. From what he could tell, she was the only child, and that only made matters worse. The performance up at the big house in the Residence had shown him that she was fully aware of what she could do, the way she could play men, and maybe women too, but he had no firsthand experience to tell him that. Okay, so she was potentially dangerous, but only in the way she impacted his clarity. How could you trust your gut feelings when your guts were in disarray? Well, not quite the guts, but close . . .

As for the other pair, he still had no clue who they might be. Pinpin had made a call to someone—unknown—and that pair had shown up. A man and a woman. Had Pinpin called them? Maybe, but unlikely. Billie had described them as big. Long dark hair and short red hair. A big woman and a big man. But anybody could be big to Billie's perception. It was all relative. *Hey, stupid again, Stein.* She'd slipped out of his awareness as someone on the periphery, but the woman who'd accompanied Van der Stegen to his offices had been a big woman sporting short red hair, and there'd been that flash of recognition, that glimpse of interest. It was possible. Had to be. Billie had said there were two of them. Would Van der Stegen's staff have the capacity and resources to doctor the records at Pinpin Dan's apartment? Probably. He remembered the sense of unease she'd generated with her presence. Time to ask a couple of questions.

Van der Stegen had left his card, hadn't he? Jack shuffled around the apartment, trying to find where he'd left it. He'd collected too many cards over the last couple of weeks. Finally he found it shoved at the back of a shelf. One of these days he was going to have to get more organized. He slotted in the card and made the call.

It took some time for the system to answer, and when the display faded into colors and life, it was only pseudo-life. An auto-answer program spoke the inevitable words. "The person you are calling is unavailable at the moment. If you'd like to leave a message, do so now. Have a good day."

Jack grimaced. "Mr. Van der Stegen, it's Jack Stein. I have a couple of things I need to verify with you. It's to do with a couple of your employees. I would prefer not to go into details right now, but if you could call me back as soon as you're free, I'd appreciate it."

Then he remembered. *Shit!* Billie's block was still on his home system. Van der Stegen couldn't call him. He ordered up the screen and called again. "Mr. Van der Stegen, Jack Stein. I'm sorry to bother you again. There's a problem on my home system. I'm afraid it's out of action right now. You can reach me via my handipad. Thanks."

So, as far as that lead was concerned, he had little option but to wait for Van der Stegen to get around to calling him. If the pair at Pinpin's apartment were those whom Pinpin had actually called, and they also worked for Van der Stegen, then that would likely tie Joshua Van der Stegen to the happenings at Pinpin's apartment. No, he didn't like it. It didn't feel right. Maybe they just had some sort of intercept on his systems. He could try to work out whom Pinpin had called by cracking through Pinpin's home system, but he didn't have the skills to do it personally. He'd need to use someone else, and with the place under police scrutiny, he didn't like his chances. He'd need someone like Pinpin to do something like that, or Billie, but Billie was gone. He wrinkled his nose and sighed. That left very few options.

Everything seemed to be coming back to Joshua Van der Stegen. And now he was working for the man.

Joshua Van der Stegen.

The guy had interest in lots of things, but he doubted that he could be implicated in the disappearance of his own handipad. That just didn't make sense. If Gleeson knew that the handipad belonged to Van der Stegen, why wouldn't he just return it?

Gleeson.

Maybe he could get something more out of the little clerk. Unifying threads, and at the moment, Gleeson was starting to look like he was sitting firmly at one of the connecting nodes.

Jack grabbed his coat, set the system on divert, and shoved his handipad in his pocket. It was pointless to sit here and wait around, going nowhere. If Van der Stegen called in the meantime, he could start down that path of inquiry, but otherwise the inactivity was getting to him. He could call, but this sort of thing he preferred to handle in person, just in case his senses told him something that wouldn't be apparent over a wallscreen. Time to pay someone another visit.

Thirteen

He was still deep in thought during the elevator ride down to the street. Gleeson. Everything kept leading him back to Gleeson, yet the innocuous little man couldn't be a major player. He just didn't strike Jack as the type, unless the flighty, nervous demeanor was just an act.

Gleeson was probably working for Van der Stegen, but there was nothing to verify it. Maybe he was working for both sides. But there were definite links to the wrong side. Or maybe just the other side. How did he know which was the right side and which was the wrong side? All he had to go on was the clue left for him in his dream. The left-hand side. But he could hardly believe that, when it came down to it, Gleeson was key. His guts were telling him that didn't make sense either. He let out a growl of frustration.

He'd barely stepped from the front door, heading for the nearest shuttle stop, when a shadow loomed up on either side of him. Jack considered making a dash, and then the uniforms swam into view. Police. Shit, he didn't have time for this. On either side of him, they took a firm grip on his arms, banishing any thought of escape.

"Jack Stein?"

"Yeah, all right. You know who I am. What do you want?" It was hard for him to take these ineffectual functionaries seriously, and he struggled to keep it out of his voice. The Locality really policed itself when it came down to it, more or less. These guys were just errand boys.

"We need you to come with us."

"Look, friends, can't this wait till later? I was on my way to see someone."

They didn't even bother to respond, just motioned him forward to the special shuttle waiting at the curbside. The police vehicles, long, low, and squat, colored an innocuous white, were about the only nonpublic transport that ran in the Locality, apart from one or two delivery transports. Everything else moved back and forth via the shuttles, or simply grew in place. They bundled in beside him, one on each side, and issued a command. Jack, sitting between the two burly uniforms, decided it would have been stupid to try to put up a fight. These guys were big, and in his current state they would have been all over him in seconds. He'd sustained far too many bruises in too short a time already. Okay, then, he'd play along.

"So what's the story?" he asked, looking from face to face. Both stared impassively ahead, not even registering that they'd heard. "I hope this isn't likely to take too long. I have an appointment to meet a client."

One of the uniforms snorted. "Well, your *client* will have to wait, Mr. Stein, psychic investigator."

Jack could hear the contempt in the way the man said his title. *Fine.* It was clear he wasn't going to get any favors from them, so he shut up and watched the way ahead. It just wasn't worth the energy trying to

get through their thick skulls. He didn't have too long
to wait. The vehicle whisked rapidly up the main avenue, overtaking a shuttle, then veered into a turn that
took it deep into the heart of Central Park, where the
police buildings were buried away from view. No
need to see the police in a perfect society, was there?

They traversed the edges of the lake, passed
through a shielding wall of trees, and then they were
there, sitting in front of square, squat, featureless
buildings that housed that which passed for a police
force in this place. He was bundled out of the vehicle
as silently and unceremoniously as he'd been herded
in. Still no word of an explanation.

He'd been inside this place once or twice before. In
his line of work it was inevitable, but usually he'd
been there by his own design, rather than being casually carted off in a police transport. Why had they been
waiting for him outside his apartment building, rather
than coming in? That question would wait until he
worked out why he was here, but it was yet another
question to add to the growing number all the same.

He was escorted past more uniforms lounging
against walls and sitting with their feet up, down a
corridor, and into a small room with a table and two
chairs. His chaperones left him there, closing the door
behind him. This was classic stuff. He'd seen it all before. Clearly he was about to be "interviewed," but
they wanted him to sweat awhile first. Well, Jack was
used to waiting. If they thought they could faze him
that way, they had a thing or two to learn. Would there
be two of them? He'd lost count of the number of times
he'd seen this old vid. Sometimes he might just as well
be living his life in black and white with a gravelly
voice-over.

They didn't keep him waiting too long.

Louis Ng. He wandered into the room, quietly closing the door behind him. Jack almost didn't realize he was there for a moment. Ng pulled out the chair opposite, sliding his slight frame between the chair and the table, and sat.

"Mr. Stein," he said.

Jack really didn't have time for this. "What do you want, Ng?"

"I would suggest a little more civility, Mr. Stein."

"You can have your civility. I've already answered your questions. What do you want with me now?"

"We have fresh information, Mr. Stein, and we'd like you to corroborate a few things."

"I've corroborated about all I'm going to. What right have you to drag me in here without any decent explanation?"

"Tell me about the girl."

"What girl?"

"The girl at Heironymous Dan's apartment. We have reason to believe he had a young girl staying with him. Would you know anything about that?"

Shit. They knew about Billie. *Think quickly, Stein.* How much should he tell them? But wait a minute. If he had been on the apartment's security records, Billie should have been there too. There was only one conclusion. He was right. *All* the records had been doctored, and that could mean only one thing: Someone had been feeding the police information. There was no other way they could have known he was there. It was the only way they could have known Billie was there too.

"Why would I know anything about that? I told you the first time we spoke that I'd visited the apartment.

That's all. Now, if you want to read anything more into it, then that's up to you, but I don't know what you want. Maybe it's about time you started answering some of my questions."

"We've had information, Mr. Stein, that you've been seen in the company of a young girl—a young girl who fits the description of the girl that was staying with Heironymous Dan."

"That's bullshit, Ng. Information from whom? And why? Why would anybody tell you that?"

"That's unimportant. It just seems very peculiar, don't you think? You visit Mr. Dan at his apartment, and he subsequently disappears. Then you're seen in the company of this young girl, and she appears to have vanished as well."

Shit again. Someone was watching him—had to be. Time to clam up in case he inadvertently gave anything else away.

"Listen, Ng, unless you've got anything other than a few unfounded rumors to go on, I've got nothing to say to you. We can sit here all day if you like, but I've said all I'm going to say."

He crossed his arms and stared across the table, daring Ng to push it any further.

Ng smiled. It was the last thing Jack expected. The special investigator leaned across the table, putting his face close to Jack's, the smile still plastered across his features.

"Well, Mr. Stein, I find your attitude very disappointing. Especially in light of the unusual circumstances. I don't quite know yet what we will charge you with, but we will charge you. It's somewhere between unlawful abduction and murder. I haven't decided quite which yet." He stretched his hands wide for emphasis, looking at first one then the other. "Somewhere in between here lies your guilt, Mr. Stein, and I'm going to find out exactly where. Until that time I've decided for the good of the community that you will remain confined here. We have a nice little room for you. Comfortable, but basic. Very basic. Somewhere we can keep an eye on you."

He took a moment for what he was saying to sink in, then sat back, looking satisfied. It was time for Ng to cross his arms. There they sat, both with crossed arms, staring across the table at each other, Ng with his self-satisfied smile and Jack with his tight-lipped mouth. For about a minute Jack's resentment overcame his rationality, and then he realized the full implications of what Special Investigator Ng was telling him.

"Listen, Ng. I can't afford to stay here. I've got work to do. Stuff I have to look after. I'm working on a couple of contracts at the moment, and things are finely balanced. I need to be out and about."

"You had your chance, Stein. Now it's my turn."

Jack lapsed into silence. It wasn't like the old vids. Ng could do just about what he liked. There wasn't any trial process. There wasn't any jury of one's peers. There weren't any lawyers. There wasn't even a judge, unless you counted Ng himself. The police went about their business and justified whatever they did through a series of reports to the people who kept the force running.

"I see you're finally starting to understand the gravity of your situation," said Ng. "Now, if you were to tell me where Heironymous Dan is now, and perhaps also his young companion, it might help, but otherwise . . ."

Jack sighed in response. "I don't know. I wish I did. Listen, Ng. You've got my records. It's not my style. Even you should be able to realize that. So why don't you let me go and I'll get on with what I'm supposed to be doing? That way we both might find out what's happened to one Heironymous Dan."

"Don't play games with me, Stein. You can give me more than that."

Jack gave a heavy sigh. "It's all you're going to get."

Ng slapped the table. "Enough!"

One of the other officers appeared in the doorway, awaiting instructions.

"Take him to the cells. Take his handipad, whatever else he has. I want him to have plenty to think about."

Ng stood and faced the wall, turning his back as Jack was led wordlessly from the room.

He was escorted in silence down a long corridor to a desk. Just as they'd been directed, Jack was searched, his handipad taken, the couple of spare patches from his inside pocket and his coat removed. Another corridor, a small door, and they led him into a small, windowless cell. The walls were bare, unmarked. One thing about the Locality: Graffiti, small scratchings saying you'd been somewhere didn't last very long. Even that small avenue of making your mark on the world had been programmed out of existence. A small cot bed lay against one wall, and a toilet in one corner. A basic hand basin was attached to the wall beside the toilet. That was it.

"I hope you like things simple," said the officer, who now stood in the doorway. "Welcome home." He grinned and shut the door. The locking mechanism slid firmly into place.

Black and silver. Black and silver. The dream was upon him. He knew it was a dream. Things just weren't adding up. Something slithered across his foot. There was a metallic rasp against his boot. It was a snake. Tiny, tiny, the serpent had a black front half and the rear was colored silver. Jack peered at it as its body wave-formed away from his foot. The rear-section scales were not just colored silver; they were actual silver, metal. The rasping had been the feeling of sharp metal against the thick, hard tops of his boots. He stepped after the snake, but it slipped away into the darkness, elusive.

For the first time he noticed how dark it was. A thick blanket of gloom sat over everything, not that he could make out what the everything was. He had to strain to pierce the velvet darkness. It *was* a dream, wasn't it? He knew it was a dream, but he was powerless to control its direction. Not good.

A sense of foreboding swept over him, and with the foreboding came despair. What was he doing here—in the middle of nothingness? The blackness trickled through his perceptions and on into his chest. A sigh broke inside him, deep, forlorn, and he took another step. There was nothing for him here. Nothing for him anywhere. Pointless.

A glimmer of light in front, or perhaps it was merely his imagination, his senses creating a visual image to make up for the starvation of the darkened void.

But no. There was something there, off in the distance. The vaguest hint of light smudged the darkness in front of him. A rush of hope spread through him, replacing the sense of desolation inside, and he stepped toward the faint beacon that beckoned him forward. All around, on every side, came the sound of rustling.

He daren't seek that sound, for inside he knew it whispered *peril*. He had to focus, to seek the light. What was beyond the thick blankness he didn't need to know. He didn't want to know.

After what seemed an eternity, the source of luminescence started to take shape. It was tall, vaguely oval, and with each step he took, its form became more defined. With each deliberate placement of each foot, forcing himself relentlessly forward, the ever-present rustling grew stronger, louder in his ears. For an instant the sound distracted him as he realized what noise it was. It was the sound of scales, hundreds, thousands of scales rasping as they slid over one another. With that understanding, Jack knew fear.

Taking a deep breath, he willed himself to ignore the noise, instead concentrating on the shape ahead. One purposeful step after the other, he drew closer. The vague light grew more distinct, silvery within the black, and he stopped. Standing defiant in the midst of nothingness was a giant oval shape, a jet-and-silver torus that stretched high above him. He allowed his gaze to track its form, and finally, as the details were lost in its vastness, he recognized the shape for what it was—a giant serpent, half silver, half black, the end of its tail grasped firmly in its jaws. Vague feathery formations projected just behind its head. A bloodred eye stared sightlessly into the blankness, faceted, a huge red jewel. Here then was Ouroboros standing in the darkness—the wyrm of old. He swallowed. His legs were shaking, and there was cold sweat on his forehead.

With an effort he tore his attention from the jeweled eye and looked down, into the interior of the vast coiled loop. He hadn't noticed it before, because it was black against deeper blackness. The serpent shape encircled a tall black door. Etched upon the door's surface were letters in an ancient script he recognized, but not that he could decipher. He knew what the letters said, what they meant, but he still couldn't read them. The doorway, the portal, stood before him, beckoning. And as Jack stood there, trepidation pounding in his chest, without a sound the door swung slowly open.

"Jesus," he breathed.

Behind the doorway a vast tunnel lay revealed, stretching off into the gloom. It had walls, but it had no walls. The surfaces shimmered and crawled with ill-defined shapes. They were shapes, but not shapes, and every time he tried to focus on the angles, lines, impossibilities, they slipped from his grasp, over, through, and between one another. The rustling murmur grew in pitch, pressing against his ears. What was he supposed to do? Step inside *there*? No way.

With that last thought came silence, sudden, complete. Vast, crashing, empty silence. And all was still.

"It's time, Jack Stein." The voice floated up to him from the depths of the tunnel. Laughter. "It's time and more than that." More laughter. He knew the voice, the laugh. The White-Haired Man was back. "Show me, Jack Stein. Where is your girlfriend now?"

Jack could do nothing but stare as a giant face took shape within the tunnel's bounds.

Dammit. He wasn't going to play with this malevolent vision. Not this time.

With an all-encompassing flash of brightness, everything changed. What had been black became white. What had been silver became ebony. It flickered and flashed, back and forth, changing from one instant to the next. He winced against the visual assault, the

strobing images, trying to concentrate on the huge
face. Flickering. Hard to pay attention. Pounding his
senses with light. But in those brief flashes, he saw. He
saw what had been hidden. The White-Haired Man
was not a white-haired man at all. He had long, dark
hair, dark, deeply tanned skin, and his eyes were normal. Dark, dark eyes—almost too dark.

The images had been reversed all along.

Look at one side, then the other. Seek the other side.
He'd had the clue all along.

Jack struggled back to consciousness, grasping at
the threads of reality. He was still groggy from the
sleep, but there was something else now—excitement.
Why his dreams should give him something now was
a puzzle, but he'd definitely gotten something. Now
he had a picture of whom he needed to find. The
White-Haired Man who wasn't. He was linked to the
snakes somehow, and if he could work out the connections or who this guy might be, then a few more little pieces of the whole would be falling into place.
Well, one thing was for sure: Whoever this guy was, he
wasn't Pinpin Dan. Bony facial structure, but the pal-
lid, pasty features of Mr. Heironymous Dan didn't fit
the picture, and Pinpin did have white hair, almost, if
you discounted those nasty yellowish-gray streaks.

Jack looked around the blank, featureless cell. Not
so different from his offices, really. Maybe his subconscious had made the connection and invoked the
dream. It didn't matter now, but the similarity stayed
with him, locking himself away in a cell to do his
work. *Great.*

He dragged his fingers through his hair. *Look at you,
Stein,* he thought. *What sort of existence is this?* Sure,

there were advantages to self-enforced solitary, but
there had to be limits, right? The sound of the door
opening halted that line of thought in its tracks, and,
making sure his face was blank, he looked up to see
who it was. Some nondescript officer stood in the
doorway, not one of the ones who'd brought him in.

"Come on, Stein. On your feet."

Jack just growled at him.

"Look, Stein, you can stay here if you want, but
you're free to go."

"What?" Jack looked at him blankly.

"You've got some pretty powerful friends, Mr.
Stein. I'd count myself lucky if I were you."

Jack pushed himself to his feet, confused. *Yeah,
Lucky Stein. Lucky all right.* Despite further questions,
he couldn't get anything more from the officer, and he
was led unprotesting out of the cell, down the same
corridor, to collect his belongings. Within moments he
was deposited outside the front doors, blinking stupidly at the expanse of park and trees and the edges of
the lake, and none the wiser. There'd been no sight of
Ng, nor either of the officers who'd brought him in.
Pretty powerful friends. He scratched at the back of his
neck. Well, someone was looking after him, but he'd
have to worry about that later. For now he needed a
shower and a change of clothes.

It was a long walk back through the park to the
shuttle stop. He strode, head down, his hands shoved
in his coat pockets, fingering his handipad. As he
touched it, his stomach lurched. What if they'd been
through it, seen what was on it? He'd just have to hope
they hadn't. He wouldn't normally give the police a
second thought, but now, suddenly, they too were
trouble. He was starting to become too complacent.

He'd been relying on his instincts, his natural luck, and a sense of wrongness to warn him, instead of using his head. It was about time he used his brains as well. That was what was wrong with this coddled existence, everything on hand at a spoken command, things delivered to you from walls and ceiling panels and little mobile drones that followed you around. You just expected things to be fed to you.

By the time he reached the edges of the park and walked along the street, nursing his preoccupation, finally ending up at the shuttle stop, he was starting to formulate a plan of action. Top of the list was keeping out of the way of the police. He had things to do, and couldn't afford their interference. He didn't really need an extra risk now, particularly if they actually had been at his handipad.

Fourteen

Back at his apartment, Jack knew what he had to do. He had to go back to the snakes, back to the Ouroboros. That was where all this had started. The dream he'd had in the cell only enforced the need, a need he was conscious of without the sleeping prompt. The ring. The symbol in the mine. That was his first clue. Sure, he'd been taken down the path of the tree of life, but somehow they were linked. Ten spheres, ten points—there was a message there too, but he didn't know what it was yet. Virtually all the dreams he'd had since the mine dream had been populated by snakes, or snakelike things. His subconscious, his other sense, was trying to tell him something, and he had still not made the connection. There was no point going to his office and invoking a dream state. A dream would just tell him the same things all over again. He was just being too stupid, or maybe just too lazy, to pick up the link. He called up the material Billie had saved for him and started scanning. It wasn't long, with his attention properly focused this time, before a new passage jumped out at him:

> *It is interesting to speculate if this stone is not the origi-*
> *nal archetype of the Holy Grail (which has alternately*
> *been described as a cup, a stone, and a light by different*
> *mystics), or the philosophers' stone, which has the ability*
> *to open up the Ouroboros or close it.**

Wait a minute. So here the Ouroboros was merely symbolic of a doorway. Some sort of gateway or portal.
The circle of the snake could open or close. That was
what the passage was saying. Exactly as it had in the
dream in the police cells. And this was a clear link to
the alchemical stuff as well. The philosophers' stone
could open the doorway represented by the
Ouroboros. Doorways, gateways, leading into what?

"The thing in the cloud place. The water place. The air
place. The place of dark earth. I don't know."

The dream had been telling him it was a place unlike any other. Okay, that was a start. The images were
implying there was some sort of gateway that led into
another . . . what? He continued scanning, and discovered another linked passage. Old, old stuff.

> *Far off, unknown, beyond the range of thought,*
> *Scarce reached by gods, the years' rough haggard mother,*
> *Stands a primeval Cave in whose vast breast*
> *Is Time's cradle and womb. A Serpent encloses*
> *The Cave, consuming all things with slow power,*
> *And green scales always glinting. Its mouth devours*
> *The backbent tail as with mute motion it traces*
> *Its beginning. At the entrance Nature sits,*
> *The threshold-guardian, aged and yet lovely*
> *And round her gather and flit on every side*

*****Frater I.A.M. *Parallels within Gnosticism, Graeco-Roman Myth-*
ology and Hermeticism, 1994, as cited in Harris.

Spirits. A Venerable Man writes down
Immutable laws. He fixes the number of stars
In every constellation, makes some of them move and
*   others hang at rest . . .*
. . . Of its own accord, the adamantine door swung
*   open, revealing the huge interior, displaying the*
*   House*
*the Secrets of Time.**

Making the stars move, eh? The Secrets of Time. A vast house? All he'd seen in the dream had been some sort of shapeless tunnel. Yet through all of this stuff there was a common binding thread. Motion. Gateways. Doors. And now there were references to space and stars. Movement. The serpent climbed the kabalistic tree, tracing a path through the ten nodes, ten spheres, to reach what? Transcendence? Enlightenment? No, that was too mystical. There had to be something rooted in reality that tied it all together. There was the mention of Nature. Nature guarding the doorway. *Interesting . . .*

The stuff Billie had put together for him was good, but he still had to find the point that unified it all, that linked it seamlessly together. He ran through the things Billie had been telling him, turning them over in his head. Formulae, chemistry, philosophy. Science and space. Science stuff. He slapped his thigh. That was it! *Stupid, Stein. Why didn't you think of it before?* Billie had uploaded the contents of Van der Stegen's handipad, hadn't she? It was right there in front of him. All he had to do was call it up. He'd scanned it

*Claudian, Claudius (Roman poet) from *On the Consulship of Stitchs*, as cited in Harris.

before, but before he'd been concentrating on the historical stuff. Easy to miss something if your focus was on an entirely different direction. The problem was, Billie wasn't here to call it up for him. What had she said? Nobody could get into it if she didn't want them to. *Okay.* He issued a command and . . . the wall blossomed into life with Van der Stegen's notes.

Jack sighed in relief. The girl was smarter than he gave her credit for. With every new event that revealed something else about her, he was impressed by Billie's natural sharpness. He was in no position to let her know that right now, and that was yet another problem. Billie was turning out to be the key to so much. Just so much more than he ever imagined. Where the hell was she now?

"Where is your girlfriend now?"

No, that was wrong. That was just wrong.

It didn't matter. He'd find her.

The contents of Van der Stegen's handipad were more complex than he suspected. Jack had guessed some of the material might be beyond him, but the extent was frightening. He rapidly skipped past sections containing mathematical formulae and instead concentrated on the text, seeking a unifying thread.

There were copies of scientific articles among the scribbled notes, some of them old, some of them new, and the notes connected one to the other by a set of unifying jump hotspots, allowing him to rove through the text following various points. The notes made by Van der Stegen himself were either commentaries on the article contents, or brief forays into one or another tangential train of thought that picked up some minor or major point throughout the text and expanded on it further. The notes were cross-linked to other sections, and a multibranching path of threads and cross-threads wove throughout the text.

These were the ramblings of someone's internal dialogue, and Jack felt a slight sense of unease as he delved further. He was starting to become impressed with the depth and breadth of the man's thought processes. Still, there was nothing that provided the link he sought. He spent two hours, stopped, and wandered into the kitchen to make a coffee, then wandered back to dive in again. It had to be somewhere here. Why else would he have the stuff? The clue hadn't been the handipad itself; it had to be its contents. It could have been either, with Jack's ability to sense things from physical objects, but he should have seen, should have known. When he hadn't gotten any impressions from the handipad in the first place, then he should have known.

Finally he came upon a thread that seemed as if it might bear fruit. It made mention of the Greeks back on old Earth. Stuff about four elements: air, water, fire, and earth. In the beginning everything was made up of four elements, but with the application of analysis and thought, these could be broken down into smaller particles and components held together by particular energies. The energies were what bound existence together. Jack frowned. Four elements. Again the dream words that Ronschke had spoken floated through his head. Cloud, water, air, earth—they could almost be the same thing. Just everything mixed up together. He returned to the text. Energies. There were different forms of energy as well. History had identified a number, and then gone further in its classification, breaking them down into different types, and seeking others. Various theories about the nature of these energies abounded, but they also stated that knowing how to manipulate those energies gave you power over the types of matter they controlled. Scientific theory up to a point had been incapable of explaining satisfactorily the interaction of the various forms of matter, until the emergence of a new theory that reduced all matter and energy into a series of tiny strings vibrating or resonating within a ten-dimensional universe.

Jack sat back on the couch and slowly read the passage again. Okay, matter, energy, he understood, but vibrating strings of energy in ten dimensions? Ten dimensions. It was that which had stopped him. There was something else that worked in ten dimensions, depending how you looked at it: the tree of life. It was the kabala with its ten nodes, each point resonating a power across a different plane. Planes, dimensions, the terms were interchangeable in certain circumstances. No, but it couldn't be. The link was tenuous at best. Or at least he thought so, until he came across the next section of scrawled notes. There was something hasty about the way they'd been written. He scanned them carefully.

Ten-dimensional geometry allows the wormhole to be!!

Jack stared at the sentence, the two exclamation marks. The wormhole—what was that? This was some sort of revelation to Van der Stegen, important enough for the emphasis, important enough to express excitement in the eagerness with which he'd written it. Wormholes.

Suddenly he had an urgent need to find out what progress Alice had made at the library. Now he had something else to add to the mix. He called up a communication link and called the library. Alice's face swam into view.

"Oh, Jack. Hello. Calling to check up on me? I was beginning to despair of your ever calling back. I've put some things together for you. I don't know how much help they'll be."

"Thanks," he said. "Sorry about the delay. Something sort of came up. Actually, Alice, I've got something else to add to the mix. Do you feel like doing me another favor?"

"Tell me."

"Okay, I've got a theory working here, but I need confirmation. Do you know anything about wormholes? About ten-dimensional geometry? I want to see how that links to the kabala stuff and the alchemy references."

"Wow," she said. "This is getting better all the time. No, nothing off the top of my head, but I can certainly put something together for you."

"Could you do that? And then can I come and see you? It might take a couple of hours to get up to the library. Will that give you enough time?"

"Sure. Come on up. I'll see what I can put together in the meantime. I look forward to seeing you, Jack." She gave a brief smile.

Jack felt himself smiling back. "Yeah, me too," he said.

"Jack, come on in. I've put together some things for you. Stuff that I think will explain it most easily. Come on over here."

He joined Alice over by her screens, trying to keep his attention away from the annoyingly distracting ranks of data cubes quietly humming around them. There was a fresh floral scent near the bank of screens.

It was Alice. She was wearing something. He was sure she hadn't been wearing any scent last time.

"First," said Alice. He dragged his attention back to what she was saying. "Wormholes are sort of like gateways in space, in the real universe. A lot of theories say that they require ten dimensions to be able to operate, dimensions that we can't perceive, hence the ten-dimensional geometry."

Jack stared at her. Gateways. Doorways. That was it! Whatever Van der Stegen was working on involved passing through ten-dimensional space, transcending normal space and passing through that place where everything was mixed up to get to another point. Shit, they were working on some type of travel. That was the connection, and Outreach was doing the same thing. Had to be. The creature passing through the rock walls in the mine, Ronschke's talk of a place where everything was mixed up, the doorway symbols, they all pointed to the same thing. Jack had just been too far away from the ideas the images had been pointing him to.

"Jack?" said Alice.

"Yeah, yeah, sorry."

And the mining crew had disappeared to . . . where? The cloud place, the air place, the water place, the place of dark earth. Wherever that might be, it was through the doorway, through the gateway that opened up a passageway through ten dimensions. If Ronschke had gone through that doorway, then he could be anywhere. The dreams had told him that Ronschke was still alive, but how could he be sure? How could anyone survive that?

Maybe the notes Alice had put together would tell him something else.

"I'm really grateful, Alice," he said. "This stuff is really good. What else have you got for me?"

She called up something on one of the screens with a couple of quick taps. "There, the easier material first," she said.

He leaned over and peered at the screen, following the text. The scent of her was stronger.

*First, the only way to hold the wormhole open is to thread the wormhole with some sort of material that pushes the wormhole's walls apart, gravitationally. I shall call such material exotic because, as we shall see, it is quite different from any material that any human has ever met.**

"Now, you see that one," she said, looking at his face. "That's interesting, because if you think about the other material you had on alchemy, I can see a parallel there. This special stuff that makes things happen. It's like the philosophers' stone is to alchemical work. A lot of alchemical writings were symbolic anyway, pointing to means of transcendence. They weren't actually literal descriptions of chemical reactions, but code for other forms of transformation. Do you follow?"

Jack nodded slowly. That was the unifying link. Exotic material to hold the wormhole open. Something unusual. Exotic material *was* like the philosophers' stone in the ancient texts. It was the key that opened the gateway represented by the Ouroboros, just like in the dream. Jack looked at the next excerpt.

*Kaku, Michio. "A Theory of Everything?" in William Shore (ed.), *Mysteries of Life and the Universe* (Harcourt Brace Jovanovich, 1992).

We also know that if an infinitely advanced civilization somehow acquires a wormhole, then the only way to hold the wormhole open (so it can be used for interstellar travel) is by threading it with exotic material. We know the vacuum fluctuations of the electromagnetic field are a promising form of exotic material: They can be exotic (have a negative energy density as measured by a light beam) in curved space-time under a wide variety of circumstances. However, we do not yet know whether they can be exotic within a wormhole and thereby hold the wormhole open.*

Jack stood back. Space and time. Interstellar travel. There it was. Just like in the earlier passage. He felt as if he were completely out of his depth, that the concepts, the materials, were more than slightly beyond him. He didn't understand any of the stuff about negative energy density or vacuum fluctuations, but the underlying threads were tenuously starting to come together. He also knew that they were starting to come together for one reason only, and that was because he was finally beginning to use his head as well as simply relying on his extended senses. There was some small satisfaction in that knowledge, at least.

"Alice, thank you. Really. This is great. You know, there's another link, and I just wanted to make sure. Some of the kabalistic stuff was talking about resonating energies along the points of the tree of life. Do you see where I'm going with this?"

She grinned. "Of course. Ten points—ten dimensions. Yes, I can see the link. No doubt about it."

"Hmmm," said Jack.

*Kaku, Michio. *Hyperspace*, (Oxford University Press, 1995).

"I hope I've been some help, Jack, but I'm intrigued. Where exactly is this taking you?"

That was the question, all right. Where was it taking him?

He reached out and put a hand gently on her shoulder. She didn't resist. "I'm not sure yet. I wish I knew. Maybe you can help me work that out."

"I don't see . . ."

"Okay, I think you might be able to access stuff that I might not be able to get to."

He took his hand from her shoulder and ran it back through his hair. "You know what would really help? If you could get whatever you can on the Van der Stegen family. There have to be records, right?"

She frowned. "Well, sure. But I don't see how that relates."

"Trust me," he said. "It may help tie everything together, but I need to be sure. Can you keep it quiet and send it to me?"

She bit her lip and nodded.

"I'll let you know when I've pulled things together a bit more. I can't really say anything just yet. And listen, Alice, I really do appreciate everything you've done."

"Oh, I'm happy to help, Jack." She lifted a hand to push her hair into place, though not a strand was out of place.

"Thanks again. I'll see you soon, I hope."

"'Bye, Jack," she said. "I look forward to it."

He really did like her, and he felt a little guilty for using her like that. There was an obvious attraction there, but he wasn't in a position to do anything about it right now. Maybe. Maybe when things had settled down a little and he'd done something about getting himself together. Maybe. He needed to do some other things first before even thinking about it. Outreach. Billie. By then, he might know where he stood.

"Answer."

He glanced up at the wall as his visitor's image bled into view. Anastasia Van der Stegen. What the hell was she doing here? He frowned, considered just letting her think he wasn't in, and then thought better of it. She had to be here for a reason. And it looked like she was alone again. Not like her father—no hired body-guards to stand in the background like moronic pillars. So what did she want? He flipped between her image and the notes, debating, and finally gave the command for the latter to be closed down, waiting for them to fade from view before he was ready to admit her. It didn't hurt for her to wait a few moments, though she probably wasn't used to waiting for anything.

"Open," he said, and headed for the front door. In a way, this was lucky. Anastasia Van der Stegen was bound to be one of his next ports of call anyway, one way or another.

"Jack Stein," she said, a deep huskiness in her voice. "I'm so glad I've found you here."

"Miss Van der Stegen, I . . ."

"No, Jack. I can call you Jack? I've already told you, it's Tasha."

This was like some of the worst dialogue from the old vids. He had to keep his head on straight, especially with his latest revelation about her floating around in his head. He wasn't going to let her know his suspicions.

"Tasha, then. What brings you here? You can hardly have just been passing by. So what can I do for you?"

"Well, Jack," she said, leaning against the doorframe sinuously. It seemed there was more than one sort of snake in Jack's world. After an uncomfortable pause, she spoke. "Aren't you going to invite me in?"

"Ah, yeah. Sure." She was certainly playing it up.

He stepped back to allow her to enter, waited as she slid past him, and then he closed the door behind them. He took a moment to watch appreciatively as she sauntered into the living room, closed his eyes, shook his head, and then followed. What the hell was she really doing here, and how stupid did she really think he was?

"Does your father know you're here, Miss Van der . . . ah, Tasha?"

"It's no business of his."

She stopped in the room's center, gave the entire area a sweeping, dismissive glance—the same sort of look her father had given Jack's offices—then turned her attention back to him. They stood staring at each other for what seemed like several seconds before Jack got a grip on himself and cleared his throat.

"Um, why don't you sit down? Can I get you something to drink? Coffee? Something else?" Not that he had anything else to give her.

"No, that's all right." She settled herself on the edge of the couch and ran her palms from side to side along the edge on either side of her. She was gazing at him, her head tilted downward so she was looking up at his face. Her features were unreadable. "So don't just stand there. Come and sit down, Jack," she said, patting the couch beside her.

"Right." He crossed to sit awkwardly in the chair

opposite her. He deliberately chose the chair rather than the position on the couch. "So what can I do for you, Tasha? Have you a job for me? Or is it something else?"

"You know, Jack Stein, ever since that day at the house, I haven't been able to stop thinking about you. So mysterious. Intriguing. I wanted to find out some more about you. You left me your card and, well . . ." She shrugged. "So here I am."

"You're sure I can't get you a drink or something?"

"No, really. I'm fine."

"Okay, Tasha. What can I do for you? What would you like to know?"

"So, you're a psychic investigator, are you? What does that mean? You play on hunches?"

"More or less. It's a bit more complex than that. They're more than hunches. And I guess a bit hard to explain. Sometimes it's just about being in the right place at the right time." He shrugged.

"But all of life's like that."

"Yeah, well, more or less. I just happen to be in the right place at the right time a little more than most. Sometimes it's the wrong place too."

Anastasia Van der Stegen watched him as he spoke, barely moving her gaze from his face. She ran the tip of her tongue over her lips before continuing.

"What else, Jack?"

"Well, some of the stuff I get comes from dreams, or from impressions given by physical objects, or even sometimes from people themselves."

"What sort of stuff?"

"I guess you'd call them visions. Dream images. Flashes that come to me when I touch something. I use those to guide me in certain directions."

She nodded and moved her hand to one thigh, leaning forward ever so slightly. "So you see things when you touch things?"

"Sometimes."

"Hmmm." It was a low, animal sound, full of suggestion, and despite everything, Jack felt himself responding.

She held the moment, and then finally continued. "So what did you see from Daddy's handipad?"

Ahh, thought Jack. Now she was getting somewhere. "What makes you think I saw anything?"

She shrugged. "Well, you seemed to think it was awfully important."

"And it was, wasn't it?"

She rapidly changed tack. "So what are you working on now?"

"You really don't think I'm going to tell you that, Tasha? Let's just say it's privileged information. I have a duty to my clients."

She gave a little pout and stood, wandering behind the couch and letting her fingers trail across its arm. He found his gaze trapped by the motion of her fingers. *Come on, Stein. Pay attention.* This was important.

"But, Jack," she said. "What harm could it do? It's not as if it's going to upset what you're working on. I'm just interested." The voice was almost a purr, and she emphasized it by leaning forward over the back of the couch. "I've come all the way to see you, Jack. The least you could do is give me something in return."

"Right," said Jack. "Right."

He stood up himself and wandered into the kitchen, leaving her standing there. He wanted to play this out now, see where it went. She must think he was very stupid if she really thought he was going to fall for this

studied little performance of hers. Coffee would be
good. Displacement activity. Get the obvious little cha-
rade out of the forefront of his consciousness. He
needed to get a chance to let his brain do the thinking
for him, rather than his body.

"Are you sure I can't offer you something?"

"Well . . . no, I'm fine . . . for now." Her voice was
right behind him. He hadn't heard her follow him into
the kitchen. And then her hand was pressing up
against his back. "Come on, Jack. You can tell me what
you're working on."

Jack swallowed. She was an immensely desirable
woman, and here it was being laid out for him. For a
moment he was torn. It had been a while . . .

No. He turned and in doing so slipped away from
her hand. She took a step toward him.

"Look, Miss Van der Stegen. I don't know what you
want. As much as I'm flattered by the implications—
and I admit, the prospect is immensely appealing—
I'm not going to play. I don't know if you're here on
your own or if someone sent you, but you may as well
face up to the fact that I'm not going to fall for an old
routine like this one."

"I don't know what you're talking about." A slight
edge in the voice.

"Listen, Tasha. You asked about what I do. Because
of what I do, the nature of my work, I spend a lot of
time alone. A lot of empty hours where I've got nothing much to do, so I kill time by watching vids. Old
movies. I know the scenes from a number of them by
heart. Have you ever heard of Lauren Bacall?"

A slight frown. "No, I—"

"It doesn't matter. But not every man is simply

going to throw himself at your feet. You want to know something, ask me. Don't play stupid games."

She took a step back, raising her hand as she did so.

"And I wouldn't do that either, Miss Van der Stegen. I'd only slap you back." He wasn't sure if he would have, but the statement helped put things in perspective.

Her eyes narrowed and she slowly lowered the hand. "All right, Stein. What do you want? Do you want me to pay you? Name your price."

This was starting to get interesting. Jack leaned back against the counter, crossing his legs before him. He looked down at his fingernails, which needed cleaning, then back up at her now-hard face. "I don't have a price, Miss Van der Stegen. Not as easy as that. You tell me what you want, and then we'll discuss what it might be worth."

"You might end up regretting this, Stein."

"I don't think so," said Jack with a snort. "I don't think so at all."

She stared at him for several seconds, her jaw working, then seemed to give in. "I know my father came to see you. What did he want?"

"You didn't seem very interested when I saw you up at that big house of yours, Miss Van der Stegen. I returned his handipad, that's all. He wanted to tell me how grateful he was."

"As if I'm going to believe that. Look, I'm sorry. Listen, can we go back in and sit down?"

"Okay, let's do that," he said.

He grabbed his coffee and followed her back out into the living area. She resumed her position on the couch, and Jack took the chair again, his mug cupped between his hands in front of him. "Okay, shoot."

Gone was the coy posture, the sultry voice. In its place was something entirely different, all business and efficiency.

"I need to know what you discussed, Stein. How much do you know?"

Jack let his gaze linger on the black swirls of liquid turning in his mug. Circles again. Around and around.

"About what?"

"About what my father's involved in. That's what. Don't you play games either, Jack."

He fixed her with a pointed look. "Yeah, right. No games . . . anyway, I know that his handipad contained some important information, that's about it. He wanted to know how I happened to come by it. That's all."

"And did you tell him?"

"It's unimportant."

"Really. Well, it may be unimportant to you, but it's important to me."

Jack sipped and watched.

"How much do you know about what's on it, Jack?"

"Some."

"How much?"

He took another sip and continued watching her over the rim of his mug.

"So, will you tell me?" she said.

Jack again said nothing, merely took another sip.

"Well, fuck you, Stein. You will tell me, you know, one way or another. I could make things very difficult for you."

Carefully Jack placed his mug down on the side table. "I don't think so, Miss Van der Stegen." He really couldn't have played. As nice as it might have been, he really couldn't. You could take conflict of interest only so far.

"And I think it's about time you left. We don't have anything else to discuss."

She hadn't been silly enough to give anything away either, and it didn't really look like she was going to.

Anastasia Van der Stegen nodded slowly. "Fine. You're going to regret this, Stein. You *will* regret this."

"Time to leave, Miss Van der Stegen."

She stood, nodded once. "Fuck you," she said, and strode from the room. He heard the door slam behind her. He waited a few moments, considering whether he'd done the right thing, before making sure the door was locked behind her.

Fifteen

Later the following afternoon, Jack had already had a fairly unproductive day, and he was running over the previous evening's visit in his mind. The implied threat had not escaped him. Anastasia Van der Stegen believed she could get what she wanted by threatening him. Easy—you don't get what you want so you stamp your foot. The spoiled little girl was going to have to learn a thing or two about Jack Stein. Granted, there were very obvious things about the woman that impressed him, but the background and the privilege didn't—well, not too much. Tasha Van der Stegen was too used to getting her own way. Her life clearly had nothing to compare with the sort of things Billie had been through. Spoiled little rich kid—she had a lot to learn.

Her visit had convinced him that she was bound up in this whole net just as much as any of the other players he'd encountered so far. She had an obvious interest in the handipad and finding how it had come into Jack's possession, despite her pretense that she didn't when he'd visited the Van der Stegen place in the Residence. Thinking about that, it was strange that she hadn't made more of a move up at the big house. Or maybe she'd just had to consult with someone first, maybe Warburg, maybe not. One way or another, she was clearly working against her father, and that gave further weight to the idea that she was involved with Warburg. Van der Stegen had an interest in Outreach, and Warburg wanted it cut off at the roots. That made a lot of sense.

Alice had sent him a package of information, as promised, but it was all pretty vague. The Van der Stegen family had been one of the first sets of investors in the Locality project. They'd been industrialists from way back, with massive resources at their disposal. There were records of corporate takeovers and ownership, but most of the companies meant nothing to Jack. Most of them didn't even exist anymore. After the Locality's foundation, information on the Van der Stegens trickled away. It didn't really help that much. But as far as the connections were concerned, things were at last gradually starting to fall into place. Tasha involved with Warburg, and also somehow to the white-haired/dark-haired man. The connections were there, but he was still no closer to finding Billie. Back to Gleeson. He had to go back to Gleeson. Gleeson held the clues to Outreach, and Outreach held the clues to where Billie was.

Jack sighed, grabbed his coat and handipad, and headed out into the early evening. Down on the street he looked up at the ceiling panels, watching dark clouds scud across a moon-filled sky. A shuttle up to Gleeson's, and then? He wasn't quite sure. He had to find out something more about Ronschke, but asking additional questions would only worry Gleeson, and the little man was nervous as hell as it was.

He could discount Anastasia Van der Stegen for now. She was nothing more than a lightweight, meddling in stuff far too deep for her. Just because she had a powerful father didn't mean she had the same sort of knack he obviously had to have gotten where he was. However, she was linked to Warburg, and if he could find out what was going on there, he'd be closer to some answers. He had to get to Warburg somehow. As Gleeson lived and worked in the heart of the Outreach, he had to be the key. Joshua Van der Stegen valued the little man's information flow, so it was time to get Van der Stegen's money working for him, perhaps in ways he hadn't thought it might.

The shuttle was slow in coming, and he was starting to become impatient. From time to time the shuttles suffered various mechanical breakdowns in the region of Old, and it delayed their schedules. Either that or the problem was with the Locality support systems that simply allowed the shuttles to grind to an inconvenient halt. They would back up all the way to Mid, and then you could spend seemingly endless periods of time waiting for them to get moving again. It looked like tonight was such a night. Finally he got sick of waiting and headed on up the avenue. Maybe by the time he'd walked a few stops, the shuttles would be moving again. At least he'd kill some time, give his head some space for more free association.

There were few people on the streets, but then there were rarely many people on the streets at night in this, the lower-middle end of Mid. Normally he wouldn't worry about walking the neighborhood at night. People were more likely to avoid him than the other way around. He cultivated the sort of bedraggled appearance that meant they maintained a wide berth, especially in the darkness of evening. He grimaced to himself. Somehow he was starting to become tired of the way everything fell apart. It didn't matter whether it was the buildings, or the transport system, or just people. Everything fell apart one way or another. His efforts to extricate himself from the job, and then winding up here, no one to care about or worry about except for himself. He'd had the organization, the job, and despite there being things he didn't like about it, at least it had been something solid. It was as if he'd made his own existence fall away, as if he simply didn't want a real life around him anymore. Instead he'd surrounded himself with mindless programmed consumption. It wasn't living. It was pretending to live.

It was time he started doing something about it. He was weary. Weary of the gradual unraveling that was the earmark of his life.

He'd walked past two stops, and still there was no sign of the shuttle network kicking back into life. Typical.

After the third stop, something started to twinge at the back of his consciousness. He glanced around, but couldn't see anyone or anything particularly that might bring on the feeling. A few more meters and the feelings grew stronger. He stopped this time, waiting, listening for some hint of what might be causing the unease. Nothing. The evening was still, just like the buildings around him. No footsteps, no voices, nothing disturbed the blanket of quiet. Maybe he was just being jumpy. He'd been off the stims for a couple of days. His nerves always got frayed when he was easing up. It was a no-win situation, really. Either he was on the stims and his nerves felt like tightly stretched elastic most of the time, or he was coming off them and he was becoming edgy. He shook his head and started walking again. Maybe it was just the lack of the familiar whir and hum of the shuttles that was making it feel too still.

He glanced up at the ceiling panels, but the display was unchanged. The moonlight, or pseudo-moonlight, glowed from above, painting everything in shades of gray. He sighed, looked back uptown, and continued his trudge.

Two more stops and there was a chunk and grind. The shuttles were coming back on line. About time. He'd passed a stop about fifty meters back, so he turned and retraced his steps, rather than walking on to the next stopping point. There, off in the distance, he could see the approaching shuttle lights heading up toward Mid Central. Good, he'd had about enough walking for one evening. Out of the corner of his eye he caught something moving in the shadows across the other side of the street. Jack peered across, trying to see what it was. All he saw were shadowed walls and an empty street. No, he was definitely just edgy. There was nothing over there. With a conscious effort he dismissed it and turned back to wait for the shuttle, only two stops down now. Two stops, but it might have been forever. The ceiling panels were growing denser with purplish cloud, obscuring the moon's surface and adding a darker pall to the surrounding gloom. By the time the shuttle neared his stop where he was waiting, glancing nervously around, Jack felt a touch of relief.

He slipped inside the doors and headed for his usual corner. The shuttle car was empty, and surprisingly free of crap that people had left behind. Perhaps most of them had simply given up and walked during the outage, just as he had. The shuttle seemed to take forever to get under way, but finally the doors slid shut—almost. Just as they were about to seal, an arm and shoulder forced themselves between the closing doors. Then a torso followed, wedging the doors open.

A solid, stocky man wearing a dark jacket and with short-cropped blond hair shoved his way into the car, holding the doors open for a companion. He was a tall guy, wearing shades, hair tied back. Okay, it was dark. That was just a bit too much slavery to image for Jack's taste. *Take the bloody glasses off.*

The shuttle was protesting now with an insistent chiming, registering the obstruction, warning that it was about to get under way. Making sure that his companion was fully inside, the blond man released the doors, stepped inside the car, and, after a passing glance in Jack's direction, stood with his back to him, masking his companion from direct view. Well, that suited Jack fine. He didn't have to look at the fashion casualty directly.

Jack watched them for a couple of minutes as the car slid off up the avenue, and then returned to his thoughts. They seemed engrossed in their own conversation, and the little he could see of them showed him nothing particularly interesting. The next stop came and went. No more passengers boarded, and the pair remained in their huddle in the doorway. Another stop, the doors slid open then closed, and the shuttle headed on. The blond glanced over his shoulder at Jack, then turned. Deliberately he strode down the length of the carriage and sat directly opposite. Jack looked him over. What was this? He was not too tall, but big, well built. He took in Jack's scrutiny and returned the stare, but with a slight sneer as well. The guy looked like trouble. Jack averted his gaze and made a show of watching the advertising displays above the man's head. That way he could keep an eye on him without hitting him with a direct and potentially confrontational stare.

Somebody plopped down in the seat beside him. It had to be the blond's companion. Studiously Jack avoided looking at him. This was not good.

"Well, Jack Stein, isn't it?"

Jack turned. He knew that voice. The companion removed his shades, pulled the tie from his hair, and shook it out. Long black hair, dark eyes, heavy tan. The bottom dropped out of Jack's stomach. It was the White-Haired Man that wasn't. He swallowed before answering.

"Yeah. Do I know you?"

"Maybe. Maybe not. But you know some friends of ours, and they know you. They're not very pleased with you. You really ought to learn to be more cooperative, Jack."

The blond one had stood and crossed to stand in front, boxing him in. The guy's face was plastered with a malicious grin. Jack'd seen that look before. It was the look of a man who enjoyed pain—someone else's. He had a nasty feeling that he knew exactly whose.

"Listen, guys, I don't know what you want, but you're not going to get it from me. So why don't you simply walk away now?"

"Or what?" said Blondie.

The dark-haired one was leaning close now, right in Jack's ear. "Everything's gonna be all right, Jack. You just tell us what we want to know."

Jack got up from his seat. The blond one took this as all the excuse he needed. He grabbed Jack's coat and flung him hard against the opposite side of the car. The apparent strength in the blond man's arms made itself felt, and Jack smacked against the opposite window, his cheek slamming up against the resilient Plexiglas with a crack. He fell back down against the row of seats, reflexively huddled into a ball, his hand cupping the burst of pain where his cheek had made contact. Blondie was over him again.

"That's just a taster. Now you're going to help us."

Jack grunted through tightly clamped teeth, grimacing against the pain. The one with black hair was crouched down in front of him at eye level.

"Did you say something, Jack? I think he said something, Mike."

"Shit," Jack hissed. This was not going to be fun.

"Now," said the dark-haired one, right up close to Jack's face so he could almost taste his breath. "You tell us where you got that handipad, why don't you? Then it'll all go away."

"Fuck you," said Jack. He knew it wasn't a smart move, but he had to say it. Circumstance sort of demanded it. He tried to struggle to his feet.

Blondie grabbed him and hit him. The blow connected with his damaged cheek, and lights exploded behind Jack's eyes. He fell, the back of his head connecting hard with the bottom edge of the window, slamming a fresh burst of light through his brain before he crumpled to the seat. Everything right now was pain. He couldn't think; he couldn't respond. He should have known as soon as he saw the pair what was on their minds. Sloppy. Very sloppy.

The White-Haired Man with black hair was back. He was leaning close again. Jack tried to focus. His vision was blurred and foggy.

"Who gave it to you?"

"Gaaah. Dunno." He mustered up his energy and spat right into the looming face.

Slam. The one called Mike hit him from above, crushing his face into the yielding synthetic seat fabric.

Through the pain fog, he could feel the saliva slipping between his cheek and the smooth, ridged material, making his skin slide across the surface. Still he tried to focus. A landscape of plastic pale orange, textured, faded off in front of his eyes. He suddenly, peculiarly, found the seat's fabric immensely interesting. The vague image of the blond one was above him again, his big fist raised above his head, ready to bring it crashing down. Jack squinted up at it. He couldn't take much more of this. It was getting to be too much of a habit.

"Just tell us."

"Gaaah."

"Tell us." *Slam.*

"I don't fucking know. I don't know!" The words hurt now.

Crack. The fist connected again, his head exploded in light, and then nothing.

A low groan brought him back to consciousness. The sound was familiar. Through the aching fog, he vaguely remembered his own voice. He opened his eyes the merest crack. He was still on the shuttle. He peered around, looking for the other two, but there was no sign in the immediate area. The shuttle was quiet. It seemed to have stopped moving, and he was alone, lying huddled on the row of seats. What had happened? Where had they gone?

Gingerly he levered himself upright and squinted out the windows, rubbing at the dried crust of saliva around his mouth. The shuttle was pulled into a siding. Blank walls faced him out one window, empty tracks out the other. It had obviously finished its run for the day. A lance of white pain throbbed, nestled in a hard point behind his eyes.

He must be in Mid Central. Two other shuttles sat parked beside his a little farther up, obscuring any direct view. *Dammit.* Stuck in the middle of a shuttle siding a long way from his apartment. He stood and his cheek blossomed into throbbing pain. Tentatively he brought his fingers up to feel the damage. It hurt. It hurt badly, but the bone underneath seemed to be intact. He wondered if there'd been any other passengers on the way to Mid Central. If there had, they'd evidently distanced themselves from the huddled and hurting Jack Stein. There was a large lump at the base of his skull beneath the hairline, and he prodded at it carefully, inspecting his fingers as he brought them away. No blood. That was good.

They had given him a thorough going-over, but he couldn't remember telling them anything. That was good too. But feeling like this was not. It was starting to become too much a way of life. He stooped, leaning against a railing for support as he collected his thoughts. Why did he continually leave himself open to this sort of shit? He was becoming too complacent, taking things for granted. His inner senses had been screaming alarm bells at him, and he'd just dismissed them. *You know better than that, Stein, or you should by now.* It was those senses that had made him what he was. He ought to know better.

The Anastasia Van der Stegen visit had prompted this. Maybe he should have been a little friendlier. God knew it would have been pleasant enough. So, confirmation: The White-Haired Man was linked to her. Names shuffled around in his head, slotting into places in the mental diagram. Another small piece of the puzzle, but it didn't do him any real good without verification. He was in no state to get that backup now, though.

There was only one thing for him to do, and that was get back to his apartment, dig out some patches, and then once they'd done their work, and he'd nursed himself back to some semblance of health, track down the pair who'd given him the going-over. Gleeson could wait. He could do with a bit of payback, but this time he'd be ready. It just showed how soft and complacent he'd become. His military training counted for nothing anymore. He couldn't even give a good accounting of himself. He staggered toward the door, hit the release, and stepped down between the shuttles. One good thing: He didn't have far to walk to catch a shuttle back to his apartment.

Another thought struck him as he crossed the sidings: The White-Haired Man did jobs for Anastasia Van der Stegen, but he was probably the same one who had been at Pinpin's apartment. Maybe he had been there under Joshua Van der Stegen's orders; it made sense that he worked for the old man. There was no reason why Van der Stegen wouldn't have a personal collection of hired muscle. There had been a pair of them at the apartment, according to Billie. A tall guy with long dark hair, and the woman with red hair. The fragments were at last really starting to click into place. The red-haired woman with Van der Stegen at the office, and this other guy. They were the ones who had seen to Pinpin.

He shuffled off between the parked shuttles, his coat pulled tight about him as he headed for the Old-bound platform and home. He grimaced at himself. He could have chosen an easier way to find out.

Sixteen

"Mr. Van der Stegen, thanks for calling back." Tasha's father had taken his own sweet time in getting around to doing so. "I need to know about someone who works for you."

"Yes?" Jack peered down at Van der Stegen's image on his handipad. The man's attention was on something off to one side. He looked up, and for the first time noticed Jack's face. "Good God, Stein. What happened to you?"

"Doesn't matter. Had a slight disagreement."

"I see."

"Back to the topic, Mr. Van der Stegen. I actually need to know about two people, really. Have you got someone working for you? I don't know his name, but he's a tall guy, long dark hair, thin face with high cheekbones, deep tan. Sound familiar?"

"Actually, yes. It sounds like you're describing Alexis Grecco. I'm not entirely sure, of course, but that could very easily be him."

"Do you have an employee record handy?"

"No. I don't keep that sort of thing to hand. I have people who look after those types of things for me."

Jack nodded. "Yes, of course you do. An address maybe?"

"Yes, as it happens. One moment." He fiddled with something offscreen, and a moment later Jack's handi-pad flashed a receipt.

"Thanks. What about a solidly built guy with short-cropped blond hair?"

Van der Stegen shook his head. "No, not familiar. Could be, though. Some of my staff come and go. I don't really have a lot to do with all of them, so I don't necessarily know all their names and faces. Only the ones closest to me. Sorry, that's all I can tell you. So, Stein, what's this about? Has it something to do with what we discussed?"

"I just think that this Alexis Grecco, if that's his name, may know something that will help me find out what happened. I think he may be involved. What does he do for you?"

Van der Stegen frowned. "What do you mean, 'you think,' Stein?"

"I'm sorry; I can't give you any more than that right now. So what does he do?"

The frown got deeper. "Security, mainly. Driver from time to time. Well, driver more than not these days. Sometimes he acts as an escort to Anastasia when she needs to visit the Locality."

"Uh-huh. How long has he worked for you?"

"Two or three years."

"And before that?"

"I don't really know. As I said, I have people who look after that sort of thing for me."

"Okay, thanks. I think you've given me enough for now. I'll be in touch."

Van der Stegen's image blinked out, and Jack

prompted the handipad for the message. It was an address farther down the Old end of Mid. So the guy didn't live out at the Residence. Made sense. If Van der Stegen had business that needed taking care of, it was unlikely to be anything out at his house. He probably had a number of people scattered across the Locality's length. Okay, time to pay one Alexis Grecco a visit, and maybe even up the score a little. This time he'd be the one with the element of surprise. The way he was feeling, he'd need it.

It didn't take long to get to the district where Alexis Grecco's address said he lived. It was a creaky neighborhood, not quite as stuttering with the marks of decay as the farther reaches of Old, but enough that the systems were obviously not functioning to full capacity. The apartment building, when Jack found it, looked like it had some sort of pink and gray-blue mold growing up the outer walls, but it was probably just a discoloration of the builders as they lost control of pigment. He stood for a few seconds out front, trying to get a sense of the place. He could feel his own nerves but nothing particularly from the building or the area surrounding it, so he stepped inside. Fourth floor. The elevator looked battered and the lobby was dim with yellowish light. It couldn't be costing this Grecco much to live here, but maybe Alexis Grecco was a man of simple tastes and it was all he needed. He punched a button, but nothing happened. He stood there for a few seconds, waiting, and then grunted. Jack gave up on the elevator and looked over at the narrow staircase winding up into the gloom. Four floors of that. *Great*.

A few years ago and this apartment block would have been one of the more modern constructions in the fashionable end of New. The building tastes changed, and as the buildings crawled down the length of the Locality, they not only became less functional, but they dated, reflecting past styles of programming and taste. The modern programs gave the blocks in New an entirely different feel. This place not only felt old; it smelled old too.

One by one he mounted the stairs, his nose wrinkling at the vague mustiness that wafted from the floors below. Somebody had used the bottom of the stairwell for more than dumping trash. A building's self-clean programs usually took care of that, but not anymore. Basic building functions started to break down as they crept toward Old. Complex routines like the automated cleaning programs were some of the first to go. Somewhere from up above came the muffled sound of someone shouting. This Alexis Grecco was clearly a man of basic needs.

He reached the landing and, glancing either way, determined which way the numbers ran. He waited, listening, then approached the right number warily. He'd already had one encounter with Grecco, and the last thing he wanted was a repeat performance. The figure populating his dreams over the past few weeks loomed in the back of his thoughts, making the sense of unease even more palpable. Was he sure he knew what he was doing? Still, there were no alarm bells. His senses questing, he stepped toward the apartment's front door and rang. Nothing. The guy wasn't at home. Either that or he wasn't answering. With the state of the apartment block, he doubted that the door screener would be working anyway, so it was more likely that he simply wasn't there.

It was a letdown. The expectation had been stringing through his body, and now the guy wasn't home. He leaned his forehead against the doorframe and closed his eyes, thinking. He could wait here. He could wait across the street, watching for Grecco to show, or he could find something else to do.

"Hey, can I help—"

Jack knew who it was immediately. The voice from his dreams, the sudden alertness flashing through him. It was Grecco. A hand on his shoulder.

Jack turned slowly.

Grecco's eyes widened, and in an instant he was gone, pounding up the corridor and away. Wherever he was going, there had to be another access. A door slammed, and Jack had his confirmation. Another staircase at the end of the corridor. He couldn't let Grecco get away. He needed some answers.

With a curse he too bolted up the corridor. There was a door just around a corner at the end, and Jack fumbled to get it open, cursing inwardly all the time. *Stupid.* He should have been ready, but why should he have expected Grecco to run? Especially after their last meeting.

He heaved himself bodily through the door, slamming it out of the way with his shoulder. There was a railing just inside. He leaned over and peered down, but he couldn't see the lower staircase. The sound of running footsteps echoed in the narrow space. There was no way now that he could go back and try to cut him off. He had no choice but to follow.

One flight, two flights. He was halfway down the third when there was the crash of another door opening below. Jack quickened his pace. Hopefully around here there wouldn't be that many people around. A running man should be easier to spot. He physically launched himself down the last flight of stairs, holding on to the rail to steady himself, and then he too barreled out the door and onto the street outside.

The doorway led to a small side street next to Grecco's building. Jack glanced both ways, but there was no sign. He closed his eyes and took a deep breath. That way. Back to the main street. He took off, running. He could feel Grecco. He was not too far away.

As he rounded the corner, he stopped and looked both ways, up and down the street. No sign of anyone. He closed his eyes again. The presence was coming from Oldbound. He turned and started walking quickly in that direction. This far down, any number of the buildings had started to become abandoned, as the residents could no longer put up with the deterioration of their living conditions.

He slowed his pace, letting his sense guide him. He passed one building, two, three. Across the other side of the road a derelict construction stood, the outside walls flaking, windows crumbling into dust. A broad, dark doorway led inside from the street, the doors themselves long gone. The pull was coming from there. Jack nodded, crossed the street, and stood outside, waiting. Grecco was definitely in there.

His mouth set into a hard line, Jack stepped inside. Just inside the darkened entranceway, inner alarm bells rang.

A figure broke from the shadows and charged past him. Jack tried to grab, but he was too late. He turned and started running. The figure ducked into a side street, long dark hair flying. He had him now. He entered the side street, wary. Nobody. Farther down the street there was a series of doorways. He raced toward them, seeing that one of them had been forced open. Jack's guts were guiding him now, pulling him toward the place. He stopped, listening. Nothing. Gently, gently, he pushed the door open and stepped inside.

Jack spun as alarms rang inside his head. With his arm out he grabbed a handful of cloth, pushing Grecco rapidly backward, slamming him up against the wall. The large piece of building material that Grecco had been holding above his head, ready to bring down on Jack's skull, flew from his hand and fell with a solid thump against the floor, bits crumbling from its edges. Jack felt the pressure, felt the wind being driven from the man's lungs. There was nothing like surprise. And now every one of Jack's senses was alive. He was running on his own stims now.

"We meet again," he said, peering into the familiar face. A cheap line, he knew, but somehow it gave him a sense of satisfaction.

"Stein! I—" Grecco tried to shrug off Jack's grip and at the same time lifted his arm for a roundhouse swing.

Jack was ready. Everything had telescoped into slow motion, and his heightened senses read the move before it came. He slipped out of the way and Grecco connected with nothing. Before he'd even finished the swing, Jack was there, delivering a swift, concentrated blow to the solar plexus. All that military training came in handy sometimes. Grecco doubled over, and Jack caught the back of his head and drove Grecco's face hard into one lifted knee. Instantly, he released and stepped back. Grecco crumpled, falling against the wall and the trash-littered floor.

Jack quickly dropped, forcing his knee into the base of the other man's throat. He grabbed another handful of clothing and lifted his other hand, ready to strike. "I owe you one, Grecco," he said in a flat, businesslike voice. Grecco tried to squirm away, but Jack had him effectively pinned, and he increased pressure with his knee just to emphasize the point.

"Now, you listen to me. I know who you are, and you know who I am. I want you to tell me who sent you after me."

Anger was upon him now, and when Jack got angry, emotion trickled away. All the impressions from the dreams had tumbled together into one hard knot of driven energy. Coolly, calmly, he pressed his knee harder into the man's throat. He could kill him now. He wouldn't, but he could.

"Get off me." A rasping, constricted voice.

"I'll get off you when you tell me what I need to know."

Grecco snarled through gritted teeth, and shook his head from side to side. Jack slapped him, hard. The sound echoed around the dank, empty space.

There was something satisfying about the look of shock. Grecco had stopped moving. His hands were up now, trying to ease the pressure of Jack's knee from his throat, trying to get air. Jack slapped him again.

"Can't breathe," said Grecco in a struggling voice, trying to shy away as Jack raised his hand for another slap. Jack eased the pressure a little.

"Listen, Grecco. I don't care about you. You can live or die here, but ultimately I don't care. All I want is the answer to my question."

Grecco used the opportunity to try to slip from beneath Jack's knee, using the wall to gain leverage, but again Jack was ready for him. A ringing slap to the side of the head, increased pressure with his knee, and the squirming subsided some. Jack decided to add emphasis to his point and he bore down hard on the man's throat. A strangled noise and Grecco went very still.

Somewhere in the back of the building there was the sound of movement, then the creak as a door opened. A disheveled head poked out, and Jack shot a glare. The face quickly disappeared and the door closed again. Jack turned his attention back to Grecco. "You know what I want. You can stop this now."

"Tasha," Grecco forced out hoarsely.

"What?"

"Tasha. Anastasia Van der Stegen."

With the mention of her name, insight flooded through him. His head filled with an image as the power flowed through his arm, from Grecco, and into his inner vision. He saw Anastasia Van der Stegen. She was not alone. She was in a close huddle with—Alexis Grecco.

So Anastasia was using Grecco as well. He wondered what she had promised him, apart from her evident charms, and it seemed Grecco was getting his own special taste of those.

"Why would she want to do that?"

"Outreach," came the croaking reply.

"So." Jack eased the pressure marginally. "Outreach."

"She's tied up with Warburg. We were going to . . ." Grecco caught himself before he said anything more.

"Anastasia Van der Stegen and Warburg, eh?"

So that was it. His head was still awash with the images of Grecco and the Van der Stegen girl in an intimate clutch. He tried to push his thoughts past it and concentrate on what Grecco was telling him.

On the floor Grecco nodded, barely. Jack eased the pressure another notch. "What's Anastasia Van der Stegen to you?"

Grecco closed his eyes tightly and shook his head. That was answer enough for Jack. This poor guy actually felt loyalty to her. Jesus, she was a classic. Exactly how many men did she have at the end of her leash? It seemed she didn't need to expend much effort to get what she wanted. He wondered if her father knew, or if he even cared.

"Thanks, Alexis. You've been very helpful." Jack briefly considered doing the man some real damage, but there was no point. He eased himself upright and stared down at Grecco, who was lying on the floor holding his throat and coughing. He turned and simply left him lying there. So much for the White-Haired Man. Which girlfriend did he want? Clearly the one he'd gotten had given him more than he'd bargained for.

As Jack made his way back out into the light he felt more at ease, as if he'd purged something from within. Action. It had been a while since he'd acted decisively. Not that he particularly wanted to go around hurting people, but this time it felt good. He had owed the guy. He didn't think Grecco would be bothering him again, blond friend or not, and if he did, Jack would be ready.

Next stop Outreach. Anastasia Van der Stegen and the chauffeur. Who would have thought it? Even though Grecco was involved with the Van der Stegen woman, he still had to find out if he got his instructions from Warburg. The readiness with which Joshua Van der Stegen had delivered Grecco's address had already ruled him out. On the surface, Grecco might work for Van der Stegen, but his allegiance lay elsewhere.

The now-familiar offices hadn't changed. Jack might as well have never left. Warburg too might never have moved, though the suit was different. He motioned Jack to a chair.

"Stein. It's about time we had some results. I hope we're nearing a conclusion to this investigation."

Jack took his time positioning himself in the chair before answering, watching Warburg's reactions, but he already knew the man was good. He was just as likely to show nothing.

"I guess you could say that, Mr. Warburg."

Warburg folded is hands in front of him on the large desk, leaning forward slightly. "So why do you need to see me?"

Jack had rehearsed what he was about to say all the way to the Outreach buildings. He chose his words very carefully.

"Mr. Warburg, I believe there are some people who are actively trying to stand in the way of my attempts to find an answer to your problem. It's almost as if somebody doesn't want me to find out what happened. I think that somebody is probably working for you."

"And who might that be, Stein?"

"A tall, thin man with long dark hair. Well tanned."

Warburg seemed to consider, then slowly shook his head. "No, not familiar."

"Well, the man I'm talking about seems to know you. Claims to work for the interests of Outreach, Mr. Warburg. As you can see, I had a little difficulty persuading him to share that information."

Warburg fixed him with a level stare. "I see. As I said, Stein, the person you describe is not familiar to me."

"He had a lot to tell me about a particular handi-pad."

Warburg didn't even blink. Jack had expected some reaction, at least, but the man was just too slick and definitely practiced—a real performer. But Jack still had one thing held in reserve—Grecco's name.

Warburg sighed. "I'm a busy man. If you want to waste time asking stupid questions, I suggest you find someone else."

"I understand how busy you must be, Mr. Warburg, but you've hired me to do a job. If you want to get to the bottom of what happened on Dairil III, then you just might want to give me a little bit of your time. Do I have your permission to continue?"

Warburg waved his hand. "Go ahead."

"During the course of my investigations, I happened upon a handipad. That handipad was secured and it contained a lot of information about some scientific research. Since that handipad came into my possession, I've been the subject of a lot of attention, most of it not exactly welcome. I believe that the handipad, and whatever it contained, is connected to what happened to the mining crew."

"You say 'contained.' Has something happened to change that? Where is this handipad now?"

"I no longer have it, but that's unimportant. What *is* important is that one of the people interested in it is a guy called Alexis Grecco."

"And?"

Not a flicker. Warburg was just too good. Either that or he really didn't know the man.

"He's the one I described, but you're telling me he doesn't mean anything to you. Well, I had a little talk with Alexis Grecco." Jack's fingers went involuntarily to his tender cheek. "He said I should talk to you. Or maybe, seeing as you don't know him, I should have another chat with his girlfriend. Perhaps you know his girlfriend, Mr. Warburg? Anastasia Van der Stegen?"

Nothing. Not a thing. Warburg was as cool as they came.

"Look, Stein. I've already told you I don't know this person, and so far you've said nothing that makes me think I want to waste any more of my time. Unless you have anything further to add . . ."

This was getting him nowhere. "No, I guess not. Except what do you know about wormholes?"

This time Warburg frowned. He had his interest now.

Jack continued. "Exotic matter. Is that familiar?"

Warburg stood and stepped from behind the desk. "Now you're starting to talk nonsense."

"Do you really want me to find out what happened to your mining crew, Mr. Warburg? Or perhaps you'd prefer me to end up with some other answer that might keep your corporate buddies quiet."

Warburg took a step forward, the fingers of one hand steepled on the edge of the desk. "It's time you left. Just get up and get out, Stein. I don't have time for this."

"So you keep saying, Mr. Warburg." Jack stood. "And maybe there's another reason for that."

"I don't have to take this from the likes of you, Stein. I suggest you leave now."

"I'm not done yet."

"Oh, but you are."

Warburg placed the fingers of one hand firmly in the center of Jack's chest and gave a little push. That small contact was all it took. Jack's head was suddenly awash with images. A broad, jagged pink landscape stretched off into the distance. The ground was littered with pink-brown rock chippings. Silver trailers caught the light and sent it in sharp arrows, casting star shapes through his inner vision.

He knew this place. It was Dairil III. He was back in the dream. The image shifted and he was inside somewhere. There was something else—a figure, tall, rangy, yellow-gray hair plastered to the top of his head. Pinpin Dan. The image shifted and there was Pinpin Dan lying dead. He was flat, stretched out, and behind him, looking on, was someone else. Jack didn't recognize the room, but he immediately knew the small figure in the background, though her features were indistinct. It was Billie. Billie was on Dairil III. Somehow it was linked to Pinpin, either via his network or some other means. But that didn't matter. All that mattered was that he *knew* for certain where she was. There was no need to play hit and miss anymore. The brief contact with Warburg had given him his confirmation.

He backed away from Warburg's hand, struggling to reorient himself. He looked hard, straight into Warburg's face.

"What are you doing on Dairil III?"

"Enough. Get out, Stein." There was restrained anger in his voice, and something else. Was it a touch of fear? He reached out to fend Jack away, but Jack was ready for it and stepped back in time to avoid another contact.

"You'll be hearing from me, Mr. Warburg," he said.

A muscle worked at the side of Warburg's jaw, but he'd managed to regain some composure. He spoke the next through gritted teeth.

"I've a good mind to dispense with your services altogether, but against my better judgment . . . you've got three weeks, Stein. That's all. I expect your report by then, and I don't want to see you. Now get out." He turned and started to stride back to his desk.

"It's okay," said Jack. "I'm going." The last glimpse he got, before turning and pacing back down the hallway himself, was of Warburg standing next to his desk, the fingers of his right hand beating a rhythm on its surface. Good, he'd finally touched a nerve. Better than he'd expected, but he also expected Warburg to sack him. Something had held him back, and that gave Jack another clue. It seemed Gleeson was right about the internal pressures within the company. Warburg was not a free agent in all of this. He needed Jack.

Warburg hadn't yet thought to see him escorted from the premises, but he knew he didn't have much time. He had to find Gleeson. And Gleeson would have to act quickly too. Warburg was alert that something was amiss now. Hopefully Warburg would be high enough up the food chain that it would take time for things to filter down through the ranks, and maybe, just maybe, those corporate pressures would be enough to give him second thoughts about shutting things down. If Jack was lucky—and this time he'd have to count on that luck—he'd be able to get away quickly enough. Jack knew exactly where he was headed now. He was going to Dairil III.

He walked quickly down the corridor, remembering vaguely which way he'd been sent last time to see Gleeson. He took a couple of false turns, but finally found the right one and headed down toward Gleeson's desk. The little clerk was in residence, and for the moment there was no one else around. He walked up to the side of the desk.

"Francis."

Gleeson continued to peer at a stack of cards he was sorting, and answered without lifting his gaze. "Hmmm?"

"Francis," Jack said more forcefully. This time Gleeson looked up and his face blanched.

"By all that's . . . what are you doing here?"

"Listen, I haven't got much time. I need your help and I need it now."

"Can't we do this away from here?" Gleeson glanced nervously around.

"No, we can't. No time. It is Dairil III and I need to get out there. I've had an epiphany, if you like. Something tells me the answer's there at the research facility on Dairil III. Have you done the things I asked you, to set me up to get out there? Tell me how I do it."

"W-well. I don't know. Wait." He shuffled through a stack of cards and slotted one into the reader. "There—there's a cargo ship leaving in a week's time. Late afternoon. Supplies and the like. That's the earliest one. But you'll need the authorizations."

Shit. A week was longer than Jack expected. It would have to do.

"You're the card wizard, Francis. Time for you to sort it out," he said.

"I suppose I . . . but . . . but what if I'm caught?"

"Let me worry about that. If we move quickly and quietly enough, it'll be over before they can do anything. I'll be on the ship, and by then it'll be too late."

"Wait, wait. Let me think." He was becoming agitated.

"Come on, Francis. We have to move. Now!"

"All right. Let me think about it. I need to work out something that will stand up under scrutiny. Please leave it with me. It's not going to be easy." Another nervous glance to either side. "Just go now. I can't afford to be seen with you. I'll come to your apartment later tonight."

Jack nodded. "Okay."

He turned and headed back up the corridor as rapidly as he had arrived. Within minutes he was out of the building and onto the wide street below, waiting for a shuttle to take him away. If he was right about Gleeson, what the little man had said was correct. He couldn't be seen talking to Jack. It would jeopardize his real purpose at Outreach.

Still, there was something chewing inside him, something not quite right. As he headed for the shuttle stop, he was working his mouth and clicking his tongue against the roof of his mouth. He was missing something.

Gleeson was good to his word, and in the early evening he showed up, looking nervous, as usual. Underneath, though, he had a self-satisfied air. Jack asked him in and sat opposite while his visitor composed himself. Gleeson could barely sit still on the couch. He was fidgeting, and a damp sheen of perspiration marked his brow. He dug in his pocket and, with a flourish, pulled out a card and slid it across the table.

"Don't lose this," he said. "Without it you're in trouble."

"So what is it?"

"It's the security pass. Allows you access to the cargo ship and to the research facility of Dairil III."

"So who am I supposed to be?"

Gleeson gave a little half smile. "Jack Stein. You're an investigator working for William Warburg on private contract to Outreach, just like you said. You've been hired to determine what happened to the miners on Dairil III."

"But you seemed to be worried about that, that somebody might . . .?"

"No. It's perfect. You see, I've thought this through. If anybody wants to check the records, that's exactly who you are. You don't have to tell any stories, and any checks will back you up. It gives you a legitimate reason to be there."

"Even the research facility?"

"Why not? It's all in the same area. Easy to justify a check, no? I've booked passage for you on the cargo ship already."

For once Gleeson looked pleased with himself, and he looked like he was even starting to relax.

Jack watched him, thinking. "Okay, Francis. It might just work. I'm more worried about somebody contacting Warburg. And after our last meeting . . ."

Gleeson waved his hand. "They're not going to bother the great man himself. Especially not from out there. I've thought about that too. If anything Warburg's name should help you if you get into trouble. People who work for Outreach know better than to question the plans of the Man."

Yes, it made sense. Warburg gave the impression of someone used to his authority and to not having it questioned.

"Thank you, Francis. Wish me luck."

"You will let me know?"

"Sure, as soon as I have anything to give you, but that's not going to be for some time now."

Gleeson nodded slowly. "Yes, I know," he said.

Jack saw Gleeson out, locked the door behind him,

and settled back to take it easy. A week to wait, and he had little else to do now *but* wait. And then there was the cargo ship. Months. It would take three months to get out there. By then the contract would be as good as dead, but he didn't really have a choice. Billie was out there somewhere, and he had to find her. Three months . . .

No, something just wasn't adding up.

Seventeen

A week of boredom. A long, deadly week with nothing to do except watch a few vids and scroll through his notes. He considered contacting Van der Stegen, but there was nothing to be gained by that at the moment. His other avenue was Anastasia, but it was better to keep well away from her in the current situation. He wanted to be right out of her sights. Any interaction and she'd be just as likely to alert Warburg that something was going on. It was unfortunate that the cargo ship wasn't leaving sooner, but there was nothing he could do about it. As an exercise, he called up the final version of his diagram and sat staring at it for something, anything he had missed. Sitra Akhar. Well, he had that right, and Pinpin Dan had to be connected to Warburg. Van der Stegen, though a silent partner in the operations, was most definitely connected to Outreach, and therefore to Warburg. The problem was, everything linked back to Pinpin Dan. It just didn't make sense. He chewed at his bottom lip, trying to work out what it was he was missing.

Everything about this case, everyone associated with it, appeared as someone they were not. Everyone he'd come into contact with had been performing—at least that, or appeared as a disguised clue within his dreams. Illusion, reality, how did you reconcile the two? His dreams were illusion, of a form, but within them lay the reality of what he sought.

Sitra Akhar. Seek the left. No, that wasn't only it. It was more than that. It was an admonition to look at the other side. Take another perspective before accepting everything at face value.

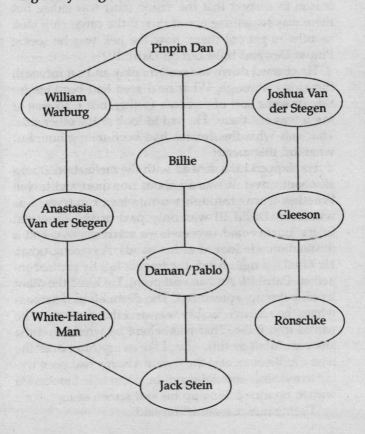

How could everything lead back to Pinpin Dan? But there he had been, in the vision provided by Warburg's brief contact. There he was, with Billie, out on Dairil III, dead maybe, but there all the same.

Wait, Stein, you're being an idiot again. So eager to look at the easy solution, he'd jumped on what the Warburg vision had given him without even looking at it. Sure, the dreams weren't logical, and he had no reason to suspect that the vision stuff was either, but there was something about this. If the cargo ship took months to get out there, how the hell was he seeing Pinpin Dan and Billie out on Dairil III?

He cleaned down the wall display and sat forward, thinking it through. What he'd seen had been the inside of some sort of research facility, but who was to say it was out there? He had to look at the other side. That was what the dreams had been telling him. But what did that mean?

He slapped his forehead with the realization. It was all about travel. It was all about transport and travel. Whether it was through wormholes or gateways or whatever, Dairil III was only part of the equation. Every journey had two ends—a starting point and a destination. He looked at his hands. A starting point. He lifted his right hand, the fingers tightly pressed together. Dairil III. And an end point. He lifted the other hand, palm up, spread flat. The destination. That was where the research facility was, and that was where he would find Billie. That was where he would find the answers to all of this. *Shit.* Like everything over the past couple of weeks, the dream visions had been trying to tell him something and he'd just failed to see. He wasted no time calling up his wallscreen again.

"Call Francis Gleeson," he said.

It took only a few moments for Gleeson's face to coalesce on the display.

"Stein!" he said. "I thought you said your system was out of action."

Jack sighed. "Long story, Francis. It's only for incoming stuff. I need you to do something."

Gleeson frowned, a touch of exasperation slipping into his expression. "What is it now?"

Jack paused for a moment, gathering the words. He didn't like feeling stupid. "We have to cancel the Dairil III stuff. I'm not going."

"But you said—"

"Yes, I know what I said, but the answer's somewhere else, closer to home."

"I told you I thought—"

"Yeah, yeah. I know what you said. Okay, you were probably right. I should have listened to you. But forget about that now. Are you listening? So this is what I need you to do."

Making sure that Gleeson had gotten over his brief sense of victory and was paying full attention, Jack continued.

"There has to be another research establishment somewhere else. It could be offworld; it may not be. My suspicion is that it's close by. My other guess is that it is not here. Some planet in system, somewhere like that. I need you to go through records, look at the time period that the facility on Dairil III was established, and see if you can come up with another destination. They had to be shipping stuff out there."

Gleeson blinked a few times, processing the information. "Yes. Tomorrow. Yes. That makes sense. But . . . I have to fix the other things too."

"Okay, Francis. If you're fine with that, I'll talk to you tomorrow."

"But how can I—"

"You can reach me through my handipad. I'm sending you the link now."

Jack sent the command and immediately cleared down the wallscreen, leaving Gleeson blinking owlishly at the other end. That done, he got up and headed in to make himself a coffee, suddenly feeling as if a great weight had been lifted from his shoulders. No real answers yet, but he was a lot closer to what he needed, in more ways than one. A hell of a lot closer.

Gleeson called him midafternoon. Jack had been sitting on the couch, dozing, when the vibration of his handipad dragged him back to consciousness. He flipped open the handipad and peered blearily down at the screen. Gleeson's face was troubled, from what Jack could see in the reduced image.

"Francis, that was quick."

"I can't talk for long," he said. "Once you'd given me the pointers, it wasn't too hard to find out. There's only one real possibility—an agricultural world about a week's travel from here called Pandora. There was a lot of equipment shipped out there around the time you said. Lots of stuff that wouldn't really be warranted in a purely agricultural operation."

For once, it appeared Jack had been right. "So what do you suggest we do?"

"It's going to be a little harder to cover," said Gleeson. "We'll have to work something out. Something that will stand up."

"So?"

"I'm working on it. You'll have to give me a little time."

Gleeson glanced to the side again. "Listen, I have to go. Meet me later. I should have something worked out by then."

"Your place?"

"Tonight," he said, and cut the connection.

Once more Jack traced the increasingly familiar route to Gleeson's apartment. Gleeson ushered him inside without any ceremony. As he closed the door, Gleeson leaned back against the wall just inside.

"I'm starting to become worried, Mr. Stein," he said.

Starting? Jack suppressed a grin. "Why, what's the trouble, Francis?"

"Well, with everything that's going on, I can't help feeling that we might be being watched. If I'm not, at least you probably are."

"Yeah, well, it comes with the territory."

Gleeson grimaced. "Well, the sooner this is over and done with, the better, as far as I'm concerned."

"You and me both," said Jack. "So what have you got for me?"

Gleeson beckoned him inside. On a side table sat a package marked with the Outreach logo.

"This is the best I can come up with," he said. "It's a corporate courier package. I've issued the appropriate authorities. You're to be a personal courier from Warburg to the administrative offices of the facility on Pandora."

Jack rubbed his neck. This time it was his turn to grimace.

"I don't get it," he said. Why send a courier at all?"

Gleeson nodded quickly. "I know, it may seem

strange, but it's not unheard-of. There are sometimes certain sensitive materials that Warburg wants hand-delivered. It's just the way it works. You have to trust me on this. Nobody is likely to question, and they're not going to want to see inside the package. That's why they're hand-delivered."

"Okay, that might work, but surely they're delivered to someone."

"Well, yes. I have a name. Only use it if you have to. I've put material in there that is likely to require personal attention, financial stuff. It won't mean much to anyone who doesn't understand it. A casual inspection will pass scrutiny, perhaps, but apart from that, you will be pretty much on your own."

Jack picked up the package and hefted it. Not too heavy, easy enough to carry with him. Gleeson had done his groundwork.

"Okay. How do I get out there?"

Gleeson nodded again. "Haulers run that way about every two days. The next one's tomorrow. With the identity card I give you, it won't be any trouble getting out there. The package will lend weight to your story. I don't envisage any problems. I've also made some rough notes about Pandora, about the administrative section there and anything else I could think of. I've transferred them to my home system."

Jack fished out his handipad. "Thanks, Francis."

"I will, of course, delete these as soon as you've downloaded them. Make sure you have them saved."

Jack nodded.

"Okay," he said. "Is there anything else?"

Gleeson looked him up and down, a slight pursing of the lips evident. "I would suggest a change of clothes, and a shave wouldn't go amiss either. Wear something dark and sober."

Jack looked down at his rumpled clothes, ran his hand over his chin. Gleeson was right. It was about time he started to get his shit together.

"Done," he said. "Okay, I'll be in touch when I return, if I return. Wish me luck."

Eighteen

It was longer than a week—more like ten relative days. He used the time to catch up on lost sleep. The weeks of surviving on stim patches and Rapiheals took their eventual toll, so with nothing else to do he let his body recuperate. He was thankful that most of the sleep was dreamless. He'd gone out and bought a new set of clothes before leaving, something dark and sober, just as Gleeson had suggested. After the shave and the change, he barely recognized himself in the mirror. He could barely believe he had let himself slip so far.

There were a couple of other people on board, administrators, engineers, cargo crew, but they kept pretty much to themselves, and so did Jack. There wasn't much to talk about. The sense of relief when they ship finally docked at the station above Pandora was enormous. Jack wasted no time in organizing the shuttle to the surface. The sooner he was down there, the better. How the hell could people do this for a living?

One more hour aboard a shuttle and he was down. The transport eased to the ground, settling first one way, then the other, and finally coming to a complete halt. He had to give the pilot credit: It was a pretty smooth landing. Jack took a long, slow breath, held it, and then let it out just as slowly. This was it. Pandora.

He waited for the signal that he was clear and unstrapped. Now to put the pass Gleeson had worked up for him to the final test. It had worked so far, but you never knew. If it came to it, he could claim he was just investigating operations on the planet. It would be a push. He had no background in the sorts of agricultural operations that occurred in a place like this, but he would have to make do. The old mining-investigation-on-Dairil III story just wouldn't cut it here. He still didn't know what he'd find, but somehow, this time he *knew* this was the place. There was more than simple nervousness working in his guts.

A slight clunk and the noise of machinery signaled the opening of the doors. He grabbed his bag from the locker next to him and stood. As the door slid open he was ready for what he'd see—farms were farms, after all—but nothing quite prepared him for the vast lines of cropland stretching on and on into the distance. It was a clear day, and he could see for miles. Everywhere was green. There was no sign of settlement, just field after field after field. No sign of people either, which was a good thing. The odd piece of machinery stood near the fields, looking like strangely metallic scarecrows, and somewhat out of place against the variegated green background.

As the stairs settled to the ground, he shrugged off his coat, looped it through the straps of his bag, and, squinting against the open sky, made his way to the doorway. He hesitated at the top, trying to work out which way he would head, but a voice came over the intercom, prompting him to action.

"You okay back there, Mr. Stein?"

"Yeah, thanks." No one there to meet the transport. That was good. "Just acclimatizing."

"Takes a bit of getting used to, doesn't it?"

"Yeah, well. I've seen worse. Thanks again for the lift." And with that he stepped out into the open landscape, scratching his head. So where in the hell was this research facility?

The pilot made sure Jack was clear before retracting the steps and shutting the door. He wasted no time getting the transport under way, and within moments it was a fading dot against the pale bright sky. Jack stood where he was, barely able to track the diminishing shape against the glare. Which way now? He had a rough idea of the layout of the landscape—where the population centers lay—but most of this world was completely automated. Gleeson's hastily scribbled notes had shown him that. The best clue they had was the location of Pandora's administrative center. Computer equipment, scientific tools, all these had been shipped out here. It made sense for that sort of equipment to wind up in the complex that ran the world for Outreach. It was also the most logical place to site whatever research effort they had going here. The planet was populated by Outreach people, no native inhabitants, and company people were likely to be less interested in what went on in the offices and hallways of company bureaucracy. They were all company people here.

The landing strip was little more than a patch of open ground, cleared in the midst of all the fields. A single ramshackle hut sat off to one side. A couple of vehicles sat parked at the edge. He considered them briefly, weighed up the options, and realized he had little choice. Shouldering his bag, he headed toward them.

The long, flat vehicles were similar to working vehicles anywhere: a cab at the front, and a flat carrying area at the back. Electric motors, by the looks of things. He felt the gravity too—not as intense as back home—somehow making everything lighter, less real. With a grunt he heaved himself up into the front of the nearest vehicle and checked it over from the front seat. The cab was dusty, the smell of fresh earth filling the interior. Jack sat for a moment, just experiencing it. He couldn't remember the last time he had smelled that particular scent. Nothing in the Locality was as natural as that. A discarded water bottle lay behind him, and he gave a wry grin. It was just as if he'd left it here for himself from the dream on Dairil III. He reached back and snagged it. The weight told him it was full. He didn't know how long the drive to his destination would take. The water might come in handy. He looked over the panel and found it was a simple button for ignition. He pressed it, and the motor whirred into life. Simple controls. He hit the shift to engage and steered the car into a wide arc across the landing strip and onto a simple dirt road that led away.

He bounced along in the car, barely skidding around corners on the loose dry earth, puffs of dust floating away behind him. It was funny; he always did things better in the dreams. In the dreams he could drive these things. The drive took around half an hour, and as he traveled the wide-open fields gave way to low rises and finally to hills. When he was at a distance he thought far enough away, he stopped the vehicle and got out, dusting off his clothes while he looked at the distant administrative complex built into the side of a taller hill, all glass and steel, and somehow strangely out of place in the middle of this fertile landscape. A series of pipes ran back up the hillside behind, disappearing over a ridgeline above. He would make the rest of the journey on foot, not wanting to announce his presence too early, not knowing quite what he was going to find. He reached into the cab and shuffled around inside his bag, pulling out the package that Gleeson had provided him. If he met anyone, and they questioned why he was on foot, he'd just say he had problems with the vehicle's engine, that it had died, stranding him in the middle of nowhere and leaving him with no choice but to walk.

It took about another hour to walk the distance to the complex, and he kept a watchful eye as he drew closer, trying to keep out of the direct line of sight as much as possible. Nearer to the buildings he tried to decide his best route, but there was nothing to give him a clue as to his best access point. Blank glass walls looked over the hills below. There was nothing else. Jack clutched the package in front of him and pursed his lips. Somewhere here lay an answer, but there didn't seem to be anything obvious. He was feeling suddenly very exposed out here in the open fields. It wouldn't be long before someone spotted him. He closed his eyes, thinking back to the Dairil III dream, looking for some sort of clue.

Slowly, slowly, he opened his eyes again. There, above the office buildings. Those pipes, whatever they were, running up the side of the hill, behind and above the office complex. They weren't usual. They must lead to something, just as there had been conduits above the mine entrance on Dairil III. They led somewhere too. Up above there was some sort of escarpment. Tucking the package under his arm, he headed that way, off to the side and above the offices themselves.

With the pipes serving as his guide, he clambered up the slope, occasionally checking behind and below, making sure there was no one to observe his progress. Finally, sweating with the exertion of the climb, he crested the lip and stepped out onto a flat, rock-strewn shelf, and there, sitting in front of him, in the side of the rock, invisible from below, sat a set of doors. Nodding to himself, the resolve growing inside, Jack walked toward the entrance.

The doors were twin, splitting the entranceway into two. Cross-banded webs of black painted metal we punctuated by a thick, smoked glass-like substance, obscuring whatever lay within from view. Jack looked at the forbidding barrier and knew there was no way anyone could shift those doors on their own, so he looked around for some means to activate whatever would open them. If he were lucky, he wouldn't need to contact anyone inside. The doors stared at him as he stood there, grimacing. Okay, then bluff it was. He searched for some sort of intercom or camera. Nothing. Still, he didn't have to be able to see it for one to be there.

"Hello," he yelled. "Anyone there?"

Silence. No sound at all from anywhere. Usually there was noise of some sort, but the world itself was deathly quiet. The only sound was that of a slight breeze, stirring the long leaves of the surrounding vegetation, marking the boundaries of the flat rock expanse. He dug in his pocket and pulled out the pass Gleeson had arranged for him, looking for some sort of clue. The card was virtually blank. Maybe he could see something through the glass, if it was glass. He walked to the doors and pressed his face up against the opaque surface, trying to peer through. As he brought his hand up to shield his eyes, a thunk shuddered through the doors' material, quickly followed by machine noises. Jack looked up at his hand and stepped back. Of course. The card that Gleeson had given him was a key. Simple. Bringing it close enough to the doors had triggered their opening mechanism. As the doors pulled apart, a wash of cooler air chilled the surrounding air and the slight dampness of his brow. Grateful that it had been so easy, he stepped inside and headed down the corridor that stretched farther into the complex, if complex it was, alert at every step in case he should meet someone.

The passage led deep into the heart of the hillside and seemed to go on forever without a break. With the vast doors sealed behind him, the sound of his own footsteps sounded loud, too loud. He caught himself trying to creep along without making too much noise, then grinned. Stupid again. He had every right to be here. His pass said he did. If he was caught skulking down a corridor, then that was really going to be believable. After a while he focused on another noise, something stirring deep beneath the sound of his own footfalls. He'd been half aware of it since he entered the place, but hadn't really noticed it. A deep throbbing vibration ran through the walls and floor, like the sound of some vast machinery. Whatever it was, it was big. Too big for a simple research facility. He headed down a side passage, in a direction where the vibration seemed louder.

Jack rounded a corner and came face-to-face with . . . Pinpin Dan.

"Dammit. Shit," he breathed.

"Well, well. Jack Stein! You look like you've seen a ghost." Pinpin gave him a tombstone grin, then brayed with laughter. "Ah, young Jack. The loook on your face. I can assure you, dear boy, I'm very much alive. Sorry to disappoint you."

Jack simply stared. He could barely believe Pinpin's casual attitude after all that had happened. He didn't even seem surprised to see him. The same old tombstone teeth, lank gray-yellow hair plastered to his skull. He was dressed in some sort of gray coveralls, buttoned at the front. If anything Pinpin's flesh looked paler and more fish-belly white.

"Come on, Jack. Talk to me," said Pinpin. "I imagine I gave you an awful scare back in my apartment, but that's all in the past now. Of course, it wasn't real, but our young Wilhelmina helped to make it more so. There's no witness like the sweet innocent, eh?" He tapped the side of his nose with one finger. "So, Jack. Is it wooork that brings you out here? I imagine that it is. Well, that's not a good thing, is it, Jack? It won't do at all."

He glanced down and saw the package tucked beneath Jack's arm, the Outreach logo emblazoned all over it and gave a slight nod. He reached out and gripped Jack's shoulder with bony fingers. "As happy as I am to see you, dear boy, and I have been expecting you to show up eventually—it was easy to get through the doors, wasn't it?—you really shouldn't be here. Company business or not, if I were you, I'd take this one small piece of advice from me. Get off this world, Jack, and don't come back. Whatever you're wooorking on—and I can hazard a guess what that might be—just drop it and get the hell out of here."

There was a feral look to his face that Jack had seen only a few times before.

Pinpin leaned forward conspiratorially, casting a glance over his shoulder, though there was no one to be seen for the length of the corridor. Pinpin's grip on his shoulder was becoming painful. "It's only because we're such good friends that I can let you do this. I like you, Jack. I really do. There are times when we might wooork together again. I don't want any harm to come to you, really. Especially after you looked after Wilhelmina sooo well."

Suddenly the image of Pinpin's face that had floated up when he'd been talking to Daman back in Old became understandable. Clearly the kids in Old had seen Pinpin since his supposed death. They had thought Jack had been lying to them. That made a lot of sense. Billie had probably been there, and not long before Jack had come looking for her. That was where she'd gone. Pinpin Dan had come to get her. Further pieces started to slot together. Jack extricated himself from Pinpin's grip and took a step back. "So where is she?" he said.

"Why, dear boy. She's here with me, of course. What did you expect?"

Jack bit back his first response. "She's okay?" he said finally.

"Of coooourse she's okay, Jack. Would I let anything happen to Wilhelmina? I don't think so."

Yeah, no more than you already have, you evil bastard. But he didn't say it. He just sniffed and clamped his jaw shut.

"Would you like to see her, Jack? Seems you've

taken quite a shine to my young friend, haven't you? I can believe that you've been awfully worried about her since I came to collect her from your apartment. Of course, you gave me quite a scare when she wasn't there, but then I found her message. It was easy to track her down from there. She's good, but not quite that good. She does, however, have a range of other talents that make up for it, eh?"

The look he gave was far too knowing for Jack's liking, but he couldn't afford to react. Not yet.

"Yes, of course," he said. "Can I see her?"

"Well, I don't see what harm it could do, dear boy. I can allow you that before I send you on your way. I need you functioning at the moment. So don't worry; no harm's going to come to you. You just need to be back home, back in the Locality."

"I don't under—"

Pinpin placed a long, bony finger in front of his lips. "Ssssst. Not now, Jack." He reached across and steered Jack forward with a hand on his shoulder. "This way. Then we'll call someone to escort you to your vehicle. It won't take too long to get the shuttle back."

Long, glistening corridors faded deep into the complex. Straight, straight lines. Everything Jack had seen over the last few weeks had involved curves, sinuous shapes, and the contrasting layout of the facility struck him now. They walked for what seemed like a good quarter of an hour in complete silence, the only sound that of their footfalls echoing from the corridor walls and the distant hum of machinery buried somewhere deep within. Finally Pinpin pulled him up in front of a door by placing another hand on his shoulder.

"Here we are. Now, before we go in. No fuss, Jack. All right?"

"Yeah, okay. I've got it, Pinpin. You don't need to worry. You're in control here."

Pinpin grinned his tombstone grin—no amusement in it, then pushed open the door.

Flat white. Clinical. But what did he expect—all the trappings of home? Billie was sitting in a chair looking at a wall display. As she noticed the door open, she quickly uttered a command and the wall cleared down. Only then did she turn to see who it was.

"Uncle Jack!"

Jack swallowed and glanced sideways at Pinpin, whose grin only broadened.

"Billie. You okay?" She looked okay, but her face was shadowed, as if she hadn't had enough sleep. That haunted look was back again. The same look as the kids down in Old—a long, tunneled deepness to her gaze.

"Uh-huh. Sure," she said. "How did you get here? What are you doing?" Question after question.

"Just wait, Billie. You're sure you're okay."

The tumbling flow ceased and Billie stood. It seemed like she wanted to cross the space between them, but something was holding her back. She nodded.

"As you can see, Jack, Wilhelmina is perfectly all right. Wilhelmina," he said, turning back to her. "Jack has just popped in to pay us a brief visit before returning home."

Jack glanced across at Pinpin. "I'm not quite ready to leave yet."

"But I'm afraid to say you'll have to, Jack. You have woooork to do, remember?"

Jack quickly balanced his options. He couldn't afford to be too pushy, but if he just let things go, it would achieve nothing.

"What work? I'd rather spend a little time with Billie."

"You have to go back and submit your report for Outreach. The one that tells them that you've come up with no rational explanation for the disappearance of the mining crew."

Jack spun to face him. "What do you know about that?"

"Why, everything, dear boy," said Pinpin, tapping the side of his nose. "Why do you think you got the job in the first place? I like you, Jack, but I'm afraid you'll never amount to anything much. You have your talents, whatever they may be, but all this fringe escapism you indulge in, it only leads to one place—nowhere. Outreach was getting pressure from within, as well as from some sources outside. Warburg had to be seen to be doing something. Take the heat off for a while so they could get on with things out here. You see, Dairil III has something that makes it very special. The miners were the first to stumble upon it. It has an immense power source buried in the heart of its mountains, something to do with the geothermal activity peculiar to that particular world. I don't understand the exact details of it, but suffice it to say it suited the program's purposes.

"And as for your involvement, dear boy, I suggested it. Hire an investigator who can be seen to be doing the job, but has no chance of coming up with any real answers. You, dear boy. The perfect choice."

"I don't buy it."

"No, of course you wouldn't. You've never been much of a visionary, Jack. Oh, that's rich." He guffawed. "And if only you'd known. When you turned up at my place with that handipad . . . it was like a gift. Miss Van der Stegen was most impressed. She and Warburg were worried about what had happened to it, and then you turn up and deliver it right into our laps."

"So she is involved with Warburg?"

"Of course she is. She and Warburg are working together. And I work for Warburg. Simple. And with the material they had on Van der Stegen's handipad, they had plenty to undermine his grip on Outreach. Why do you think she showed up at your place, Jack? I suggested it too. We had to find out exactly how much you knew, where you got the damned thing in the first place. A pity you weren't a little more cooperative."

"Dammit, Pinpin. How much of a sap do you think I am?"

"Listen, Jack. You like to think you're good at what you do, that you're endowed with some sort of talent. Well, I don't buy that. I've seen you work. You plod away. You've always been lucky, though. Occasionally you get really lucky and come up with a few answers. Occasionally the answers are staring you in the face. No, Jack. You were the perfect choice. Jack Stein— going nowhere. It's ironic, really, considering. The very people you were looking for were going nowhere too." He brayed right in Jack's face.

Jack hit him then. He didn't mean to, but the condescension, the sheer arrogance of Pinpin's tone, and the implications of what he was saying, along with the thought he'd been having himself over the last couple of weeks, all bundled together in the back of Jack's head in a tight ball of anger, and he hit him. Behind that blow lay all the force of the last few weeks' frus-

tration and pain. He hit him hard. The blow snapped
Pinpin's head back. Jack hit him again.

Somewhere in the background he could hear a
voice crying out for him to stop.

At the second blow Pinpin crumpled. One knee
buckled as he raised a bony hand to protect his face,
and he tumbled backward and sideways. There was a
table behind him—a long, low thing with hard
edges—and as he fell Pinpin's head connected with
the corner.

A crack. A thud. Slow motion. And then Pinpin was
lying there, his gangly, awkward form looking all the
more awkward.

"Oh, shit!" said Jack.

"Uncle Pinpin!" cried Billie.

She was down leaning over him before Jack had finished contemplating his fist. What had he done? The
burst of fury had hollowed him, and he stood there
uncomprehending.

"Uncle Pinpin!" said Billie again, shaking him. A
growing pool of bright red, contrasting with the shiny
white, smooth floor surface, started to snake from beneath Pinpin Dan's head. A red, wet bloodsnake,
crawling across the floor. Billie was still shaking him.
She didn't seem to have noticed the blood.

"Billie, leave him." She looked up and glared at
him. He crossed and pulled her away. "I said leave
him."

Jack was going to make sure this time. He knelt and
felt for a pulse. Nothing. *Shit*. He checked again. Billie
was standing looking down at him accusingly.

"Billie, listen. You shouldn't feel anything for this
bastard. You really shouldn't."

"He's dead, isn't he?" she said. "You killed him." Her voice had gone flat, devoid of emotion.

"Yeah, he's dead. I'm sorry, Billie."

"But you said he was dead before."

Jack couldn't deny that. "Yes, I did. I was wrong. But I'm not wrong now. He really is this time."

He stood staring down at the body. Just what he needed. A corpse, and a fresh one at that.

"But now we have a problem," he said.

And they did. Jack was feeling a hollow in his guts. He'd killed him. He'd killed Pinpin Dan. He hadn't meant to, but there was the stark reality lying on the floor in front of him. He couldn't bluff his way out of this. "What's through that door?"

"Living rooms. Bedroom. Bathroom."

"Listen, you've got to help me. Open the door. I'll have to drag him through there. Put him in the bed and clean up this mess. Maybe I can think of a way to get us out of here."

"But what about him?" she asked, nodding at Pinpin's body.

"What about him, Billie? There's nothing we can do for him now. We have to worry about ourselves."

She stared at him for a couple of seconds, then slowly turned, crossed the room, and opened the other door.

"Get me something. A towel or something that I can hold under his head."

She disappeared and returned a few moments later with a towel. Jack wadded it beneath Pinpin's head and, holding it in place, started dragging the body across the room. For all his boniness, Pinpin Dan was not small, and it took some effort. The shiny floor helped matters a little, and Jack finally managed to get him into the next room. Two other doors were in that room, a living room, and one of them lay open. Jack guessed that was where Billie had retrieved the towel from. "Billie, the other door."

Showing not even a shred of emotion, she proceeded to cross to and open that door as well. A couple more minutes and a good deal more effort, and Pinpin's body lay covered in the bed, the towel wadded beneath him, partially stemming the further flow of blood, but it wouldn't be long before it started soaking through. They needed another towel. He said so to Billie, and she quickly returned with another, which Jack slipped under Pinpin's head. He arranged the pillows so the worst of it was hidden from direct view. With the covers pulled over him, maybe no one would notice, at least for a while.

Billie stood in the doorway, watching.

Who was he kidding? It might just last for a while, but after that? He gave the back of his head a rapid scratch. "Billie, is there anywhere else we could put him?"

"Grow a wall."

"What?"

"Grow a wall. Where the door is. Nobody will see him if there isn't a door."

It took him a moment; then he realized what she was saying. "This place works like the Locality?"

"Uh-huh."

"Can you do it?"

"Easy."

Maybe it was shock, maybe it was something else, but she was taking this all too calmly. She seemed to have completely switched off all of her emotions. He didn't have time to analyze it now, but her reactions spoke of too many things.

She went back into the front room, called up the screen, and started issuing commands. In the meantime Jack went to the bathroom, found another towel, and started wiping up the remaining blood. He hid the towel in the disposal unit in the bathroom. By the time he'd finished, the edges of the bedroom door were already starting to blur. Okay, that took care of Pinpin for the time being, but in the meantime, that didn't solve how they were going to get out of this place and back home, off Pandora. He had to think about this. He'd hardly been here long enough to warrant a full investigation. It was going to appear suspicious even to a shuttle driver if he called the vehicle back so soon. He'd have to have a reason. No, he wasn't thinking straight. He was a courier.

"Uncle Jack."

"Hmmm?" She'd finished with the programming and now stood next to him, just inside the doorway.

"You know that guy you were looking for?"

"Yeah, not now, Billie. And it's just Jack, okay? I have to work out how to get us out of this place before somebody notices our friend in the next room's missing. How often do other people come here?"

"Not at all. Well, not much."

"That wall's going to take a while to grow, though. We can't take the risk. You can tell me on the way out."

She narrowed her eyes, glanced across at the other room, and shook her head. "Nuh-uh. You'd better listen to me."

"What is it?" He turned and glared at her. She barely flinched.

"He's here," she said.

"What?"

"He's here. That guy, Ronschke—the miner guy. I found out some stuff while Uncle Pinpin was looking at some other things." That particular use of Dan's name still gave Jack a shiver. "He gave me access to the systems," she continued. "I could have gotten in there myself, but anyway, I had plenty of time to look around."

Jack quickly crouched in front of her and took her by the shoulders. "Why? How do you know it's him?"

"Why do you think, stupid? You gave me all that stuff to look at, to find things out. I remembered. I remember most things. His name came out and I followed the links. That's all. Pretty simple really." He could barely believe she was being so matter-of-fact.

"And?" he asked.

"They called him a test subject. Vortex case number one-thirty-two. He's being kept here somewhere. They're running a whole lot of different tests on him. Something about passing through the null space and coming through the other side. There were others, but a lot of them just had blank records. Nothing there. There was only about, I think, eight or nine other records with the same sort of detail as the one you're looking for."

Null space? What did that mean? "What sort of tests, I wonder?"

"Oh, all sorts of stuff. Medical records. Things like that."

Medical. That made sense. It worked right into the dream image of Ronschke. And null space? . . . A picture of Ronschke floated up in his mind, strapped to the chair in the room with the translucent glass. "*The thing in the cloud place. The water place. The air place. The place of dark earth. I don't know."*

"Do you remember if there were any other names there?"

"Uh-huh. You want to know if any other names from the mining crew were there. Right?" Billie looked pleased with herself. She nodded. "All of them. I didn't have time to check all of them—the records were pretty hard to get into—but the names were there. I think it was all of them."

Vortex case number 132. And who was to say Ronschke was the last? How many had there been? There was nothing to say the numbering was sequential, but all the same. . . . Easy. They had a ready supply of miners with few ties, and probably Outreach had the means to control the information flow anyway. If there were anyone back home who cared, they could feed them anything, keep the funds flowing if necessary. Easy test subjects, but test subjects for what? And what Pinpin had said—they were going nowhere.

"Billie, what else did you find out? Do you know why they were testing him?"

"Not right away. That was harder. Uncle Pinpin didn't want me getting into some of the links, so I had to be more careful. He was on some sort of ship. A ship that traveled into . . . I don't know. There was more of that mathematics and science stuff. It sounded like the ship was going somewhere, but not going somewhere at the same time. I didn't understand it."

"Tell me some more. . . ."

She shrugged. "I don't know. Something about exotic matter, about dimensionality. It sounded like some of the ships—there was more than one—went wherever they were supposed to go and didn't come back.

Something about instability. That's right—I remember. They were trying to test the effects of the vortex, the null space, on human subjects. Like an experiment."

Shit. That was what they were doing. Outreach was using the miners as subjects to test the effects of some sort of travel. He had been right. Some sort of new ship. Gateways. A place where everything was all mixed up. Something that passed through matter like the dream beast living through the mine walls. Everything was clicking into place. Warburg knew full well what was going on. He'd hired Jack, just as Pinpin had said, to help cover up what was going on out here to give himself time. And what was going on? Ships, transport—all that logistics stuff had to be important to their business, didn't it? And Van der Stegen? Van der Stegen had to be involved somehow. It was his handipad, after all. All those formulae, scientific notations, everything else, it all pointed to the same thing. Van der Stegen had to be just as involved as Warburg.

"Uncle Jack?"

"Huh?" *Right.* A lot of good the knowledge would do him if he couldn't get them out of this place. Billie was looking at him expectantly. "Listen, all that stuff's great, Billie," he said. "But I have to find some way to get us out of here."

She frowned. "How did you get here?"

"In a shuttle. I had a pass organized for me saying I work for Outreach." He said it as much for his own benefit as for hers.

"So? Use the pass."

"Yeah, but what about you?"

"I'm just a girl. Nobody takes any notice of a young girl. Don't you know that?"

"Yeah, but what if somebody questions? We just

can't walk out of here. I don't even know how to get the shuttle back."

She pursed her lips and shook her head. "Still not very good, are you? I can do that. Wasn't Uncle Pinpin going to call a shuttle?"

"Yeah, but—"

"You've got a pass, right?"

"So . . .?"

"Well, I haven't got one. Never did have. I just came with Uncle Pinpin."

Jack stared at her. This kid was just too good.

Wouldn't they be suspicious, though, if he called the shuttle back in so brief a time? He'd been here only a few hours. If that. But no, there was nothing to say he had to stay. He was a personal courier. There was nothing that the shuttle pilot had to know. That was what the pass said. Maybe, just maybe . . . Billie was unauthorized. She was just here, and as she'd said, she had never been authorized in the first place.

"Billie, call the shuttle," he said.

Nineteen

As it was, Jack needn't have worried. Billie was right. The shuttle crew, the people on board ship, all of them, barely registered that Billie was there. She was just a kid, after all, but a very special kid, as Jack was starting to realize. He'd laughed and joked with the shuttle pilot about having another package to deliver, and that had been that.

The cabins on the ship were small, utilitarian, but with enough space not to give you a sense of being fully enclosed. Jack made sure from the outset that Billie was clear about the sleeping arrangements. He didn't want any repeat of the earlier events, especially just after she'd spent a few weeks with Pinpin Dan again. He looked at her sideways, noting the age that had crept back into her face in the intervening time.

"Billie, you okay?" he asked.

"Uh-huh," she said, giving him a brief frown in response.

All right. He could leave it for now. He didn't want to push it just yet. There would be plenty of time in the couple of weeks they had together on the journey back. Then they'd be back in the Locality, and what then? He clearly had some decisions to make.

They quickly established a routine, killing the long, endless spaces with discussions about the notes and things that Billie had found out during her time on Pandora. They'd get up late, breakfast together, work through the notes for a time, have some lunch, and maybe take a walk around the limiting space of the ship's inside. Jack began to understand some of the benefits of nearly instantaneous travel. This long, dark time between the spaces was mind numbing. You'd have to be someone pretty resilient to put up with this time after time. It was good that Billie was there. He could bounce ideas off her, and her sharp perceptions nearly always came back with something that made sense. Piece by piece, the bits started falling together.

The voyage also had other benefits. He had no access to his patches out here, and slowly, gradually, with the combination of the trip out and the extra, period back, he began to feel the effects of the chemicals filtering out from his system. There was an extra edge of clarity, of energy. There were headaches too, but after a few days they passed as well. As he reached some sort of level, with Billie's help Jack managed to put together a plausible picture of events surrounding his involvement with Outreach and Van der Stegen.

He sat across from her on the narrow bunk. "So weren't you surprised to see Pinpin?"

"Uh-huh. A bit. But he told me he'd been playing a sort of game with you. He just pretended to be dead. He said he needed to do that so you could work on the case."

Jack nodded. "Yeah, that makes sense. So where did he go?"

She shrugged. "He stayed at Outreach for a while,

but then he came and found me. We caught a flier to the port right away. Then came out here."

"So where were you? Down in Old, right? With Daman?"

She gave a brief half smile. "Uh-huh. I like Daman."

"Well, I don't very much. He and some of his friends worked me over. I think they had metal bars or something."

She seemed totally unconcerned by this revelation. "They have to look after each other. Sometimes the people who come down are trouble. They don't come back."

He decided to let it pass. "So why didn't you let me know where you'd gone?"

"Uncle Pinpin didn't want me to. I asked him, but he said it'd be better if you didn't know."

"Hmmm."

So it seemed that what Pinpin had said was right, as far as it went. It looked like he'd planned the whole thing. Jack knew there was little point questioning her further about what Pinpin had intended. Whatever story he'd told her, it had seemed to satisfy her, and it would give him few further clues about the entire setup.

Toward the end of the voyage he decided to talk to Billie again about the serious stuff, work out what she was really feeling. They'd made some progress during the day on the notes, and he thought that the sense of achievement might just act as a counterbalance to the things he needed to discuss. Not that he wanted to take the edge off her accomplishments, but he had to deal with it eventually. Here, at least, she wouldn't be able to disappear. He sat her down on the edge of the bunk.

"Billie, we need to talk about some stuff."

"What?"

"How come you ended up with Pinpin Dan?"

"I don't want to talk about that. I don't want to talk about him."

"Okay, well, what were you doing down in Old?"

"I told you when I left you the message."

"I don't mean then. I meant before. Before you got together with Pinpin."

She shrugged. "It was a place to be."

"But didn't you have anywhere else?"

"Nuh-uh."

"But what about your family?"

She gave him an accusing glare. "I told you I didn't want to talk about them. I told you before."

"Yes, I know you did. But we've got to work out what we're going to do. You must have somewhere you can go, someone you can be with."

Her face hardened. "I'm okay with you."

"Yes, I know you're okay with me, but for how long, Billie? What makes you think that that's right, that you can stay with me? Look, you keep telling me I'm not very good, that I keep on forgetting simple things. You've seen how I live. What sort of life is that, huh? Do you really want to live like that?"

"It's okay."

"It might be okay, Billie, but I can't look after you forever. I just don't know how."

"You don't look after me. I look after me. Nobody has to look after me. It's you who needs looking after."

It was going nowhere. Every time he tried to broach the subject of parents or family, she'd just clam up. There was something else there, in the background. He remembered some of her strange reactions, particularly that first night back in his apartment. There was that blank acceptance when he'd mentioned her father, and again the walls had come slamming down.

He sighed. "Okay, Billie. We can talk about it later. We can work out what we're going to do once we get back to the Locality and I sort out things with Outreach and with Van der Stegen. Then we'll work it out."

He was saying it, but really he had no idea what he was going to work out. There just didn't seem to be an answer. Not within the confines and the systems so deeply entrenched within the Locality. There simply weren't the mechanisms for dealing with it. There were child-care facilities, services that allowed the Locality to tick over, but there were no institutionalized social services, nothing to really cope with a kid Billie's age. That was supposed to be the province of the parents, and with no parents . . . And Jack knew better than to bring that topic up again. He couldn't even hazard how deep the wound might be with Billie. Perhaps that stuff would come out with time, but not now. As far as the Locality's ownership was concerned, to have anything in place that would effectively cope with the population of waifs and strays would have simply been too great a drain on resources. That was probably why the group of kids had made their home down in Old, surviving however they could. The corporate authorities didn't care, because they didn't get in the way of how things worked. If he thought about it, as distasteful as the thought might be, they actually helped the way things worked.

The decision about Billie would keep, but not for too much longer. He knew that.

He stared across at her. There was even more he had

to consider. He realized that without her he wouldn't have solved even a small part of this great puzzle, and he wondered what that might mean. Perhaps they were meant to be together. Natural synergies like that happened in life. They just happened, especially to Jack. It was hard. He didn't quite know whether he was trying to decide what to do with her for her, or purely for selfish reasons, because he knew deep down he was unable to cope. What was he, Jack Stein, supposed to do with a young girl? Maybe what she said was right. Perhaps it had been Billie who'd been looking after him all along.

He spent long hours that night and the following three or four thinking about the problem. By the time the voyage was over, when eventually they got back to the Locality and his apartment, he still had no answer.

He didn't know what to expect when they arrived. Anything could have happened in the weeks that he'd been gone—break-in, Warburg's people, police, any-thing—but the apartment was still there just as he'd left it. The self-cleaning macros had been working, de-spite the empty trays of ready-cooked he'd forgotten to clear before he'd left. Home, such as it was.

"Billie, toss your things over there. It's been a long trip, and I guess you want something to eat, right?" She nodded. "Okay, Molly's, then back here. We put the final pieces together and decide what we're going to do."

"Who are you going to tell?" she said, looking up at him. "Warburg or Van der Stegen?"

"Good question. I'm not sure yet. Who do you think?"

"Van der Stegen." She said it with certainty.

"Okay, sit down and let's sort this out before we eat. What makes you so sure?"

"Warburg doesn't care about anyone. All he cares about is his stupid science stuff and his company."

"But what about Tasha?"

"Her!" Billie snorted.

"What?"

"The big woman and the guy with the long hair were working for her. What about what happened at Uncle Pinpin's place? She doesn't care about anything."

"But Pinpin was okay that time. They didn't really hurt him."

"It doesn't matter. They beat you up, didn't they? And that was because of her. I don't like her."

"But you never met her."

"Don't have to. I know."

"Listen, you should hate me more than you hate her. What about what I did?"

"You couldn't help it. It just happened." She shrugged.

"No, maybe you're right. And you're right about the other two. And maybe about Warburg too. He'd already given the question some thought, and really he was just seeking confirmation. He'd felt what both men were like. There was nothing about Warburg that gave him comfort. Van der Stegen, on the other hand, felt more neutral. At least with the latter, he might have some chance of helping Gleeson get what he wanted.

"So Van der Stegen it is."

Although he didn't like it, the decision was clear. Warburg and Anastasia Van der Stegen had both played him for a fool. Maybe under the advice of Pinpin, but they'd done it all the same. He did have a few shreds of pride left. He could probably take the money, walk away from it all, but in a way that'd be legitimizing what they'd done, the way they'd treated him. Was Van der Stegen any better? He didn't know. It was funny; a couple of months ago and he wouldn't have given a damn, but Billie, the stuff going on in Old, the mass-marketed regimentation, and the featureless Locality life were all beginning to stick in his throat.

He spent some time chewing it over with his Mollyburger, but by the time they got back to the apartment, he was certain. First he got Billie to take the block off his system as he looked on, and then he invoked the wallscreen and made the call.

The wide driveway, the gardens, the wall of windows and doors, it was all just as he remembered it. This time, though, the opulence stuck in his throat. Joshua Van der Stegen was not that different from William Warburg. Their methods might be a little different, but in the end there wasn't too much to separate them. Van der Stegen was just a little bit less public about the things that he did.

As he approached, the front door swung open, and an anonymous man in a suit beckoned him inside. It looked like when Mr. Van der Stegen was in residence, he had his full complement of staff with him. He was ushered through the vast tiled hallway, past the polished wood staircase, and farther back, into the bowels of the vast mansion that served Van der Stegen as his headquarters. Just for a moment Jack wondered what it would be like to live like this, amid all this grandeur, then dismissed the thought. It was never going to happen.

Van der Stegen was waiting for him. He sat, legs crossed in a high-backed, leather-upholstered chair. Jack guessed it was real leather too. The genuine article, just like everything else in the house. The room was decked out in hues of deep red and brown, matching the rich tones of the leather furniture. A pair of similarly covered low couches sat opposite each other with a long, low table between them. Floor-to-ceiling shelves covered two of the room's walls and they were full, end to end, with books. They were real books. It had been a while since Jack had seen those—the paper-and-binding type. One of the other walls was graced with a broad stone fireplace, and above, surveying all that was theirs, hung a portrait. The painting showed Van der Stegen sitting in exactly the same chair, and behind his right shoulder, standing, Anastasia Van der Stegen, one hand on the chair's back, an imperious expression on her face.

"Ah, Stein. Come in. Sit. What's your pleasure? A brandy? This one's particularly fine." He lifted a balloon glass to his face, swirled it, and took a healthy sniff. "It had been so long, I thought we might have lost you."

"No, I'm fine, Mr. Van der Stegen. Let's just get down to business."

"Come on, Stein. It's not going to hurt you." A liveried butler already stood close by with a glass standing in the center of a silver tray. Van der Stegen waved him over and Jack took the proffered glass, cupping it between his hands. Van der Stegen waved the man away and they were alone.

Jack found his gaze still drawn to the painting. Tasha Van der Stegen, the power behind the throne?

Maybe not yet, but it couldn't be too far off. Van der Stegen noticed his thoughtful look.

"A good likeness, eh, Stein? She reminds me so much of her mother. I think it captures Tasha quite skillfully."

"Uh-huh." Perhaps more than he knew.

"So what is it you have to tell me? Have you a report?"

"I will, of course, upload the report in its entirety to your home system, but I never do that without briefing the client first, Mr. Van der Stegen. I find it cuts through a lot of wasted time—gets to the heart of the matter."

"I understand."

"Before I go into detail, Mr. Van der Stegen, I think you should be aware that I know most of what the operations on Dairil III and Pandora are all about. I know your involvement with Outreach, and I know what your research boys are trying to achieve out there."

Van der Stegen paused and took a moment to compose himself before speaking. "All right . . ."

"Well, I just don't want there to be any surprises in that regard."

"Fine. Continue."

"There's some pretty weird stuff in what I have to tell you, but it all centers around the mining operation. The nature of my work may make some of the things I have to say seem a little peculiar, but that comes with the territory.

"I'm sure you're aware of the research effort under way on Dairil III and Pandora and what it's trying to achieve, just in the same way William Warburg is. I'm not one hundred percent certain of your involvement with Warburg and the extent to which it continues, but both of you are seeking the same thing, and the bottom line is making the logistics of your operations more efficient. There are also other, commercial benefits to be had from holding a monopoly on portals, gateways, whatever you want to call them, and the means of traveling through them."

Van der Stegen nodded. "I don't think there are any surprises there, Stein."

"No. It's all pretty logical. The thing I haven't quite worked out is how far you're involved. How much you actually know about Warburg's activities out there on Dairil III."

Van der Stegen leaned forward and fixed Jack with a narrowed stare. "What's this got to do with who took my handipad, Stein? That's what you were employed to find out."

"It has everything to do with it, Mr. Van der Stegen. It was the contents of that handipad that motivated its theft. And the contents have everything to do with the operations on Dairil III. It also has to do with the eventual ownership of Outreach and the ambition that drives that. The handipad was merely a key to a far broader plan."

"I see. Continue."

Jack took a moment to compose his thoughts before continuing. The subject of Anastasia Van der Stegen was likely to be sensitive.

"It also has to do with your daughter, Mr. Van der Stegen."

"Tasha?" He frowned, his thick, dark eyebrows emphasizing the depth of his scowl. "What's this got to do with Tasha?"

"Quite a bit, I'm afraid. You know she's involved with Warburg?"

The frown relaxed, and he sat back in the chair, looking thoughtful. "Is she now?" He laughed.

It was not the reaction Jack had expected at all.

"I believe your daughter to be a very ambitious young woman, Mr. Van der Stegen. That ambition stretches to Outreach and well beyond, I would imagine. She and Warburg have been working together to take full control of the Outreach operations, cutting you out of the picture. Your handipad was part of that scheme. The material you had on it was going to be evidence enough to force you into a position where you would have to effectively retire and hand your interests over to her.

Together she and Warburg would then be free to take over completely."

"Hmmm." Van der Stegen gave a wry grin. "She always was impatient. Just like her mother in that regard." He quickly became more serious. "How far does this involvement go, do you know? Does she love the man?"

"Warburg? I don't know. Does it matter?"

"No, probably not." Van der Stegen leaned his head back and rubbed his throat slowly with his fingers. "So how was this supposed to work? I don't understand how the simple contents of my handipad could be used to do as you claim."

"Okay." Jack leaned forward. "I believe that both sides, you and Warburg, were following the same path of investigation. You, on one hand, had a team working on the gateway question—how to open the vortex. Warburg at the same time was treading the same route, but he went about it in a slightly different way. He'd actually come farther but he was keeping that fact secret. They'd managed to open the gateway. The only question remaining was how to use the gateway effectively. To be able to do that, they had to be able to pass people through unharmed. That was the key. He was using the Dairil III mining crew as experimental subjects. Some of them made it through, and some of them didn't. Just to confirm what I'm about to tell you, can you answer me one question . . . ?"

"Which is?"

"Francis Gleeson. He works for you, right?"

Van der Stegen hesitated, and then nodded reluctantly.

"Well, you see, one of the things that let them down was that one of the miners, Gilbert Ronschke, was involved with Gleeson. Ronschke was one of the crew that disappeared, that I'd been hired to locate . . . or not locate, as it happens. They couldn't have known that. It was a detail that escaped them. Gleeson was very sensitive about his relationship with Ronschke and didn't want it advertised within Outreach. Gleeson was in charge of the personnel records of the mining crew, so it was easy enough to manipulate the data to hide that fact. When Ronschke disappeared, there was one interested party at the heart of their operations that they could not have known about. Francis Gleeson. Gleeson came to me. That tied one of the threads together, but only one.

"I actually got the handipad from Gleeson. He'd passed it on to me because he wanted me to find Ronschke. He couldn't afford to pass it back to you, because he couldn't be sure that you weren't involved, knowing your connections to Outreach, even though he was working for you. How he got it, I never found out. It didn't matter in the scheme of things. Somehow it came into his possession, either directly or indirectly from your daughter. I have to assume that your daughter had passed it on to someone on Warburg's team and somehow it came into Gleeson's hands. He obviously knew what it was, and was using it as a means to try to manipulate my involvement in the case and to point to your involvement without giving anything away about his own association with you. Gleeson always claimed that it had come from Ronschke. I eventually worked out that that couldn't be true, that it was simply a ploy on Gleeson's part to further tie Ronschke into the investigation. Gleeson's a lot smarter and a lot more devious than he might appear on the surface."

Van der Stegen finally placed his brandy glass down on the table and leaned forward. "Yes, he is. All that is highly plausible, Stein," he said. "So we don't know exactly who took my handipad. Whether it was Tasha herself or not is unimportant. I still don't see how they could possibly use it to do any damage."

"Ahh, that's where I come in. I'm fringe. I recognize I'm fringe, Mr. Van der Stegen, and I've already been told directly by one particularly unsavory character who worked for the other side that William Warburg intended to use that to his advantage. He had no expectation that I was going to come up with any real results from my work on the case. He was going to report back to the board that the investigation into the crew's disappearance had drawn a blank. Due diligence and all that, but nothing that would tell anybody anything. That would also buy him enough time to complete the experiments on Dairil III. To Warburg's mind, psychic investigation, psychic anything, is a waste of time, and that would be used to prime the board."

"I don't see how—"

"That was just the first step. With that sitting in the back of their minds, Warburg was going to distribute the contents of your handipad to the board. There's a lot of stuff there, Mr. Van der Stegen, that is just as fringe as anything I'm involved in. Alchemy, the philosophers' stone, Ouroboros, all of that. Warburg was going to use it as evidence that you'd lost your grip. He'd come up with real results because of hard scientific work, and you, dithering around with this suspect philosophical stuff, had gone nowhere, throwing away company resources along the way. His argument would have been that you'd obviously lost your grip on reality, perhaps become a little senile, and had become a risk to the company's operations, wasting funds with nothing to show for it. One research effort is a significant drain on company resources, but two, when the second one is highly suspect and undertaken in secret, without the board's approval . . . well, that would hurt.

"No doubt you're pumping Outreach funds into your effort. You would be seen not only to be wasting money and resources, but to be losing your mind. Faced with that evidence, you'd have no choice but to cede control to your daughter. Warburg would have suggested it, and he would have gained full backing of the Outreach board. Then, in partnership, she and Warburg could continue unhindered. You'd be out of the picture, Tasha would have what she wanted, and Warburg would be free to carve out his empire. The perfect union. Until, of course, Tasha decided to take how much she really wanted. But that would be another game to be played out accordingly when the time came."

Jack sat back and spread his hands. "That's it. That's the whole story."

Van der Stegen said nothing for some time, and then he grinned. He actually grinned.

"Very good, Stein. I'm afraid Tasha and William are going to have to wait a while longer. I always knew he was a sly, calculating bastard. It was my work that put him onto this path in the first place. Just like him to ignore that and deny any connection. He probably doesn't realize that I have complete records of our initial discussions about this problem. When I confront them with this, they're going to have to sit back for a while and learn some patience. I'm not ready to retire yet. Not by a long way. And now that I have the full information about the mining crew, I'm the one who'll have the upper hand."

"And what about the crew? Aren't you going to do anything?"

"What? What should I do, Stein? They're not my responsibility."

Jack had had enough. "Don't you feel anything, Mr. Van der Stegen? Anything at all? You're acting as if this is just some big game to you."

Van der Stegen said nothing, just shrugged.

"Dammit," said Jack quietly. There was nothing he could do to influence this man. Nothing at all. And there was nobody he could tell either. No one who would make any difference. He leaned forward, slapping his hands on the tops of his thighs. "Fine," he said with finality. "Look, there is one thing I want to know. Call it my own curiosity, but can you tell me something?"

"Hmmm? What is it?" Van der Stegen was only half paying attention now.

"I don't understand, Mr. Van der Stegen. What is all this stuff about alchemy, about the kabala? What relevance does it have to any of this research your people have been involved in?"

"Fair question, Stein, and actually one I'm prepared to answer. As a race, we've made enormous advances over the last centuries. Science and technology have moved at a pace that's almost impossible to track, and yet we remain ignorant. As we've advanced, as things have become easier for us, we've moved farther and farther away from true knowledge. How many of us really understand the way things work? How many really know the way things fit together? I have long believed that we, humanity, have known things far beyond the accumulated scientific and technical knowledge we profess today."

"I don't understand. . . ."

"And nor do we, Stein. Fundamental beliefs, accumulated knowledge of being, these have fascinated our race since the dawn of time. We, my people, were stagnating in the smug hubris that surrounds our own accomplishments. I wanted to go back, explore those areas of knowledge that perhaps went beyond the boundaries that we had set ourselves. The ancient mystics and churchmen were the true scientists of their day. In our modern technical viewpoint, their endeavors were little more than superstitious nonsense. But if we *really* analyze their texts, their knowledge, we find pointers to other, more basic and practical truths.

"They had answers to the big questions that we were seeking. The philosophers' stone is nothing more than a pointer to exotic matter. I don't expect you to come to grips with the technical details, but the underlying message was held there in coded form. With the right key we could open the gate to transcendence, moving beyond the material world. That's exactly what we've been doing. Exactly. In that respect, we are no different from the ancient alchemists and kabalists. Where they received that knowledge originally, who knows? Maybe some ancient race, maybe some other way, perhaps there had been a fall, but their problem was that they just didn't have the resources or technology to exploit it. But we do, Stein. We do. Imagine if someone like Newton had had our resources. . . ."

There was a light in Van der Stegen's eyes, and Jack almost found himself being caught up in the man's evangelical vigor—almost. He swirled his drink and looked down at the intricate pattern in the woven carpet beneath his feet. He still didn't quite understand what it was about, but Van der Stegen clearly believed what he was saying. He looked back up at the older man sitting across from him, his gaze firmly fixed in the distance.

"You've got a pretty strong set of beliefs there, Mr. Van der Stegen. Or at least it sounds like you do."

"Certainly, Stein. It's about our future, about our advancement. It's about progress. When it comes down to it, I don't mind admitting I'm an idealist. If it turns out to be profitable along the way, then all the better."

"And what of the people who get hurt along the way? Don't they matter?"

"It depends, Stein," Van der Stegen said slowly, clearly annoyed with the line of questioning. "You have to look at the bigger picture. You have to look at the net result. What people anyway? Do any of them *really* matter in the broad scheme of things?"

"People get hurt. You had that pair of thugs, Alexis Grecco and his sidekick, working for you. I know. I know intimately. How can you seriously justify that?"

Van der Stegen shrugged. "They're good at what they do."

Jack sniffed. He knew pretty well firsthand how good they were.

"And the Locality. What about what goes on there? What about the corruption, the kids down in Old, all of that? What about the mindless patterned consumption?"

"Listen, Stein. My family built the Locality."

Jack knew that full well from the background on the man that Alice had sent him from the library, but he said nothing.

Van der Stegen continued. "Where would those people be if we hadn't? Safe, secure, a modern and serviced environment where they can be assured a quality of life, every convenience at their fingertips. Where else would they get that if it weren't for what we'd done? I can't be responsible for what people do with their lives. Nor can I be concerned about what they do to entertain themselves. As long as the system keeps ticking over and it doesn't impact me, why should I care?"

"But you know it goes on."

"Know *what* goes on? The same things that occur and have occurred throughout history wherever people congregate in numbers? Is that what you're talking about?"

It was clear Jack was going to get nowhere following that path. He didn't want to alienate Van der Stegen just yet. He knew what he should be doing was standing and shouting at this man, with his smug confidence and glib answers.

"And what if I were to tell people what you're doing, what your people are doing?"

"What, Stein? What are you going to tell them? More to the point, who are you going to tell? The police? Who employs them?"

He was right. Van der Stegen did have a responsibility, whether he'd admit it or not, but there was not a thing Jack could do about it. Were the people in the Locality victims? Were they victims because they chose to be so?

"What about Gleeson? He's working for you."

"And will continue to do so until he no longer proves useful."

"Well, then, will you do something, Mr. Van der Stegen? Just one small thing." Jack let the question hang heavy in the air between them while Van der Stegen sized him up, perhaps assessing whether he was really going to make trouble.

"So . . . what is it?"

"Find Gilbert Ronschke. He's somewhere in the facility on Pandora. Let him go home."

"I don't think I—"

"Listen, as long as you want Gleeson to remain of use to you, Ronschke's your key."

Van der Stegen slowly rubbed his upper lip with one finger before finally speaking. "All right. Yes, I can see the value in that. I can have my people see to it. There's no point in upsetting the machinery. It takes time to put these things in place."

"Fine. Thank you."

"And now, Jack Stein, with that, I think our business is concluded. There will be a flier waiting to take you back to the Locality. One of my people will see that your needs are accommodated on the way out. I truly am grateful for what you've done, and I have notified my people appropriately, but I don't really expect to see you again."

Don't worry, thought Jack. *I doubt you ever will.*

He'd clearly been dismissed, and, placing his glass carefully on the low, carved wooden side table—real wood—next to the leather armchair, he got to his feet.

"One last thing, Mr. Van der Stegen. What will you do about Tasha?"

"That's none of your concern, Stein. Suffice it to say, Anastasia will have learned a valuable lesson by the time I've finished with her. It will make her stronger in the long run, and that's a good thing for her and for the Van der Stegen name and the future of our interests. We all need lessons, Stein."

Van der Stegen barely seemed to notice as Jack left the room.

Twenty

All the way back to the Locality, Jack was deep in thought. His mind floated with images of the past few weeks, of Pinpin, of Van der Stegen, of Billie. He hardly noticed the broad landscape passing beneath his gaze. He'd finished at least one side of the contract, the Van der Stegen part, and brought it to a conclusion. Regardless, it still left a sour taste in his mouth. The one real point was that maybe he'd managed to satisfy Francis Gleeson, or at least put the things in place that would make it happen. He was sure Van der Stegen would make sure Ronschke was found and returned. He needed Gleeson, and therefore he needed to keep the little man satisfied. At least Jack had achieved that much.

What about Van der Stegen, though? Van der Stegen owned the Locality. He didn't own any title to it; there was nothing saying it belonged to him, but he owned it all the same, and a hell of a lot more besides. Yet, despite that ownership, Van der Stegen held no responsibility. He was above accountability for his actions. The man was right, in a way. How could he be held accountable for the things people did to each other, the things people always did? The real question was, did Jack want to stay as part of the collection of

trinkets that belonged to the Van der Stegen family
and those like them? That was all the residents of the
Locality were to them—playthings. And it didn't matter whether it was Van der Stegen or Warburg. On a
scale, there was probably quite a bit to separate the
two, but ultimately they were part of the same game.
What could he, Jack Stein, do? There'd always be a Van
der Stegen or a Warburg, and there would always be
victims who suffered the consequences. By living
there, by being a part of all that, Jack bore as much of
the burden of passive responsibility for its continu-
ance. Well, he wasn't going to be passive anymore.

And what about Billie? She was as much a part of it
as any of them, but did that mean she had any debt?
No, in the end, he guessed she was a true victim—a real
victim. Others, many others, were really little more
than casualties of their own design. But not Billie.

And as he sat there, the air rushing past the flier as
it soared toward the belly of the beast, Jack came to his
final decision.

He barely hesitated to nod his thanks to the pilot as
he descended and made his way past the locks into the
landing bay shoved up at one end of the Locality like
a blister. There were some practicalities to attend to,
but first he needed to get back to the apartment. When
he finally got there, a wary Billie let him in.

"Billie, will these things work outside the range of
the Locality?" he asked, digging out his handipad. He
guessed they must. He'd seen them used in the Residence, which was a fair distance from the Locality, a
distance that must change daily with the Locality's
continued crawl across the countryside.

She frowned. "I guess, but what do you—"

"It doesn't matter right now."

He knew she was ready. Billie didn't really have anything to take. Jack stood and scanned his apartment. A few clothes. A few assorted patches in the bathroom. Nothing much else. Where were the traces of his life? No bric-a-brac. No personal memories. Maybe it was time to change all that. He needed a bag, and some food and supplies. No matter about his equipment back at the office. It could be replaced easily enough, and he felt somehow, now, that it was tainted anyway, tainted by the Locality and everything that existed inside it.

"Wait here, Billie. I've got to get a few things, and then we're leaving."

"Nuh-uh. Leaving where?"

"It doesn't matter. We're just getting out of here."

She said nothing, just stared at him.

Jack sighed, then crouched in front of her. He owed her some sort of explanation. Did he have any right to force her to leave with him?

"Billie, listen. This place is no good. The Locality's no good. As long as we remain here, it can't get any better. We'll go on, the same old things. Sure, I'll get work here and there, make a living, but what about you? What do you want?"

She frowned, then shrugged. "What are you talking about, Jack?" The question was framed in a peculiarly adult way.

"I guess I'm talking about the fact that you deserve better than what you've got here, what we've all got here. Are you happy?"

Again, she shrugged.

"I want you to be happy, Billie."

She looked at him blankly and he looked away. Just for an instant he couldn't meet her eyes.

"Okay. I'm going to get some things. You think about it while I'm gone." There was no going back now. "And while I'm gone you can decide. You think about whether you're happy here. You said you were okay with me. You either come with me or stay, but I'm not going to hang around in this place anymore and just let all this crap happen. I can't do anything to change it. The whole place belongs to people like Warburg and Van der Stegen. Maybe somewhere else I can make some sort of difference, but I can't change things here. This place, everything in it, it changes you, not the other way around. It's time I took some responsibility."

She watched him carefully as he prepared to leave, a frown clearly etched on her forehead.

As he left the apartment, Jack knew there was a risk. He could come back and Billie would be gone. Then he'd have his answer. And what would she do then? Maybe drift back to Old. He hoped it wouldn't be that way.

He didn't know how long he could rely on his hand-ipad outside of the Locality. It had to have some range. Food, provisions, a couple of tools. What else? Maybe something that he could trade, or convert. That still worked. He hadn't been out of the real world that long. And then? He'd have to rely on the instinct that had served him so well over the years. He didn't know where he was going or where he'd end up, but it was somewhere in the real world. Of that much he was sure.

When he got back to the apartment, she was still sitting on the couch. He felt some relief. At least she was still there. That was something.

"So?" he said.

"So what?"

"Have you made up your mind?"

She narrowed her eyes at him and crossed her arms. "Where are we going, Jack?" she said.

"Um . . . I don't know, really. I thought we could get outside the Locality, and head in whatever direction felt right."

"Nuh-uh," she said flatly. "What's wrong with you?"

"I don't know what—"

Billie fixed him with a stern look. "You really do need looking after, Jack Stein," she said. "Did you get paid?"

"Well, yeah . . ."

"Are there fliers that go to other cities?"

"Sure, but . . ."

Billie sighed and rolled her eyes. "Well, pick one."

She was right, of course. What with Van der Stegen's payment, the stuff from Gleeson, he had enough for a ticket for both of them, enough to spin things out for a couple of months after that. He should be able to find something in another city. It might take a few weeks to get started, but the work would start to come.

"Yeah, you're right, Billie." He met her gaze sheepishly, feeling slightly stupid. "Tell you what. You pick somewhere."

She shook her head and sighed again as she stood and crossed the room to call up the wallscreen.

Jack looked down from the flier's window. Out across the landscape, a broad escarpment overlooked the valley where the Locality currently crawled. Cliffs, rocks, escarpments—they'd all featured heavily over the last few weeks, and here he was looking down on another one. No White-Haired Man this time. No dream to sweep him away, but he'd come full circle all the same. Full circle. He'd had his fill of circles.

Below lay the Locality, inching its way across the plains and valleys, shimmering with its own obscene opalescence, and strangely reminiscent of the sinuous tentacles extruded from the mine walls on Dairil III what seemed like so long ago. Down there was the real beast—nothing more than a doorway into a hive. And inside lay the remnants of what had been promised to everyone who had lived there, gradually falling apart into inevitable corruption. He glanced across and put his hand on Billie's shoulder. They still had a lot to work out, Billie and he, but now they had the opportunity to do it somewhere else. Maybe somewhere better.

"You ready for this, kid?"

"I guess," she said. "What are we going to do when we get there?"

He looked up at the sky—the real sky—then back at the Locality. As above, so below. That was the alchemical rubric. You had to know the depths to ascend to the heights. Well, they'd both been there, Billie even more than he.

"I don't know," said Jack. "I don't quite know."

But he knew it didn't really matter that he didn't know. It never had.

"You know what, Billie? I think we'll work it out together."

There was the barest shake of her head, and just the hint of a sigh. Her lips slightly pursed, and giving no other response, Billie turned to look out the window at the landscape crawling slowly past below them.

About the Author

Jay Caselberg was born in a country town in Australia. He graduated with Honors from the University of Wollongong, then pursued a Doctorate at the University of New South Wales in Sydney, claiming that his postgraduate degree was simply practice to write large, cogent volumes of material. After he realized that academia wasn't going to fulfill his ambitions, he joined the workforce. His job involved extensive travel, dealing with internal management systems in over fifty-four countries for a global accounting firm. In 2002, the firm for which he worked ceased to exist. Since then, he has continued to write and publish, both as Jay Caselberg and James A. Hartley. He currently lives in London. This is his first novel. You can find him on the Web at www.sff.net/people/jaycaselberg.

ROC Science Fiction and Fantasy
COMING IN NOVEMBER 2003

TRICKSTER
by Steven Harper
0-451-45941-5

The telepathic communications net, known as "The Dream," has been shattered. And the majority of the Silent who used it are unable to reenter. But Kendi Weaver has more pressing concerns: finding the family that slavers tore from him more than a decade before.

PATH OF FATE
by Diana Pharaoh Francis

0-451-45950-4

In the land of Kodu Riik, it is an honor to be selected by the Lady to become an *ahalad-kaaslane*—to have your soul bonded with one of Her blessed animals, and roam the land serving Her will. But Riesil refuses to bow to fate—a decision that may have repercussions across the realm.

MECHWARRIOR: Dark Age #6: Service for the Dead
Book Three of the Proving Grounds Trilogy
by Martin Delrio

0-451-45943-1

MechWarrior Tara Campbell faces two ruthless enemies. Should she be defeated, Terra is sure to follow.

Available wherever books are sold, or to order call: 1-800-788-6262